my first time

Gay Men Describe Their First Same-Sex Experience

EDITED BY JACK HART

ALYSON PUBLICATIONS
LOS ANGELES

Typeset and printed in the United States of America.
Printed on acid-free paper.

This is a trade paperback original from Alyson Publications Inc.,
P.O. Box 4371, Los Angeles, California 90078.
Distributed in the United Kingdom by Turnaround Distribution,
27 Horsell Road, London N5 1XL, England.

First edition: May 1995

5 4 3

ISBN 1-55583-283-0

Contents

Introduction

In my previous book, *My Biggest O,* I asked gay men to describe the best sex they'd ever had. A number of contributors identified their very first gay encounter as also being their best. That surprised me. I had assumed that greater experience would bring greater enjoyment, and that first-time encounters would rarely qualify as best.

By the time I had finished that book, first-time experiences filled an entire chapter. They were some of the most interesting stories. And so I decided that my next book should focus entirely on this intriguing topic.

The publisher and I solicited stories by placing notices in gay newspapers around the country, asking gay men to write about their first consensual same-sex experience. Then, I sat back and waited to see what came in.

While waiting, I admit that I had some misgivings. Would a whole book of these stories prove repetitive? But I needn't have worried. As you're about to see, there's an enormous variety here. The earliest accounts are set back in the 1930s; the latest, in 1994. Sometimes the first-timer is seduced; other times he takes the initiative. Most of the stories carry a sense of delight; a few convey pain. Many are sexy, or exciting, or romantic.

I left it to contributors to define "first-time." Did casual adolescent sex play with their peers count? As you'll see, men interpreted the phrase differently, but a large number independently arrived at the same criteria: they selected the experience with which they came to think of themselves as gay, or different, or at least when they realized that male sex had an emotional component for them that wasn't felt by other boys who were just messing around.

I would like to thank Alistair Williamson, at Alyson Publications, who invited a number of Alyson authors to contribute. Several took the challenge, and they brought some high-caliber writing to this collection. For example, after reading James Russell Mayes's story "Teen for the Day" in the "Post-Stonewall" section, you won't be surprised to learn that his recent book *Small Favors,* with its stories about coming out in rural America, has won high praise from critics.

With strong, established writers like Mayes, any editing on my part would have been superfluous. For others, I often applied light editing to help the writer get his story across better. Largely, however, I've tried to allow each contributor's voice to come through. I never changed content, even if I or someone else might disagree with it. Several contributors conclude that their first experience might have made them gay. I'm skeptical that sexual orientation is determined this way, but if that's what they believe, they're entitled to say so here.

Originally I planned to arrange these stories according to each contributor's age at the time. I later decided it was more revealing to break them up based on the era when each one took place. It was too late at that point to contact everyone who had not included a date in their story. Using clues in the text and the cover letter, I was generally able to assign each piece to a section with a high degree of confidence. The story that was hardest to pinpoint was "Show Time." The narrator refers to getting a $1.40 payment plus a ten-cent tip as a newspaper boy. That struck me as a midsixties amount, so that's where I've placed this story. Conceivably it could have been a decade earlier or later.

▼

As we began soliciting stories, I wondered if a lot of men would make up something fun, rather than describe their actual first experience, which may not have gone as they had hoped. A few accounts did have all the flavor of a porn magazine submission: The coach and the high school football quarterback in the deserted locker room, for example. I omitted these stories. My apologies to the former quarterback if, in fact, this all really took place. In that case, you've had more than your share of good fortune in life, and I trust you won't be too hurt at being left out of this book.

For the most part, my sixth sense tells me the accounts I received and have included are all true. There are too many unexpected details and nuances. Take this — from one of my favorite stories, set in the 1930s after a sixteen-year-old boy finishes an encounter with a Bible salesman on the bus:

"He gave me a vest pocket Testament bound in artificial red leather and told me, 'Have a good life.' I thanked him, but thought it a mite peculiar that a Bible man was the first person, besides myself, to jack me off. I still have the Testament. It's not been used much."

If that was made up, then somebody missed a promising career as a novelist!

▼

As I read and reread these stories, several themes emerged.

Card games (notably strip poker) and other games of chance make repeated appearances. It doesn't take a Ph.D. to figure out what's going on here. The element of chance removed personal responsibility for making the crucial decision. "I didn't really *want* to get undressed — the cards made me do it," you can imagine these characters saying. Two other standby icebreakers, wrestling and backrubs, also get their share of use.

I was struck by how many men feel certain that cock sucking came naturally to them, right from the start. Yes, a few had to be cautioned to "watch those teeth," but nearly everyone who comments on this issue seems convinced that the act was instinctive. I wonder how they will announce the discovery of *that* particular gene?

Several stories are set in the context of a birthday. I can think of two reasons for birthdays to make a disproportional appearance. First, attention is focused on you at your birthday. It disposes people to be nice to you and think favorably of you ... perhaps even to give you a present. In addition, I suspect birthdays provide an impetus, a sense that "I'm getting older, it's time to find out what I'm missing."

A number of contributors, many years later, re-encounter the man (inevitably now married) with whom they had this first encounter. In most cases, he genuinely seems to have forgotten all about it. A moment of awakening for one of those partners was no more than a little recreation for the other. This certainly supports the theory that sexual orientation is already determined by puberty, and that actual experiences may help one recognize it, but don't set it.

A trend that emerged after I had grouped all the stories chronologically is that overall, stories from the more distant past are more upbeat than recent ones. It appears that first-time gay sex is usually enjoyable, in and of itself, but coming out is more likely to be painful. In the thirties and forties, it was easy to have sex while postponing any recognition that you were gay. Today, the two experiences are often nearly simultaneous. I've speculated further about this distinction in the introductions to some of the sections.

▼

My greatest regret, in compiling this book, was that I received far more engaging stories than I had room to use. In the end, I chose those that were well written, while also portraying a variety of experiences. Many good stories set in the 1970s and 1980s, for example, couldn't be used because those sections were already too long. Thank you to all the men who sent me a story. I'm sorry I couldn't run them all.

Jack Hart

1. Before Kinsey (1930–1948)

Those of us born after World War II all too easily think of the prewar years as the dark ages. How awful it must have been to be gay then!

And in many ways, I guess it was. The word "gay," in its modern sense, hadn't even entered the language. Gay people were invisible to the population at large. There were no gay organizations or newspapers. The Kinsey report, which startled America by revealing that homosexuality was far more commonplace than anyone had imagined, didn't appear until 1948. A gay person could easily go through life feeling utterly alone.

So why are there so many happy and joyful stories in this section? Some of it may be self-selection. Only men with a great deal of inner strength could have acknowledged their feelings, found others, eventually come out, and survived through it all to submit a story for this collection. Those for whom the guilt became too great presumably got married, and repressed their truest feelings.

▼

In addition to the generally upbeat tone here, I was struck by the male camaraderie of several stories. Repeatedly, we see a boy passing along what he knows about sex to a less experienced friend.

In a world where formal sex education was rare, you got information and encouragement from your peers. In the first story, which is one of my favorites, K.R.B.'s older friend tells him: "'Kenny, that's a fine dick. From the size of it now, it's going to be a real beaut' in a couple of years...' He made me feel proud and I was no longer ashamed to have Harley see my youthful nakedness."

In this context, it didn't much matter whether you might ultimately be homosexual or heterosexual. You *did* need to know why your dick got hard, and nobody else was volunteering that information. To quote K.R.B. again: "All boys did the sorts of things we did. It was the expected way of growing up and becoming personally aware of your maleness."

Sort of an apprenticeship in malehood. Like any good apprentice system, it offered something for both parties. Such relationships seem much rarer today.

These pre-Kinsey stories consistently showed a high caliber of writing and a real diversity of experiences. I think you'll enjoy each of them, and learn something about a different era. I certainly did.

Farmboys

K.R.B.

My childhood in the 1930s was spent on a farm in rural Kentucky, in a family consisting of two loving and authoritative parents, three older sisters, and myself. Fewer than a half dozen boys within a year or two of my age lived near enough to pal around. For entertainment we went fishing, or swimming, or hiked the hills, or just messed about. Much of our time was spent in the barn where we had privacy and occasional opportunity to observe stock animals copulate.

Sex always was uppermost in our minds. We often invented excuses to whip out our dicks so we could compare sizes, or observe who was growing the most cock hair. We naturally got hard as part of the contest to see who was biggest. From the age of ten, I got hard whenever I saw the smooth outline of a rod in another boy's pants, or glimpsed a naked dick in a public john, or when anyone cruised me as I pissed.

As early as I can remember I was obsessed with seeing male sex organs on men and animals. It was particularly exciting to see one when it was uncut or hard. I fantasized for hours about skinning back a hooded dick. Indeed, my first orgasm, at about the age of twelve, came as I played with myself and thought about doing just that to the boy who had come over to my house that afternoon to play. Cumming that first time scared the shit out of me. But it was instant addiction. I have, on average, jacked off once a day ever since.

Later, at ages thirteen and fourteen, when we held dicks together to compare size, it sometimes led to a circle jerk, though I don't recall any mutual masturbation at those times. The winner was the one who could shoot first and farthest. I almost always won because the sight of the other guys pumping their stiff rods got me hot and pushed me to the brink in no time.

My first shared gay sexual experience occurred when I was thirteen. It was with a boy of sixteen my father had hired to help with chores on weekends and after school. Harley was blond, tanned, slender, muscular, and manly in every way. He knew how to do everything with animals and farm equipment. He was my hero and first love. Harley taught me about the care of animals, harness repair, and many handyman skills that have remained useful to me to this day. When he occasionally put his arm

15

around my shoulder in a friendly way and I felt the heat of his body next to me, I always got a hard-on.

A couple of weeks after Harley came to work for us, we were in the barn helping a neighbor who had brought his cow over to be serviced by Old Max, my father's Jersey bull. I always tried to be around at those times because it's a hot thing to watch a big bull hump a cow.

When Harley brought the bull up behind the cow, his huge sac alternately swung like a church bell or pulled up tight against his crotch. His slim crimson rod slid in and out of its sheath and dripped pre-cum. Max sniffed and licked the cow's rear end a couple of times. Then he reared up, with prick sticking out about a foot and a half. It probed around, but when the tip finally touched the cow's hot, wet cunt Max lurched forward and gave two or three thrusts that almost knocked the cow to her knees. Two feet of stiff rod slammed in and out of her. It was all over in less time than it takes to tell. Old Max pulled out, got down, stretched his head out, and gave a long moan. Then he climbed back on and humped the cow all over again. The cow, the farmer, and Old Max all seemed satisfied with a job well done.

After helping the farmer get his cow back in his truck, Harley and I were hot and sweaty. The barn was shady and cool so we went into a horse stall and flopped down to rest on some bales of hay. Watching the bull service the cow always got me horny and I had sprung a rod. Harley had too. I sat opposite him where I could look straight at his crotch. His tight jeans were damp with sweat and clung to his legs. A smooth round ridge, bigger around and longer than a hot dog, ran diagonally across his upper thigh. It gave a jerk.

Harley watched me stare at his crotch and said, "You know what that is, don't you?"

I nodded and reflexively my own stiff cock jumped against the front of my overalls.

He said, "Little buddy, you want to see my dick, don't you?" I couldn't say a word, and could feel my face going beet red. He went on, "There's nothing wrong with wanting to see another guy's dick. I like a look-see too." After a moment he said, "I'll show you mine, but then you've got to show me yours. Fair is fair. Okay?"

He stood up, loosened his belt, and slowly unbuttoned the front of his pants. He wore no briefs. His right hand went in and fumbled around for a moment before coming out with his hooded, half-hard dick. His hand went back in and returned with his ball sac. His entire male pride was now hanging outside his open jeans and some of his golden cock hair showed above and beside it. He stood silently and let me stare as his cock bobbed up and down and lengthened to full erection. The head and crown of his cock were only slightly concealed by the thin short foreskin. His tool was beautiful, far and away the biggest one I had ever seen — about a seven incher.

"Now it's your turn," he said. He saw I was almost in a trance and added, "Relax. I'm your buddy. It's no big deal to show meat."

I stood, took two steps to stand before him, opened my fly, and took my prick out. It was stiff, with its naked shiny head glowing red. He said, "Kenny, that's a fine dick. From the size of it now, it's going to be a real beaut' in a couple of years. You're going to be big balled and heavy hung or I miss my guess." He made me feel proud and I was no longer ashamed to have Harley see my youthful nakedness.

Then he said, "Do you just want to look at mine, or do you want to hold it too?"

Struck dumb, I nodded my head. He took my hand and put it on his stiff rod. It was silky soft, springy hard, and beautifully shaped. I palmed and squeezed it, then slowly pushed down to skin back his cock head. I could feel the throb of his heartbeat as the cock swelled and got stiffer. My other hand moved in to cup his balls. Holding his dick and balls was the most wonderful sensation my hands had ever felt. Automatically one hand moved up and down, skinning and unskinning his cock head; the other kneaded his balls in their purse. He got harder and harder. Harley began thrusting his hips back and forth, fucking my hands, slowly at first, then faster and deeper.

He whispered hoarsely, "Squeeze it harder. Faster! Faster!" Then he closed his eyes tight, threw his head back, and thrust his hips forward, saying, "Duck! I'm cumming!"

He shot a long string of creamy cum out over my shoulder onto the straw. The first spasm was followed by four or five weaker pulses. He breathed heavily for a minute and then said, "God A'mighty, Kenny, that was as good as I ever had." After a bit he asked, "Do you jerk off? Have you ever cum yet?"

I nodded and said, "Yeah. Lotsa times."

He asked, "Do you want me to do you? I owe you one."

My dick was still out and hard as a rock. Anything or any way Harley wanted to do me was all right. I was in heaven. He grasped my dick and began jerking me off. Almost immediately I shot as heavy a load as I had ever cum before. He kept on squeezing my dick and sliding its skin up and down. Without ever going soft, I shot again, but without much cum the second time.

That's the story of my first-time gay experience, although, at the time I didn't recognize it for what it was. It was one of the best I ever had — something to jack off by for the rest of my life. In the next year and a half, following our first enjoyment of mutual masturbation, Harley and I had many other intimate experiences. We rarely talked about what we did together, nor did we discuss it with other boys. They may have suspected we were sex buddies, but it wasn't common knowledge and we didn't brag about it. Insofar as I know, we kept each other's confidence and never spoke about what we did to anyone else.

Our silence was not so much secrecy as the fact that we didn't think our behavior in any way unusual or unnatural. In those days, being 'queer' simply meant you actively sucked cock or you passively let someone fuck your butt. Since Harley and I neither sucked nor fucked, we had no occasion to think what we did was homosexual. In those days, in my part of the country at least, mutual masturbation between men was okay for heterosexual enjoyment. It was part of the normal framework of sex experimentation between boys — just an expected part of growing up to be men. In the language of the day, mutual masturbation was "just helping a buddy get off." I might add that passive oral sex (letting yourself get sucked off) and active anal sex (sliding your cock up another man's butt) were also acceptable forms of heterosexual male behavior and not in the least considered gay activity.

I lost track of Harley after he finished high school and got married. I suspect Harley was gay like me. Back then, getting married was the expected thing. Just as now, getting married shut off a lot of questions about being gay, but that changed nothing. Most of my old gay friends were, or still are, married, had kids, and served well in some branch of the armed services. But, same as me, closeted or not, they always were, and still are, fruitcakes.

What I said about my sex life between ages ten to fourteen was pretty much true for all boys I knew. Our curiosity and sex play had nothing to do with being straight or gay. All boys did the sorts of things we did. It was the expected way of growing up and becoming personally aware of your maleness. During those years I assumed that all the rest of my buddies had thoughts about sex exactly the same as mine. I did not realize I was actually gay until I was about seventeen. That's when it struck me that I was always having crushes on older boys at a time when other guys my age were having exactly the same kinds of emotional attachments to girls. That's when I knew something was different about me.

My sexual orientation surely has been imprinted in me from the beginning. My gayness must be an innate quality because I can't remember when I wasn't obsessed with seeing dicks or thinking about them. I am reasonably sure I was never sexually molested by any older person during my early childhood. My jack-off fantasies and wet dreams always involve images of intimacies with men and their sex organs — never of women or breasts and pussies.

Harley and I did not think of our relationship as something special or that we were in any sense "lovers." That was too sissy. It was *maleness* that appealed to both of us. We could be friends and buddies, but not lovers. We did not challenge the accepted attitude that to be lovers or to be married demanded that partners be of different sexes.

In some ways, things were simpler, but not necessarily any better, when I was young. Then it was *what you did,* not *what you thought,* that made you homosexual. The idea of *sexual orientation* (your reflexive erotic response to opportunities for sex with a male or female partner) had not been invented. In a way it was better back then because, unlike in the armed forces today, gays could not be discriminated against and deprived of civil liberties simply for the set of their minds. What went on in a man's head as a result of sexual desires was his business. You couldn't be penalized for thoughts alone. That's the way it still should be. On the other hand, back then everyone had to stay in the closet. That was bad. On the whole, little by little, I guess things are getting better for guys like you and me. It's tough, but it's going to take time to gain full acceptance and the personal rights straights take for granted.

Boots and Saddle

Anonymous

My "first time" took place at an English-style, Catholic boarding school to which my grandparents had sent me. While I deeply resented being uprooted from the comfortable abode where I had lived since my parents' divorce, it was decided that I should shed the protection offered by the large brownstone house, its seven servants, old Irish nanny, and English tutor. It was feared that I might be "spoilt" unless I left all that. Of course, it was already too late, as I was so secure in myself that I came across as arrogant and overbearing.

Upon arriving at school, filled with trepidation, I soon discovered a group of little guys exactly like myself of which I soon became the leading light. Although I was a less than perfect model, they followed me because I put up a bolder front than they did; at fourteen I was pretty showy and foolhardy, which they admired enormously.

Among the seniors, who were for the most part typical Eastern seaboard prep-school prototypes, there was one who stood out. The son of a Canadian industrialist, he was tall for his age, blond, blue-eyed, ruddy-faced, and strong as an ox. For sixteen years old he was quite a specimen indeed, and he could have put down any other boy in the school had he wanted to do so. Apart from all these pluses, there was the fact that his accent was unusual and his clothes looked as though he was fresh off the farm. Particularly unusual were his high-topped, laced, tan shoes, which he called boots, and which I made the butt of many rude jokes. The fact that I knew he heard my jokes and did nothing about it made me even cockier.

I forgot to tell you that in the English tradition older boys could use the service of younger ones, who were called "fags." And so it came to pass that one day when I was in the hall outside Bartlett's room, he called out for me to come into his quarters. As I entered I felt somewhat apprehensive, even more so when he ordered me to shut the door. He stared at me for a minute or so before saying, "My boots seem to have a fascination for you, Gerard, so I'm going to permit you to shine them for me. Fetch the bootblack box from my closet which I bought just for this occasion. I decided long ago to teach you manners and humility. Now kneel down and start learning."

Although I had never before knelt before anyone and I certainly had never cleaned boots, I realized Bartlett meant business and I obeyed him at once. Knowing that I was at a loss how to begin, he dictated my every movement. He showed me how to rub the polish into the leather with my bare hand and how to brush and snap the cloth at the end of the process. Surveying his boots carefully when I had finished, he expressed himself satisfied, stating that it wasn't bad for a start and that I'd do better next time. He commanded me to lick the toe of each boot to give them an even better shine.

Bewildered by a situation over which I had lost all control, I did everything that he bade me do. "That's your first lesson in bootblacking and humility," he said, "and you didn't do too badly. Come again tomorrow afternoon. You have a lot more to learn. You can go now, and thanks." Strangely enough, I felt no resentment or defiance toward Bartlett. In fact, I had a warm feeling for him and looked forward to the next episode.

▼

When I arrived at his digs next day he was waiting for me, wearing a pair of good-looking knee-high riding boots. "Okay, Gerard, you know the routine. Let's go." As he placed his foot on the stirrup of the box and I observed the extent of the job ahead, I suddenly felt a strange sensation. I was getting a hard-on! I had been mastered and subdued and was enjoying it!

When I had polished and licked Bartlett's boots he declared himself pleased and stated that I was about to receive my reward, at which point he produced an enormous cock and commanded me to caress it. I did so with pleasure, although I knew absolutely nothing of sex at that time. I fondled and kissed it until he made me take it between my lips. He worked my head back and forth a few times and suddenly his cum gushed into my throat and all over my face. I didn't quite know what had happened until he explained it to me. After that he fondled my small erection in a manner that excited me more than anything I had ever experienced.

This became a daily occurrence and I counted the hours between visits. When we ran into one another during school hours, just a glance down at his boots gave me an instant erection. I thought of nothing but bringing Bartlett's boots to a high gloss and receiving my reward. He fellated me as often as I did him.

One day, however, he made me strip and lie facedown on the floor. Then, placing one foot on my back, he said, "You're a beautiful little guy, almost as pretty as a girl, and you're my own fag. Today I'm going to show you what my riding boots are for." Slowly he mounted me, applied some sweet-smelling salve to my ass, and entered me. I had never know such pain, nor such pleasure. My master fucked me brutally and remained astride for quite a while before dismounting. "Too good to be true," he said and I agreed with him wholeheartedly. I think of him every time and it's never gotten better.

Shooting Par

Anonymous

I had numerous sexual encounters before "The First Time." My prepuberty childhood in the late 1940s was in a neighborhood of contemporaries where all sorts of sexual encounters were made. There were heterosexual encounters, homosexual experiments, a little bondage, and some incest thrown in for good measure. I can't remember a period of time after the third grade when the neighborhood gang wasn't "playing nasty" in some shed, field, or abandoned house. And I remember quite clearly that I always thought sex with the boys was much more interesting.

I count the "first time" as the time when there was an actual climax involved. The first time was when we were no longer kids experimenting with our bodies, but old enough to go for an orgasm.

His name was Jack, and I thought he was quite sexy for his fourteen years. I was twelve. He had the hots for my best friend's sister, and it was rumored they had "gone all the way." I thought the girl unattractive, and wondered why Jack was interested in her. I know now that I was just envious of his attention to her.

In the seventh grade, I went to a new school and met Jack coming home on the bus. He was giving all the new students a bad time and hazing them. I tried to stay away from him, but when we got off the bus, he chased me, pushed me up against a telephone pole, and pulled out a tube of lipstick. I begged him not to paint my lips. The humiliation would have been too great. Instead, he slowly marked my forehead and face, calling me bad names as he did so. When he was finished I had a raging hard-on. He noticed it, grunted, and walked away.

A few weeks later I saw him driving balls on the golf course. I remembered the hard-on I got when he hazed me, so I went to him and started talking. He was quite good at hitting golf balls. I asked what would happen if he hit one in the woods to his left. He said that he could easily find it in the woods. I said he could not, and he challenged me to a bet: if he found the ball, I would suck him off. I could feel my dick getting hard. I said the bet was on, and he hit a ball out of sight into the woods. We followed.

In no time he had a golf ball in his hand, swearing it was the one he had hit. The next thing I saw, his pants were down and a nice, straight, hard six-inch dick was pointed at my mouth. I said no. He said yes, and we argued. He said he was not going to let me go until I had fulfilled my part of the bargain. I must have been the most reluctant cocksucker of all time. There was his dick: big, beautiful, hard, and looking delicious. I wanted it so badly, but feared it so much. Somehow I knew I was no longer playing nasty with the neighborhood gang anymore. This was for real and maybe forever.

When I finally took it in my mouth, I had no regrets. It was the most exciting thing I had ever done. It was a passage in life. Suddenly this sexy older guy who had fucked girls now had his dick in my mouth. I had him by his most tender organ, and he was enjoying it. He kept telling me how to do it better; he yelled not to bite him and to watch my teeth, and I begged him not to come in my mouth. Of course, he did anyway. When it was over, he walked away with a golf ball in his hand and two empty balls in his pants. It did not occur to me that I should also have an orgasm.

A week later and after much guilt and fear of social and divine punishment, I could stand it no longer. I went back to the golf course. He was in the same place, hitting balls. I spoke. He grunted. I asked if he would like to look for a golf ball in the woods. Without even glancing at me, he hit a ball into the woods, and I eagerly followed him in. Only this time he did not have to coach me to give him pleasure. After all, this was my second time.

For the next year, Jack broke me into the world of male-on-male sex. We had quickies in the woods, in public bathrooms, and when no one was home, we made out in his house. I'll never forget the first time he fucked me. It was so painful that I begged him to quit. Thankfully, he did not quit, and in time it became his favorite thing to do when we were together. One time during a session, we lay in a sixty-nine position and for a few minutes he took my dick in his mouth. He never did it again, and I thought it strange that he would do such a thing. After all, I was the "queer" one. It did not occur to me until much later that he was repressing his own sexual feelings.

A few years after high school we ran into each other on the street. I asked if he remembered me. He looked at me for a second, grunted no, and walked away. I was not upset by his rejection. He had given me a thorough education in male-on-male sex, and I will never forget the first time and the first person in my sexual life.

E.J., First Love

Robert Mahoney

It was during CYO baseball the summer I was
halfway fourteen, my jeans straining to conceal
the evidence, and E.J. gone thirteen that
month, not long budded and impatient with
nature's pace, that we sensed the attraction.

Neither of us could put a name to it or
define it, but we understood its power and
design as it drew us back from the pack on
the long walk home from games, diverting
us behind fences and hedges, and luring us
to grass blankets, there to entwine and
grope the forbidden places — adolescent
horseplay to the casual observer, but we
knew its secret dimension.

One afternoon in September we lay side by
side on E.J.'s bed enjoying Notre Dame whip
old Purdue, when the halftime whistle
signaled my call, but E.J. stilled my hand,
reminding me the younger children of the house
were about and might wander in and out.

"Spend the night," E.J. told a face betraying
disappointment in a mission failed; the invitation
a first, though we'd camped together bound up
in zippered bags and fully clothed, our bodies
never touching.

I had no experience of an advanced nature in
our preoccupation, nor did E.J.; instinct alone
guiding us in the pillow fight that left us
naked, mingled, and rampant; E.J.'s sex urgent
against my lips and (I assumed) requesting entry;

24

so, I parted them (never thinking to request the
password) and E.J. slipped in.

The choreography seemed right for the music
and after the *finale* I expected a bow, but E.J.
swept from our stage, neither word nor gesture
his gift, leaving me confused and alone in that
unfamiliar setting to ponder what went wrong.

Early Sunday morning I awoke to confront E.J.
framed in the doorway, arms folded and eyes
accusing, who greeted me with: *"You* knew *I had
to serve ten o'clock mass!"* implying I had
lured him into *mortal* sin, and that our less
sophisticated performances of similar nature
(and result) were merely *venial* and no impediment
to his receiving the Host in a state of Grace.

If E.J. felt his soul in jeopardy that morning
at solemn mass it failed to register on his
cherubic countenance as his tongue accepted the
sacred wafer from the hand of the monsignor, an
inquisitor who would have probed deeply any
refusal — on balance, the greater of the two
evils, E.J. must have concluded.

That same afternoon in the broad backseat of his
mother's Roadmaster, at rest in its garage safely
hidden from view and door bolted against siblings
(the lady of the house at the Bridge table), the
hypocrite advised his devil, *"It's okay if you
want to do again what you did last night."*

We became at that moment secure in our roles,
the casting consistent — for, you see, on
whichever baseball teams we ever played, E.J.
was always named pitcher and I, his catcher;
and he did not offer, then or ever, to exchange
that certain gift in kind *(a bridge he was
reluctant to cross),* though E.J. was never,
then or ever, ungenerous with an alternative
expression of fondness which sent me home
drained, if not completely satisfied.

We had three years together, midsummer to
midsummer. E.J resigned as altar boy and
I from choir; we no longer dwelled on sin,
its wages, and soon forgot our Latin.

In high school we entertained girls, E.J. and I
double-dating; but that was a time when virginity
governed and a boy might come home with lipstick
on his collar and an ache in his groin (on such
occasions, E.J. a most ardent partner once we
dropped off our dates).

Our parting had nothing to do with falling out
or conflicting orientations, though I suspect the
latter was on the horizon as E.J.'s needs and
mine diverged; the culprit was a divorce (my
family, not his), followed by relocation to
another city of a mother and her anguished son.

Though I returned to visit from time to time
during those early months of our separation and
found E.J. warm and obliging, it became clear
that my character would have a diminished role
in the chapters he was about to read — so I
wrote myself out of his story.

What remained to me were mementos, among them
a photo, since enlarged, which captures E.J.'s
essence at the peak of my obsession; a picture
in which he is: *fifteen, blond, and grinning,*
full of himself in Shetland sweater and wide
wale cords, posed to best display the fruits
of his ample basket, already promised at the
snap of the shutter to the boy behind the
camera, almost too excited to focus.

I never saw E.J. again in life, his casket
sealed at the request of the family; a highway
accident claiming their oldest child just four
days into his twenty-first year.

I had lately seen death in a different guise
and attended the funeral in a soldier's uniform;
returning alone to the church from which E.J.

was buried and had once served mass, and where
from above I had chanted my hymns.

I climbed to the loft of distant memory, and
looking down upon the communion rail I imagined
E.J., silver plate in hand poised to capture
the wafer should the priest misjudge, glancing
up and smiling at me as if to confirm a promise.
Then softly, so no one else could hear, I
sang a *Requiem* for my first love:
E.J.B., 1931–1952

Peer Knowledge

Anonymous

We were seated side by side on a low wooden platform, amidst a forest of oil field equipment, on a deserted spot at the edge of the little Oklahoma town of Seminole in 1939.

I was an innocent thirteen. Weldon, my ninth-grade neighbor, was a year older and quite worldly in my eyes.

"Do you know," he asked with a smirk, "why a woman's cunt is like a frying pan?"

"No," I said.

"Well, you have to grease them both before you put the meat in."

I pretended to understand.

"Have you learned how to jack off yet, Billy?" he asked.

"What's jack off?"

"You take your cock in your hand and stroke it up and down until you come."

"Until you what?"

"Come, stupid."

"Oh."

He slid his hand onto my leg and moved it purposefully up to my crotch, then wrapped it around my small but swelling penis.

"I'll show you," Weldon said.

We both unbuttoned and he placed his hand over my rigid dick. He first stroked downward, causing the foreskin to slide down, leaving the glans exposed. Then he reversed the motion. Up and down, up and down. I was making little whimpering noises and squirming with delight.

Then he bent over and put his mouth over my tiny cock. The feeling of the warm saliva, the movement of his tongue, and the tugging suction sent a hot thrill up through my groin and into the head of my dick. I felt myself swell even more.

After a bit he sat up. "You don't have much down there yet but it'll grow."

"Here," he said, and placed my hand on his hard cock. It was considerably bigger than mine. He helped me move my hand down and up, down and up, exposing the head, then concealing it with his foreskin.

"Go down on it and take it in your mouth," he commanded.

"What does it taste like?"

"Like a piece of fat."

I leaned over, placed my mouth tentatively over the end, and, liking the taste, lunged downward — too hard because he said, "Don't use your teeth."

I got the hang of it quickly enough (as if I were meant to) and Weldon began to get excited. He had me work on his rod more and more rapidly, finally placing his hand on the back of my head and pushing my lips and nose all the way down into the black hair that enclosed his penis.

Then he announced: "I'm gonna shoot." He gave three quick thrusts and his cock seemed to jump and salute in my mouth. "I'm coming," he moaned.

My mouth filled with liquid spurts of a warm saltiness. He grunted, sighed, and relaxed. Slowly his prick started to soften. I pulled away and dribbled his cum onto the ground and spat.

He said, "When you jack off till you come, your cum spurts out like milky white stuff."

After a moment he said, "Okay, your turn." He bent over and again took my penis into his mouth. Thrill after thrill coursed through me until I reached a climax of delicious intensity. My cock pulsed and throbbed and jumped in his mouth and exploded in my first orgasm. I let out a shout of delighted wonder. I had no idea then that this was the beginning of a life of total male sexual commitment — if not always contentment.

He sat up and wiped his lips.

"Nothing came out, though," he said. "You didn't shoot any cum. Maybe it'll take a few times jacking off to get your milky cum stuff started."

"Oh," I responded.

"But don't do it too often."

"Why?" I asked. "Will you run out?"

"I don't know about that," Weldon said. "It's supposed to cause pimples and if you do it too much it'll eventually make you go blind and drive you crazy."

Big Red

William Parker Vaughn

1940s, age 15

I was twenty-five months old when my father was killed in a train accident. My mother was only twenty. We had returned to my hometown to live with Mother's parents.

I was close to three cousins who were about the same age as I was. Rolena, Billy Joe, and I experimented with sex from the age of five or six until we all went to high school. Billy Joe and I were about the same age and I considered him handsome and would always try to get him to undress in front of me. While riding our bicycles, the three of us shared our ever-changing but always-growing knowledge of sex.

Like most youngsters of that era, we never were taught any sexual facts by any adult family member. Our information came only from our peers.

My freshman year in high school, I continued to be fascinated by the young men around me much more than by any of the girls. I loved the physical contact in health and physical education classes. I loved the smells associated with the boys' gym and the locker rooms. Like most freshmen, I soon began to associate with just a small number of fellow classmates. One redheaded boy by the name of Vern appealed to me more than any other. His bright red hair fascinated me, and I got strange feelings in the pit of my stomach when I saw him naked in the shower and dressing room. I followed him around as much as I could. We shared homeroom and several other classes during the day.

Our school was an old four-story building built before the turn of the century. The main locker rooms were in the basement. The boys' locker room was at one end and the girls' at the other. There was a restroom right next door to both. During breaks before or after each class, Vern and I were often in the locker room changing books or just preparing to go home in the evening. The lockers were two-tiered, lined up in rows with benches in the middle. My locker was on the lower level and Vern's was on the upper lever just about three doors down. On several occasions I managed to make contact with what I considered to be some of Vern's most impressive body parts. I would manage to touch his butt, grab him from behind and press my front side up tight against his backside, and let my hand brush against his large penis.

One afternoon we had both been involved in some after-school affair and were in the locker room getting ready to go home. It was empty except for the two of us. I could feel the tension building up. I was down on one knee putting books in my locker. I had already put on my winter coat. To this day, I remember the blue-green color of that coat. Vern was watching me and I returned his gaze. His eyes were staring right at mine and I saw him lower his hand to stroke his groin. The words coming from his mouth were what I had wanted to hear for a long time. He said, "You really want this, don't you?" My head nodded and he proceeded to unzip his trousers. He reached in and pulled out his beautiful and very erect penis. I immediately leaned forward and put my lips on the head, then let it slide into my mouth and throat. I never gagged at all and the whole action seemed to be something that I had been destined to do.

An empty locker room is not a particularly safe place to be doing what we both knew was not a usual activity. Vern pulled his cock out of my mouth and said we could go into the boys' restroom for more privacy. He zipped up and we walked into the empty restroom area and into one of the stalls. Vern lowered his pants again.

I got a real close-up of that beautiful cock and very red pubic hair. The manly aroma coming up into my nostrils was sexually exciting.

I started to suck and lick my way from the head of his cock to its base, fingering his balls and letting my other hand touch the cheeks of his fuzzy ass. Next I took both hands and reversed his position, giving me a full view of his backside. My tongue moved to the crack that separated the cheeks of his ass. I licked my way down and he bent over to receive the special attention that I was giving him. My left hand was between his legs, gripping his hard cock. I held up his shirt with my right hand for a better view of his backside. When he turned back around, I saw something I had never seen before or since. The head of his cock was so big, so shiny, so slick, and so purple it looked as if it would burst at any moment. I put that beautiful cock back down my throat and moved it in and out as fast as I could.

Almost immediately I heard the sound coming from within and felt the muscles of his body react to my movements. He was really getting pleasure from my actions, and I was pleased to be serving him. I knew that something was about to happen and that I was going to enjoy it immensely. I had masturbated many times by myself and with my cousins. While I had never tasted any man's semen before, I was ready for it. The first gush shot out on my tongue and I savored the taste as I tried to swallow it and all of the gushes that followed.

As I finally released Vern's cock from my mouth, one last spurt of semen dropped onto my blue-green coat. I took my finger and rubbed it into the material. Vern pulled his trousers back up.

This was the first of many sessions to follow, always after school and always in that same stall. Did Vern return the pleasure? Yes, and once he brought his friend Paul for me to service.

31

Our relationship continued throughout our freshman and sophomore years in high school. Following my sophomore year, my mother and stepfather moved us out of the city and I never saw Vern or Paul again. I never will forget Vern. I can still close my eyes and bring back a clear image of his body as he turned to show me that beautiful big cock with the huge purple head. They say that each man's semen has a different taste. Even after fifty years, I rub the roof of my mouth with my tongue and taste Vern all over again. I have tried without success to find him several times during my lifetime. Red hair still does things to me. I should have kept that old blue-green coat with the spot of semen that never faded.

The Bible Salesman

T.B.F.

My first time was with a Bible salesman the summer the war ended, 1945. I met him on a bus trip from Greensboro, North Carolina, to Culpepper, Virginia. I never saw him before or after that one time.

School had let out and I was on my way to stay with a great-aunt, Granddad's older sister, where I would help with yard and garden chores for the summer. It was between my second and third years in high school so I must have been sixteen. I had been jacking off regular for about two years and had now and then played grab-cock with boys in the gym showers — nothing heavy yet — not that I wasn't into cock-watching a'ready. But I hadn't started making out with either boys or girls before that summer.

When my bus left Greensboro, it was packed without a seat to spare. At Danville, Virginia, several people got off, including the fat woman in the aisle seat beside me. A muscular gray-haired man, old enough to be my pa, moved from across the aisle to take the seat. He carried only a flat sample case and light raincoat.

Right away, after the bus started rolling, he asked questions. Where was I from? Where was I going? How old was I? He'd get my attention by patting my thigh and drumming his fingers. I was conscious of him all the time he talked, and of the way his hand kept inching up toward my crotch. He spread his legs wide so his knee bumped mine. I pulled my leg away several times until I got tired of holding it back, then I just let it rest alongside his. He didn't seem to mind, and it felt good even though I could feel myself getting horny from his patting and my leg resting up against his.

Then he began saying things like "Those cows in that field sure look like they could use a bull about now," or "I'm wearing a new pair of Jockeys and the way this bus swings around them curves they sure are riding up on me." He'd grab his crotch and pull down, saying, "I've got to get me some ball room." I didn't know how to answer, him being an older man.

We had a rest stop when we got to Lynchburg. I needed to get to the restroom real bad. The men's room was crowded and we had to wait our turn. I was able to cruise a fine collection of cocks — some short, some middling, and some nice thick ones with foreskins too. I like the way men with foreskins always skin their dicks way back so the pink cock head shows before they let fly. When our turn came, we stood side by side. I unbuttoned and immediately let go with a heavy head of pressure. My friend stood watching me piss and under his breath admired the size and shape of my dick. He wasn't making much progress himself. I looked over and saw that, although he was not full hard, the rim and head of his dick were puffed out and flaming red. He shook and skinned it back several times trying to make the piss flow, but it just seemed to stay the same, or maybe even get a little thicker. Watching him made my dick start to rise. I tucked it away but it pushed out the front of my pants, so I had to keep my hands in my pockets to hold things down as I walked back to the bus.

It was dusk when we got rolling again. To my disappointment (because I thought he might start something interesting) my old gentleman friend said he'd try to get some sleep. He put his seat back and spread his raincoat over his knees like a blanket. I looked out the window for a while, but after it got dark there was nothing much to see — just lights going by. The driver turned out the interior lights and everyone quieted down and soon appeared to be dozing or actually sleeping. So I put my seat back too, covered my lap with my jacket, and fell asleep almost immediately.

In my dreams I went to all manner of familiar and strange places. Finally I wound up in the shower room at the high school gym with my wrestling partner. We stood under showers and I had a hard-on. His back was to me at first. When he turned, his hard cock stuck straight out at me. I reached out to feel his boner and he moved his soapy hand to my belly and began rubbing it around and moving closer to my crotch. When finally he took aholt of it, I felt my wet dream coming to a head. I struggled to awaken because I was just enough aware of where I was to know I didn't want to mess up my pants with cum.

I awakened to find it was not all a dream. The old gentleman had spread his raincoat over my legs and his right hand was feeling me up and squeezing my dick under my jacket. I froze up and did nothing while he went on playing with my privates and getting me hot all over again. I am not sure when he became aware that I was again awake. Finally he whispered, "Unbutton and take it out so I can hold it. No one will see with your jacket on your lap."

It never crossed my mind to say no. I unbuttoned and my prick jumped out. He wrapped his fingers completely around it and pressed. It felt wonderful and sent goose bumps from the back of my neck down to my toes. At sixteen you can get a powerful hard-on fast, but it comes with a short fuse. He twisted and jacked my cock skin and rubbed my cock head with his palm. In less than three minutes — bam, bam, bam — I practically shot my cum through the back of his hand. He enjoyed it as much as me. We used his handkerchief to clean my prick and his hand.

We didn't have time to do anything more, because by then we were entering Lynchburg and would be at the bus station in a minute. My companion stood up in the aisle and got his small sample case down from the overhead rack. The case was full of all kinds of Bibles. He gave me a vest pocket Testament bound in artificial red leather and told me, "Have a good life."

I thanked him, but thought it a mite peculiar that a Bible man was the first person, besides myself, to jack me off. I still have the Testament. It's not been used much. It brings back memories of when I was just beginning to be a man.

That's about it. It was a good session, but far from the best memory I ever had about gay sex. One-on-one, fifty-fifty sharing is way better than just being done by someone else.

That experience was the first in a long chain of gay action, but I doubt it made me gay. If it wasn't the Bible man on the bus, it would've been another man someplace else. Later that summer I had my first whack at sex with a girl in Culpepper. She had been around the block many times before I met up with her. It was a disaster. I lost my hard and was shamed almost to death. If I had been straight by nature, wouldn't you think that being with a naked girl and offered every opportunity to have your way with her would override the experience of an old man jacking you off in a bus? That hardly makes sense to me. No, I would have been gay whether or not I'd met the Bible man.

.

A Snowy Night in Vermont

Anonymous

1930s, age 20

From my perspective as an octogenarian, I'd say I've been gay for all of my life. Early on, I learned to masturbate by frenetically humping the mattress of my crib, and I know that before I was six I got a kick out of seeing penises on museum statues. When old enough to clip pictures from movie magazines, I always went for actors — Richard Barthelmess or Wallace Reid — never pretty actresses.

Before puberty I fantasized myself in a prone position with somewhat older boys lying on top of me. The picture later substituted burly truck drivers for these youths. And at thirteen, studying photographs of handsome Charles Lindbergh wearing macho boots and breeches, I masturbated to the fantasy of myself kneeling in front of him, taking his penis in my mouth.

I didn't label myself till fourteen, and then only after listening to a strange conversation. Our family was driving home to Connecticut from a visit in New York. My older sister and mother were discussing theater. "Eva Le Gallienne's a lesbian," said my sister, and my mother asked, "What's a lesbian?" to which the reply was: "A female homosexual." Grace went on to explain that Josephine Hutchinson's husband had sued her for divorce, naming Le Gallienne as correspondent. I inferred that a guy who liked guys must be a *male* homosexual, and that must mean me.

I checked the dictionary when we got home, and concluded that I was indeed a homosexual. There followed a series of visits to our local library, checking the indexes of every book on psychology. I found few references to homosexuality, most of them classifying it as a disease. Not too encouraging, but at least an indication that I wasn't the only one.

It wasn't till my senior year in college that I had a real consensual encounter. True, I'd fantasized a good deal through the intervening years. I jerked off several times a week while thinking about good-looking classmates, some of whom I suspected of being gay, but I never dared make an overture. We sometimes might talk about homosexuality, yet wouldn't risk revealing ourselves.

There were rumors that the dean of men had gay inclinations, and I gave some credence to them. Well, it turned out that the dean had his eye on me. Using one of my instructors as intermediary, he invited me to dinner in a nearby town. On the appointed night, as it started to snow, we set forth in his car. When we'd gone a couple of miles on the ten-mile trip, the snow got heavier and heavier. So we turned back. There was no talk of sex — just the idea of a compatible, conversational dinner.

Back at the dean's apartment we raided the fridge and he prepared a pleasant meal. We talked about unimportant college matters. The evening passed quickly.

At about 11 p.m., when it was time for him to drive me to my dormitory, it was still snowing — typical of northern New England, where we were — and there was too heavy an accumulation for us to move the car. There was no alternative to my sharing his double bed.

During the night we were both restless, and at one point, when I rolled around, my hand touched his cock, which immediately sprang to life. I didn't withdraw. He rolled over on top of me, so that our cocks rubbed against each other. We gradually gained speed, and in short order we both came.

This proved to be the start of a relationship. Although he was forty-two and I only twenty, we really hit it off. For the next six years, I spent several weeks of each summer visiting his place on Cape Cod. In those days Nauset Beach was a deserted area of sand: we could bathe nude without an audience, and even enjoy a sixty-nine in the dunes. Nights were marked by a drink and sex.

Our affair lasted through the summer of 1940. In the spring of '41 I was drafted into the army. But I had learned enough from Burt to give myself an active sex life. The bashfulness that had marked my early college years was supplanted by a confidence that made cruising easy. During the ensuing war years I had lots of sex in New York, London, and Paris, with civilians as well as members of the Royal Air Force, Royal Artillery, British navy, and our own U.S. forces.

After the war I lived for a while in Greenwich Village, cruising bars and Washington Square. Eventually I lost interest in one-night stands. I'm now in the eleventh year of a loving relationship that I trust will last the rest of my life. It's even better than the one that started on a snowy night in Vermont.

Climb on Top

Jack Austin

1948, age 26

I met Cal on shipboard where I was a deck officer and he a radar man. I'm not sure what attracted me to him, but I liked him the instant I saw him. Maybe it was his laughing eyes, flat across the bottom and arched across the top.

I contrived to talk with him many times and, one day, I urged him to climb a small mountain with me and fry some steaks. After work, we set out. It wasn't much of a mountain, but it was fun scrambling up it, building a fire, and frying up dinner. I had also brought a bottle of good Canadian whiskey along, and after eating, we did some drinking.

I got pretty woozy and managed to tell him that I liked guys. He told me he had thought so but he liked me and was going to see if a good lay wouldn't cure me. I managed to get pretty sick about this time, but he got me back to the ship okay.

The next day was a trial. I was not accustomed to strong drink, and I went about my duties on shipboard with an air of abstraction, interrupted with a number of trips to the head, where I vainly tried to throw up some more.

When our ship returned to the States, Cal and I hung out together and he tried to interest me in a succession of women. While I played along, the women he fancied did not appeal to me, and nothing seemed to work out. I wanted *him!* During this period, he told me a lot about himself and of how he would screw any woman in sight. He told me of trying to get into a ten-year-old and getting caught; of the time he came nine times in his girl with the same hard-on after having been abstinent for almost six months at sea; of one girl he had and then, a week later, of having her mother; of the girl who was so tight he was unable to penetrate her; of the girl who finally and most reluctantly, after much urging, applied her mouth to the end of his cock and how hard he tried to come after promising her that he certainly would not come in her mouth. In short, it was a revealing sexual history.

He and I, though worlds apart in background, education, and morals, became firm friends. I did manage to awaken in him some urge to better himself. I made him a present of a dictionary and on the flyleaves I hand-lettered several sayings that I had always enjoyed, such as, "No man is an island..." and "This above all, unto thine own self be true..." He was pleased with the gift and we even went to a performance of the Philadelphia Symphony, which he also seemed to enjoy.

▼

I had borrowed my mother's car while our ship spent a month and a half in Baltimore, and as the time for our departure drew close, I had to get the car back to Connecticut. And so, about a week before we sailed, we arranged for a couple of days off, drove to New York City, and went barhopping until 3 a.m., when we decided to begin the drive to Connecticut. We were both tired so I drove into a residential section near the George Washington Bridge, parked on a side street, and we prepared to sleep for a while. I placed my legs over to the right of the car, and he stretched his legs under mine toward the left. I pulled an old army blanket over us.

I sank into sleep and began to dream that someone was trying to slide their hand up my pant leg. I liked the feeling and felt frustrated that the hand couldn't get far up, because my pants were too tight and they bunched up. Then I became aware of a hand on my erect cock jerking me off, and that my right hand also held a cock which I was enthusiastically pumping. As I fully woke up and realized what was going on, I came to a great, shuddering climax and immediately felt myself preparing for another. At last, I opened my eyes and realized it was daylight. Though we were still covered by a blanket, anyone looking in could tell what was afoot. With regret, I stopped caressing his stomach and let go of his cock. We straightened ourselves out, buttoned our flies, and proceeded to my mother's home.

It was a beautiful drive, with little traffic. We did not talk much, absorbed in our thoughts. When we arrived I introduced Cal to my mom, then took him on a tour of the lovely old town. We returned to the house, had lunch, and went up to my room to take a nap.

There was a twin bed and a daybed in my room. I gave Cal some pajama bottoms, put some on myself, and told him to take the twin bed. I started to take the stuff off the daybed so I could stretch out too.

Cal lay on his back and watched me slowly take the books and papers off the daybed. I guess my wish to be on the same bed with him came through clearly. He smiled and said, "If you'll be a good boy, you can join me on this bed." I immediately stopped my desultory work, and climbed onto the bed beside him. I lay on my left side facing him and he lay on his back next to the wall. It was getting dark in the room and I was fully erect. My cock stuck out the fly of my pajamas and as it got rock hard, the tip touched his leg. There was silence, then he said, "You've got a hard-on, haven't you?"

"Yeah."

"Turn on the light. I want to see it."

I rolled over and pulled on the light at the head of the bed, then pulled my hard dick entirely out of my fly. He pulled his out also, and we compared equipment. He said, "Gosh, you're big. It'll take some woman to handle all that." Then he insisted I get a ruler to measure my seven-odd inches. (Actually, my dick is pretty thick, though to judge from all the men I have seen, not unduly long.)

I turned out the light, and lay down again. I was on my left side, but almost on my stomach. Cal was lying on his right side. After a long pause, Cal suddenly threw his left leg over my legs, his left arm over my shoulders, and said, "You know what I'm going to do?"

"No," I said, "what are you going to do?"

"I'm going to go to sleep and have a wet dream and come all over you."

There ensued a long pause. "Well," I said, "if you're going to come all over me, you're going to have to climb on top of me."

Cal got on me and lay with his stomach on my back. It felt warm and good. I could feel his hard-on on my butt, and after a moment, I twitched my butt so the crack of my ass kind of gripped his hard cock. He whispered in my ear, "You devil, you."

I sort of chuckled and twitched again. Then we lay quietly for a while and I finally said, "You know, it would be a shame to get both of these pajama pants messed up when you come."

We took off our bottoms. I lay down on my stomach and expected Cal to lie on top of me again, but instead, he spread my legs apart, knelt between my knees, and, supporting himself with one hand on the bed, grabbed his erect cock with his other hand and began to poke at my asshole. Naturally, I tightened up and the more he pushed, the tighter I got. I gasped out in a whisper, "Wait. I've got to relax." He continued to push and it hurt a little, then he backed off and put a lot of spit on the head of his dick and went back to pushing. This time, as I relaxed somewhat more, and with the lubrication, the head of his cock gained entry and he slowly pushed himself all the way into me. Incredible feeling! I liked it and never felt closer to Cal than I did at that moment of full penetration.

Once he was fully in, he lay down on top of me again and slowly began the old in and out. I contrived to rise up to meet his thrusts and to pull away during his withdrawals. I also tightened my sphincter as he withdrew, and loosened it as he thrust in. The sensations were tremendous and exciting. This went on for ten to fifteen minutes and both of us were breathing heavily and somewhat raggedly, when he whispered into my right ear, "I'm going to come. Do you want me to pull out?"

"No. Stay right in there."

Shortly after that, he increased his tempo too much for me to keep up. I just lay there and enjoyed the sensations that brought me to a trembling pitch. He finally grunted, thrust as deep as he could, and stayed there. His body tensed and I could feel his stomach and pelvic muscles quivering as he came inside me.

He lay on top of me for a few minutes while our breathing settled down. I twitched my butt and tried, using my pelvis and sphincter, to rouse him again, but it was not to be. He pulled out. I rolled over on my back and said, "Cal. Jerk me off." He sat on the edge of the bed, grasped my rigid member with his right hand, and began pumping. I asked him to tighten his grasp a bit and, in due course, I orgasmed, spewing my cum all over my stomach and chest. It was as good a sensation as had been the morning event.

We continued to hang out together and he even got me together with a lady of the evening once. She tried and I wanted to, but I was unable to get an erection, so the event was a fizzle. Eventually, our time together came to an end when I was transferred to another ship, though we did keep in sporadic touch.

Our paths separated. I taught school in New England and Cal got married and became an electrician. I saw him only once again and, except for one phone conversation after I married, I have not heard from him. Since my divorce and coming out I've tried a number of times to locate him, but without success. I really blew what might have become a real relationship, though I do not know, given his tomcatting background, if it might have had a chance. But not to have seized the moment is a sad thing to look back upon from my seventy-some years. Carpe diem!!!

2. The Wonder Bread Years (1949-1959)

I've divided this book into six eras. I had hoped, in the introduction to each section, to broadly characterize that period. But life doesn't always cooperate with such goals. Experiences in the fifties were so varied that it's impossible to briefly sum them up.

For guys in their early and midteens, there's not much change from earlier years. You could still mess around with a buddy. You knew enough to be discreet, but it was no cause for heavy guilt trips or worry.

I commented earlier on what I call "apprenticeships in malehood" of the thirties and forties. Such relationships are rarer in the fifties. The narrator of "Tokyo Awakening" recounts an experience of this sort, but there weren't many others. Instead, there is more fumbling and experimentation by two inexperienced boys, rather than one showing the other how things work.

For men in their late teens and beyond, there is also more furtiveness. Joseph Itiel not only used a false name for his first encounter, he even claimed to be from Denmark. This wasn't mere paranoia. Thousands of people lost their jobs during the McCarthy witch-hunts because of homosexuality or alleged homosexuality.

Fortunately, the fifties weren't grim for everyone. There's a good bit of rapture, for example, in Bud Berkeley's recollections. Those who enjoy his story "White Nights" will be happy to learn that he later founded the Uncircumcised Society of America, and has written an entertaining, erotic, and quite informative book on what is clearly his favorite subject: *Foreskin*.

Perhaps most remarkable, two contributors had their first experiences with men who were comfortably and openly gay; those stories are told in "Finding the New World" and "Poetry."

In all, this was a varied and fascinating set of stories. I have great admiration for all the men who were able to come out during a period when the rest of the country was determined that they shouldn't.

Jacking Cousins

Lynn Jeffries

My first sexual experience was in the summer of 1957, when I was five. My partner was my cousin Sam, who was thirteen. Those facts alone would suggest he molested me. Nothing could be further from the truth.

Sam was born in the midst of World War II, while his father was in the army. His father saw him only a time or two, because he was ordered to Europe shortly after Sam's birth. A month before VE Day he and some buddies went looking for souvenirs in a Belgian farmhouse they thought had been liberated from the Germans. A sniper was still hidden inside, and Uncle Randall died instantly in the yard.

Sam spent his fourth birthday, Veterans' Day 1947, standing between his mother and mine, who were sisters, on a Kentucky hillside at the reburial service when his father's body was moved from Flanders stateside. Shortly after, his mother remarried, and for reasons I've never been told, he lived with our grandparents, even though his mother and stepfather lived just down the street.

That information is relevant because it led to our sharing the bed where our sexual encounter occurred. Sam put up a good front to the world. He seemed happy-go-lucky, running around with a big bunch of guys, getting into all sorts of mischief, participating in various sports, starring in basketball early on. Still, those of us in the family knew the secret he kept from the outside. Suppressing his response to a fatherless childhood had led to a problem: he was a bedwetter. He may still be; he was when he married and moved out at nineteen.

To keep from having the mattress ruined, our practical grandmother bought a rubber sheet. At five I was spending alternate Friday nights at my grandparents'. Since kids that age often have bedwetting problems too, Ma decided that night I would sleep with Sam instead of my usual spot in her bed.

I didn't mind, because Sam had always been my hero. Most of our relatives are short and fat, and I was already showing signs of moving toward the 360 pounds plus I am today, and I'm not the largest in the family. Sam, on the other hand, took after his father's family: tall, thin, with dark brown hair and deep brown eyes. He was lots of fun. I adored him, even though he teased me constantly. As an only child, I suppose I relished the attention.

Sam also had no modesty at all. He slept in white briefs and ran around the house in them each morning when he got up and each evening as he prepared for bed. I can still see him prancing through the living room wearing his clean shorts as a hat, his large, young genitals bouncing for all the world to see in the yellow-stained ones he'd slept in. Apparently he also takes after his father's family in the development of that part of his body. I've come to realize that my early fascination with his crotch was the first stirring of my gay sexuality. I didn't know how to explain it, but I really, really wanted to share his bed.

Sam always got to stay out a couple of hours after dark on Friday, so Ma put me to bed before he got home. I was asleep when he crawled into the double bed, waking briefly as the rubber sheet rustled. Then everything was quiet for a while.

At some point I awakened, probably from the gentle rocking of the old bedsprings. To my surprise, there lay Sam, his briefs below his knees, the full moon flooding through the open blinds over his rock-hard adolescent cock, which pointed at his chin as his hand moved slowly up and down. I had never before seen a hard cock, and my own teeny weenie got stiff as I contemplated how much bigger his was.

What Sam was doing looked exciting and fun, and my reaching over to join him seemed the perfectly natural thing to do. He hesitated as I clasped my smaller hand around his shaft, clearly surprised I was awake and shocked at what I was doing. But apparently my hand felt good, for he lay back and let me play for quite a while, with both his cock and his balls. Then he replaced my hand with his, and I watched until he came, pulled up his shorts immediately, rolled away from me, and went to sleep. Then, of course, we both wet the bed before we woke up.

The next morning I followed him into the bathroom as he took his morning bath. I reached down into the water and tried again to grasp his big balls. He grabbed my wrist, stopping me short. He looked me in the eye and said, "You can't do this. What we did last night is wrong and dirty, and you'd better never tell anybody."

We never had sex in any form again, but he continued his nearly nude parades for the next six years, and I continued to watch and want.

The summer I was nine, I found his wet swimming trunks hanging on the line. Since no one was around, I took them behind the smokehouse where I knew the box from our grandparents' new refrigerator was waiting until the trash collector came. I crawled inside, took off all my clothes, and pulled them on. Because of the difference in our builds, they fit almost perfectly. They were blue-gray stretch fabric, wet and cold. I winced as their clamminess touched my balls, which instantly tried to retract from the chill. Still, I wore them for a half hour as I played with my stiff little prick, recalling that night four years earlier. Then I was afraid someone would find me, so I pulled them off, dressed quickly, and sneaked them back unto the line.

I attended every basketball game he played, ogling those long legs in their white shorts trimmed in green, remembering what was between them.

I later had a three-year sexual thing with his half brother, two years older than I. He taught me oral sex, and I was the group cocksucker for him and all his buddies. When he taught me how to masturbate the year Sam was in college and I was ten, I had my first complete orgasm in the same bed where I had helped Sam get off. It was Sam, not his brother, I was thinking of.

I continued to fantasize about him until I had finished college, but I never even saw him totally naked again. And we certainly have never talked about that night.

Today, Sam is fifty-one, with three daughters and four granddaughters. He retired two years ago after thirty years in an auto factory. Most of the brown hair is gone (another genetic gift from his father's family), and the tall, thin frame now carries a bit of a gut. He attends one of the most conservative Baptist churches in town.

I live a few miles away and see him at all family gatherings. I haven't fantasized about him in years, but I do notice he still looks hot in his jeans, and their basket is still well packed. He'd make some guy into water sports a fine, sexy lover. For now, though, I tend to look more at his sons-in-law.

Eyes Closed

David R. Matteson

Perhaps my grandmother meant well. But she sure could be snoopy.

My grandparents, my aunt, and I had returned from a hell-and-brimstone tent revival meeting. I had been feeling a little guilty for masturbating the night before, and when, in the final prayers, the evangelist asked, "Every head bowed, every eye closed ... Now, if there is something you feel guilty about, raise your hand" — I had raised my hand.

Now Grandma was giving me The Inquisition about what I had done that I felt guilty about. At first I said nothing; I was only eleven, and I didn't know what to say. But she asked again. When, trying a third time, she said, "David, I think it's important that you tell me so I can help you," a wave of anger went through me. The words were out before I'd thought. "Grandma, you were supposed to have your eyes closed, and it's none of your business."

▼

That had been a year earlier. I'd seriously considered not spending the usual two weeks of summer on my grandparents' farm this year. But when my family came to the farm over the Christmas holidays, I met Chris. He had come up with his father to go deer hunting. The farm was in a hilly, forested area of Pennsylvania, and deer were plentiful. Grandma supplemented the family income by renting rooms in the big farmhouse to hunters.

Chris was less than a year older than me, but already he was developing a broader chest, and the hair was getting thicker on his legs. He had a Huck Finn smile that turned me on. And, unlike the guys at my school, he was willing to spend time with me. I wasn't that interested in guns — in fact they scared me — but when he offered to teach me how to shoot his shotgun, I was delighted.

So by the time my folks were ready to leave for home, Chris and I were talking about spending a week on the farm together, come summer. I think my parents were relieved to see me finally making friends with another boy, so they persuaded Grandma to tell Chris's father that he could spend a week on the farm; of course they'd ask him to do some chores with me.

I'm sure Grandma had no idea of the kind of "chores" I was fantasizing. The week Chris joined me on the farm, Grandma's "Tourist Home" had every bedroom booked. So we would have to sleep on two roll-away cots on the sunporch, away from all the bedrooms. During the afternoon, when we were working together with Grandpa in the cow barn, I was conscious that Chris's arms were already tan, though summer had just begun. And he was already developing muscular arms. I wished my body would shape up.

When bedtime finally came, I could hardly believe, as Chris pulled off his shirt, that I could see the line of black pubic hair running clear up to his navel. I had pubic hair by then, of course, but only around my genitals. God, did he look manly! When he caught me glancing at him, that Huck Finn grin brightened his square jaw. "Let's push the cots close together," I suggested. "Then we can both listen to country music on my little radio. If we keep it soft, the folks'll never hear it."

"Neat!" he replied. I was sure Grandma's eyes were closed by this time.

"It's clear tonight," Chris said. "I'll bet we can bring in WWVA. That's my favorite station." Though I was getting into my pajamas, he simply stripped to his undershorts, and crawled in bed. He turned his back to me and held the little portable radio in his hands — giving me an excuse to snuggle close to his bare back in order to look over his shoulder to see the radio dials.

I wondered, did he like me pressed up against his back? He didn't move away. Finally we found some good country music, and he lay down on his back. By now my eyes had adjusted to the dim light of the moon, and I lay on my side looking at his developing chest. My eyes slid down to that enticing line of black hair leading from his navel into the undershorts.

We made comments on one or two country songs, and I started to doze off — and half deliberately, as I rolled onto my stomach, I let my hand fall onto his belly. I left it there limply, pretending to be asleep, but felt myself become more aroused. I could tell he was not sleeping, just playing it cool. He didn't move any closer; but he didn't move away. It was hard to wait, but another song went by. Then an announcer feigned excitement as he delivered an advertisement — and I feigned to be slightly awakened, and jerked my hand to his penis and balls. I could feel the thickness of hair — and could sense that he was becoming aroused. That was all the response I needed. I knew he wouldn't resist now — as I snuggled a bit closer and allowed my hand to fondle his genitals, until his erection was full.

I wished he would touch me, as well. And as he became more and more aroused, I reached with my other hand and placed his right hand on my hard penis. He let it stay there only a few seconds, then moved it away gently. But I was so turned on by his responsiveness, that it didn't distract me from continuing to please him. He was terribly aroused — I don't think he'd ever had sex with anyone before — and it wasn't long till he came. And I came spontaneously.

Not a word was spoken. We each rolled a bit apart. I could hear him relaxing, and beginning to fall to sleep. Suddenly I started snickering. "What's so funny?" he said. And though it was too dark to see it, I could tell by his voice that the grin was back on his handsome face. "Next Sunday's revival," I started to answer, but I was snickering too hard to finish. "I don't get it," Chris said.

But he got it when next Sunday came. In the revival tent, on the hard metal folding chairs, I sat between Chris and Grandma. The sermon was too long, but finally we got to the prayers at the end before the altar call. The evangelist intoned his usual instructions, "Every head bowed, every eye closed." And soon he was asking about "anyone who feels guilty." I touched Chris on the leg, and then looked Grandma straight in the eyes. Sure enough, her eyes were open. I continued to look at her, and just grinned silently. Chris giggled.

Bodybuilding

Elliott D. Pursell

Year not given, age 12

I was twelve the first time I had sex with another guy. I was extremely mature for a twelve-year-old. My cock had fully matured, and I had all of my pubic hair. I was about five feet ten inches, and weighed about 145 pounds. Everyone thought I looked at least eighteen years old.

I had known that I liked to look at nude guys since I was six. However, at age twelve, though I still liked to look at them, I didn't know what it meant. I knew nothing about sex. I had no idea what cocks were for — except for pissing. I did not know that cum existed, and I knew nothing about jacking off or orgasms.

I loved to look at two bodybuilder magazines that were in retrospect clearly aimed at the gay market. The magazines only had pictures in them, and the guys wore G-strings or somehow covered their cocks. Otherwise, they were nude. One of the magazines was named *Bodybuilder*. They were tiny magazines — much smaller than *Reader's Digest*. Usually I stopped at a drugstore on the way home from junior high to look at them. Many years later, I found out that the owner of the drugstore was gay. These magazines are the beginning of my sex story.

To my surprise, I had found some of these bodybuilder magazines at a magazine stand inside a department store in Richmond, Virginia. I was leafing through one when a 21-year-old guy came up and asked if I liked what I was looking at. Of course, I said yes. He was incredibly cute and superbly built, just like the models in the magazines. He told me to follow him, and he took me into a stall in a men's restroom.

After locking the door to the stall, he took both of our cocks out. Of course, we both were rigidly hard. I had no idea what was going on. His cock was enormous, and he had huge balls to go with it. My cock was a respectable seven and one-half inches long and six and one-half inches around, but it looked tiny compared to his. He was uncut, and my cock was cut. He started jacking us off, and it felt great. I didn't know that it was jacking off, but I thought anything that felt that good couldn't be bad.

Eventually, he shot a huge load of cum into the toilet. The cum was a total mystery to me. I knew it wasn't piss, but I wasn't sure what it was. I didn't cum then, and we left. I wasn't sure at all that I would ever see him again. That night, I went home and jacked off in the bathtub, and shot my cum for the first time. I'll never forget how great that felt.

The next week, I met the same guy in the same department store, and we went to another men's room. On our second or third meeting he introduced me to cock sucking. I loved getting my cock sucked, and I loved sucking his — even though I could never come close to getting all of it in my mouth. Since those were the days prior to AIDS, we usually ate each other's load. He never mentioned fucking — oral sex was the only thing that we ever did. Nor did he ever mention rimming. In retrospect, I would love to have tongue-fucked his hairy bubble butt. Occasionally, he liked to get a third guy. It was a big turn-on for him to have me watch him getting a blow job from another man. He never wanted me to participate when this happened, only to watch and jack off.

I saw this guy three or four times a month from the time that I was twelve years old until I was nineteen. I'm certain he had no idea that I was twelve when we first met, and I never told him. He probably thought I was eighteen years old like everybody else did.

This story has a funny twist to it too. Since I had never seen another hard cock before, I assumed that he was normal-sized and that I had been seriously shortchanged in the dick department. I had no idea he was extraordinary. It took me several years to figure out that my cock was fine and that I had been comparing myself to a King Kong.

I would love to know where this guy is today. He was a great sex teacher, and he was always slow and gentle with me. The first time was one of the best things that ever happened to me.

Field Trip

Oscar A. Romero

I can still feel the chill of the morning. Gray skies on a gray day. The humidity so high, one just can't feel dry. It would be such a depressing day except for the field trip.

Victor comes up next to me. Since he invited me to his birthday party he's been trying to be closer to me. I usually hang out with the others ... the better students. But he's okay. He's nice to me.

We board the bus. We are headed for the flower show. The nursery is near the ocean. The sun breaks through the clouds every so often there, but the clouds still hide the majesty of the Andes.

Victor taps my back. He is seated behind me in the school bus. His coat is on his lap; he wears a mischievous grin. I think I know what he wants. My stomach tightens. In the school bus!? He reaches for my hand and I let him guide it around the seat. His fly is open and I touch him there! He's hard and has pulled his foreskin back. It feels wet. This is thrilling! I've never really done that with mine. My foreskin is tight and it hurts to pull it all the way back — particularly when I'm hard. But Victor doesn't mind. Instead he urges me to go on; to pull his skin up over the head and then down again. He tries to do the same to me but I slow him down.

Our coats on our laps make for clumsy cover. Damn! My head is somewhere else! I want to see more, to learn more. I'm ten. Victor is almost thirteen. The older boys know so much more! At times it pisses me off that I'm the youngest, you know.

We are getting there. I bring my hand back to my lap. It's sticky. I hope I don't soil my clothes. I close my fly and straighten out, hoping that I lose my erection. Victor does the same. I look back and he's smiling. I like him. I'm shaking. I smell my hand. It smells strange; dirty yet exciting. That is weird!

We all walk off the bus and onto the sidewalk in a single line. Victor stands behind me. There's a lot of noise, but I can't see who's talking. My focus is closer to me.

As we walk around the nursery and its aisles full of beautiful flowers, Victor presses against me. I feel his erection against my butt. I like it. I like the attention he gives me. I like that he likes me. I like that he's teaching me. I ask him if we can take turns; if I can go in line behind him, from time to time. He agrees. I like feeling his ass too. It's firm and round. It feels good against me.

Damn! It's time to return to school. I don't remember seeing any flowers. I'm still walking on air. I still feel Victor hard against me. In the bus, Victor sits next to me. I'm nervous now. I don't want to be caught. My mom caught me playing doctor once with the neighbor girl and beat me. He knows so much, and it feels good. No; don't touch me now, maybe later.

Back at school Victor is asking permission to go to the bathroom and motions me to follow. I ask for permission also. We walk down the dark corridor and into the boys' room. He asks me to pull my pants down and let him get in back. Victor tells me to spread my cheeks and I obey. I don't really understand it. He holds me by the waist and I feel his moist sex enter me completely. What a new sensation! I'm confused, but I like it. He's hugging me with both hands now as he moves in and out. I'm liking it too much! He asks if I like it and I say yes, but at least I've got to pretend that I want to do it to him too. So I ask for my turn. Victor complies. I try to penetrate but I'm not sure if I'm in. When I try to go in too far, my foreskin gets pulled back and it hurts. I let him take his turn again. He pulls out and tells me he's done, that we should leave. We join the rest of the students and my first experience is over.

I know that I feel different now. I know something now. I will want to experience more. The feelings are confusing. I'm not cold anymore. Gray sky, gray day, even the streets are all gray. Maybe gray is the color of beauty.

Tokyo Awakening

Jean-Paul Vallombrossa

1958, age 13

The year 1958 was special for me in many ways. It was the first year I lived on my own since my family was forced to leave Japan as a result of a coup d'état in our homeland. Father had been an ambassador at the time of the coup, but Japan's diplomatic rules called for us to depart. By way of Canada, where we'd previously been posted, we ended up in the United States where my attempts at school (both private and public) were disasters. I'd been an honor student in Japan, and I finally got parental permission to return and finish high school there.

My mother's sister and her husband were permanent residents in Tokyo so I'd at least have family nearby. I was overjoyed to be going back to the city I thought of as home.

Since my aunt and uncle lived across town from the school, I was allowed to live in a tiny rooming house near campus. My room was in a house filled with college-age students from the university, which was just one train station down the line. I was in heaven, being the youngest by far (only thirteen!) and each of the guys took a brotherly interest in me. It didn't hurt that they included the swim and track team members from the university.

Those who haven't lived in Japan perhaps wonder about the lodging houses, most privately run by older couples as income-producing businesses. They've all but disappeared with the affluence of contemporary life in that wonderful country, but in the fifties, sixties, and seventies they were a definitive part of student life. To find myself at thirteen an intimate of college-age athletes was a heady experience. Each student had their own tiny apartment (at least back then they were thought of as apartments), about 10 by 14 feet. Most of the houses were postwar, wooden, two-story constructions that had long corridors down the middle with a bank of toilets at one end and a cooking alcove at the other. Bathing was done at the local *sento* (public baths). If you timed it right, that visit was a nightly feast of naked flesh that made the infrequent erection a strong possibility.

At thirteen I was only beginning to understand my longings and desire for the golden flesh of my housemates. I'd been in seventh heaven since coming to Japan four years earlier, because of my fascination with how sexy the young men looked. I would have truly loved be in the country when it was "opened" to the world just because of the visions that I felt would have been a normal daily occurrence — near-naked and erotically robed men of all sizes and shapes. I have to admit I never thought then that one could or should actually touch another man intimately or have sex with them. It was purely a mental image of their finely sculpted bodies that intrigued and aroused me.

Kenji, a sophomore swim team member at the university, was a neighbor to one side of my room, while the other wall was shared by Hiroaki, who ran track for the same school. Hiro was a junior and a sinewy Adonis, with a short-cropped haircut that fitted him perfectly. Ken was tall, especially for that era, and had a graceful way of walking and talking. Being closest in proximity to my room, they both seemed eager to make sure I was happy and not too out-of-sorts over being so far from my family. Every night when they went to bathe, one or the other would stop at my door and ask me to come along with them. At first I was ashamed of my hairless body, but they cajoled me into making bathtime a regular event on my daily schedule.

Japanese families seem quite open sexually and *en famille* bathing was quite common nationwide until use of public baths declined in the last two decades. Bathtime was a relaxing event where you chatted with your friends while looking at a sea of naked bodies. Most sento were separated into male and female in the larger urban areas, but out in the countryside it was common to find the whole family bathing *au naturel* with their neighbors, with everyone quite adept at being modest while being so blatantly naked.

When they were divided into men and women, the modesty element was mostly dispensed with at public baths frequented by college students. One saw a lot of uncut beauties with tight black bushes and wonderful views of firm globular buttocks. It was common for friends to wash the backs of one another while bathing together and I was soon doing the back of either Ken or Hiro while they returned that favor by washing mine. They both agreed that I needed to become more athletic and recommended tennis. Our school included spacious grounds replete with two excellent clay courts, so I took their advice. I practiced every day and began building a body I was less and less ashamed of showing off at bathtime.

One cool winter evening I was sitting at my *kotatsu* (a quilted, heated table) studying when I became aware of a regular tattoo of sounds coming from Ken's room. It was a regular beat I'd never noticed before. I wondered what was going on, and after several minutes of its continuing unabated, I went to his door and called his name. Japanese generally just call out and open any door without waiting for an invitation to come in. And that's what I did, to find myself face-to-face with a sight I'd never seen or imagined possible. Ken was lying completely naked on his futon, oblivious to me, since his eyes were tightly closed. His hand was flying

56

up and down on a hugely engorged cock that seemed three times its normal size. I was amazed and aroused at the same time. When I stepped in and closed the door, Ken opened his eyes, noticing me for the first time. Never stopping, he smiled one of his winning smiles and beckoned me to come and lie down alongside him on the futon. It took a second "come over" signal before I moved from my spot. As I lay next to him, all the myriad desires I'd felt so long seemed to enter my mind and concentrate in my quickly hardening cock. Though I was still fully clothed, Ken reached over and put his free hand on my crotch. He gave it a gentle squeeze and said, "Make yourself comfortable."

I undid my belt and trousers and slid them down to my knees, keeping my newly arisen member hidden behind white briefs. Ken realized that I'd probably never touched another guy sexually before, and he was sweet about making sure that I felt what we were doing and going to do was a normal thing for good friends to share. He whispered all sorts of encouraging words into my ear while manipulating my cock inside its thin cloth prison. I rubbed my hands all over his hairless chest while staring into his eyes, falling deeper in love with each passing moment.

When he reached into my briefs and pulled my cock free of its restraints, I glanced down to see that I had grown to surprisingly different proportions than I was used to finding each morning when I awoke. That had been happening for several months, but I never felt close enough or sure enough to discuss it with anyone. And now I was lying next to a golden-skinned beauty who had one hand on my cock while stroking his own. He leaned over and kissed me, which just about stopped my heart for good! I never wanted that feeling of his tongue forcing its way into my mouth to end, nor the feeling that was tingling between my legs. Kenji seemed to realize that I wanted him to continue and went on kissing me long and hard, even while he stroked both of us.

My own hands were moving everywhere over his naked torso, something I'd dreamed of doing for as many years as I'd been in Japan, but never thought remotely possible.

The minutes, if they were truly minutes, sped by and with a shudder Ken began to spurt come onto my exposed waist. The heat of it and the realization of what he had just done, combined with the fact that I was being deeply kissed by someone I'd admired and dreamed about for months, made my own cock erupt with a massive dose of semen, which mixed with the load already on my naked belly. He continued to manipulate me, all the while French-kissing me.

It took several minutes to calm down enough to understand what I, or rather we, had just done. It was my first ejaculation and I never even had my hand on my cock. Kenji was sweet and kind and reached over for a towelette by his futon and wiped my stomach clean and dry. But just before finishing he leaned over one remaining pearly droplet and tongued it into his mouth. I grabbed him by the shoulders and forced my own

57

tongue into his mouth, searching for a share of that tiny droplet. I knew then, even without knowing anything about being homosexual, that Kenji was the type of person I would love the rest of my life. A life which really only began that winter evening when I was still thirteen. Change had come into my life and there was no going back.

Duncan

Anonymous

When I was twelve, Duncan came to live with his grandparents, our neighbors. Duncan was sixteen, and had moved to our small town from Gary, Indiana. The ubiquitous rumor-mill informed me of some kind of trouble necessitating his move. I wasn't certain of the trouble, but heard the phrase "smoking that reefer" used several times.

This was 1959, long before marijuana had invaded the staid middle classes of our country. I knew what it was from overhearing my oldest brother's friend talk about it. It was, I thought, something reserved for blacks and jazz musicians. It was mysterious.

Duncan's coffee-and-cream skin, processed, slicked-down hair, and musical accomplishments on a mean set of drums definitely qualified him as exotic for a naive kid like me. Too, he had gray-green eyes, definitely an anomaly on a black person, The first I'd ever seen. He intrigued me the very first day I met him.

He came to live next door during a transitional period in my life. I'd kissed Mary and touched Daria's budding breasts, and found pleasure in neither activity. I had, however, found intense pleasure watching John, my best friend, take a piss. I had experienced unexplainable dizziness when trapped beneath Toby's knees, pressing into my shoulders; his ass straddling my chest, his undefined crotch only inches from my face. I had already found pleasure in playing with myself, though had yet to discover the complete satisfaction of ejaculation. Most disturbing of all, I had unsettling dreams.

Dreams of Toby unzipping his pants while sitting on my chest had shocked me awake several times. Nothing had ever happened in the dreams, and I had no clear image of what he looked like unzipped. After secretly watching John take a piss, I began dreaming about holding his dick while he did it. I also started looking at other boys in my gym class and dreamed about touching their dicks, too. I didn't understand it, really; but knew it wasn't something to be discussed. I felt strange, alone, confused, lost, and worse — dirty and bad. Instinctively I withdrew from the world and pretended to be someone else.

Duncan terrified me. He'd become friends with my older brother. He even joked around with me. I loved his bright white-toothed smile, particularly when focused on me. I had constant dreams about him, wondering what he looked like taking a piss. Watching him play his drums, legs spread wide, always interrupted a peaceful sleep. All of my dreams centered on what his dick looked like, especially when hard. I hadn't seen it, but had sneaked a feel or two when we wrestled around. It felt huge! The size ignited a new flame of desire in me, never before experienced. Not only did I want to see Duncan's dick, I developed an overwhelming desire to suck it.

The first time I dreamed of sucking his dick (with no clearer image than having it in my mouth and sucking it like I would a finger) I awoke to an aching hard-on. I gripped myself, starting my usual rubbing motion. This time, however, the ache did not subside. I gripped myself harder and moved my hand up and down, tighter, harder, and faster.

Soon something captured my mind and I wanted to scream. Something was wrong! I wanted to stop what I was doing, but couldn't. I thought I needed to take a piss, but knew I couldn't (having already failed at trying to piss through a morning hard-on). Just when I thought I was going to die, a hot, sticky, pungent fluid flew out the tip of my dick. It coated my hand, my underwear, the sheets, and even left drops on my naked chest. I was terrified, thinking I'd broken something inside me and was bleeding. Quickly turning on the light, I discovered a milky and sometimes clear liquid all over me. I'd heard my brothers talking about cum — now I understood.

Calming down, remembering the feeling and the thoughts which had created it, I again played with myself — fully awake. The next eruption was even better! Those feelings compelled me to consider how much better the *real* thing might feel — and to make a decision.

Although I had decided to ask Duncan, I was too scared to do it. I dreamed, jacked off, and daydreamed constantly, but did nothing. With youthful innocence, I decided asking him on the phone would be easier. I finally got the opportunity when I found myself home alone. When Duncan answered his phone I disguised my voice and said, "Can I suck your dick?"

There was silence on the other end. Then Duncan laughed. "Sure." The phone clicked.

I was elated, then frightened, then terribly disappointed. Duncan was willing, but didn't know who had called him. I was too afraid to call back. I decided to wait and see if he mentioned it to my brother. Weeks passed and nothing was said. I began calling Duncan at every opportunity. The conversation never varied, on either part. I never identified myself, Duncan never asked, but somehow I knew he knew it was me.

In the fall of my thirteenth year, things changed. One night the entire family, except for Grandpa, attended my brother's basketball game. Duncan had come over. We wrestled around for a bit and I, as usual, copped a feel of his dick. It got instantly hard.

"What's that?" I teasingly asked.

"What you keep calling me and asking me can you suck," Duncan quietly answered. "I keep saying yes, but you never do it. So, you better stop playing around with it, before something happens."

I was silent for a long time. "Like what?" I croaked out. Excitement made breathing difficult.

"Keep touching it, and you'll find out. Do you want to suck it, or not?"

"We can't do it here. Grandpa's in there watching television. Let's go to the garage and I'll suck it for you. We can hear the car, if it comes."

In the garage, Duncan stood and I knelt before him. "Well," he said, "are you going to suck it or not? It's getting cold out here."

"Well, take it out then."

Duncan unzipped, reached in, and pulled out a long thick object. The darkness and shadows in the garage made it difficult to really see. It was enough, stunning me with the reality of what was happening. At first I just looked, because the smell had instantly intoxicated me. I still recall its combined aromas of locker room, sweaty feet, stale piss, and moist funk — with just a hint of soap.

"Well?" Duncan's voice was different.

I opened my mouth, leaned forward, and my lips touched Duncan's dick. Something really did snap inside of me with my first taste of dick. I moved forward on Duncan, completely oblivious to anything happening above me. To this day, I have no recollection of Duncan's reaction. I was totally lost in engulfing his dick and sucking on it forever. That's all I wanted to do. Time stood still for me. I was in a totally different world. I felt like I belonged for the first time in my life. My mouth felt familiar and comfortable with the dick invading it. I knew, without a single doubt, that nothing could or would ever replace the pleasure I received from sucking dick. It's not easy to explain.

"Would you hurry up and finish? I'm starting to get cold. Let's go in the house. Maybe you can find a way to do it without getting caught."

I reluctantly released his dick and eagerly followed him into the house.

We played around a little longer. I got to see his dick in the light and I got to suck it two more times. He never came. I don't even recall him saying anything about how it felt. Despite being able to suck him, I was disappointed in the experience. I couldn't really put my finger on it. Yes, it had been terrific. Yes, I knew I would always prefer sucking dick to any kind of sex with anyone. I hadn't eliminated girls from my plans yet, but already knew a girl could never offer me more than a guy. And I was already thinking about Lee across the street. I wanted something — something more, but didn't know what it was. Then.

Duncan and I never again got together. Once, the following year, I asked, we both talked about where, but nothing happened.

Eventually he graduated from high school and left town. I graduated, went to college, and moved away. There have been a few since Duncan. I enjoyed servicing each one of them, all those times they honored me with that pleasure. I will always remember Duncan. From him, that very first night, I learned I could never be satisfied with just sucking a man's dick. I need to make love to it. I need to give him maximum pleasure in order to receive maximum benefits. I need to make my man come.

Seven months ago, on my annual visit to the cemetery to pay my respects to my past, I noticed a new headstone. The carved name stunned me. Duncan had been in the navy and had served in Vietnam. I never knew that. I rushed home and asked my sister if the "Duncan" grave was who I thought it was. She confirmed his death and told of his dying of a heart attack after returning to Los Angeles from burying his grandfather. His wife and kids had flown his body back home to lie at the feet of his grandparents.

I never forgot Duncan. I've jacked off numerous times to the vivid memory of that first time. The shocking discovery of his death has saddened me. I'm grateful for this book, however, for allowing me to publicly remember him and say: Thanks!

A Sight in the Attic

Dean W. Barickman

1956, age 13

Most of my growing-up years and my first fumbling explorations with male sex occurred in Columbus, Ohio, in the 1950s. My family lived in several different apartments and houses, but my favorite was the brown, three-story house on Summit Street. It was there that I finally had a large bedroom to myself — just in time for a teenager exploring his body and learning to jack off.

However, the attic of that house was the place I loved most. It was no dark, dirty, spiderweb-filled storage area. It was a large, finished room with plastered, light blue walls and beautiful hardwood floors. It ran the length of the house. With two windows at either end, the attic was bright and airy. From the back windows I could look down upon my father busy in his flower beds — my father who never could bring himself to speak about sex to his younger child and only son. The front windows opened into the leafiness of ancient trees that arched the quiet, shady street far below. Pushed against the walls to the side of the front windows were single beds. Here I escaped on hot summer nights to the cooling attic breeze. Here too I found a great deal more privacy for playing with my young cock. At worst someone might open the door at the foot of the curving stairway and yell up a command that I get up before the day was half over.

So, when relatives came to visit and an extra bedroom was needed, I never minded sacrificing my room for the delights of sleeping in the vastness of the lovely attic.

In the summer of 1956, when I was only two months into my teens, an aunt and her daughter and son came to stay for a week. My cousin Harry Joe and I were banished to spend our nights at the very top of the house. On the second night of the visit, I finished in the bathroom first and had preceded my cousin to our attic beds. I was peacefully lying on top of the sheets, staring upward into the darkness, wearing only Jockey shorts. I took no particular notice when Harry Joe came to the attic and climbed into his bed on the opposite side of the front windows.

However, my attention soon was drawn toward his bed by soft rustling sounds. The moonlight filtering through the trees allowed me to view the slow, steady rise and fall of movement halfway down the bed under the sheets. My twelve-year-old cousin was obviously playing with his dick.

For several minutes I watched and listened in fascination, and then I innocently asked what he was doing. Without hesitation or sign of shame, he replied that he had thought that I was asleep so he was beating his meat. As he did at home, he had grabbed a handful of toilet paper before coming to bed and was going to cum onto it so as to avoid leaving any evidence to be discovered later by an adult.

Then came our comparison of masturbation styles. My point was that toilet paper left such a mess on a sticky, cum-covered cock. His defense was that he washed it off first thing in the morning. But the idea of having to sleep with such a mess on my prick bothered me. I put forth my preference for a handkerchief or a sock, despite the danger that my mother might discover them under the bed if I forgot to get them into the dirty clothes hamper early the next day.

When Harry Joe asked if I were jacking off too, I realized that in my fascination with his activities, I had ignored my own possible pleasures. With his question, I felt obligated to begin jerking on my dick. Moments later my cousin proudly announced his climax; shortly after, I quietly responded in kind.

Although I was one year his senior, I had always suspected that my cousin was far ahead of me sexually. The lower-middle-class influences on him in Youngstown, Ohio, were quite different from my more sheltered life in Columbus. At that moment he seemed to confirm my belief by asking if I had ever given a blow job. I said I had not; but to hide my ignorance in matters of sex, I pretended to know all about such things. I had now placed myself in a position from which I could not gracefully escape.

Without giving me a moment to contemplate what was happening, Harry Joe proposed that we blow each other's dicks. I could not protest. That would uncover my innocence. Also, I had no time to protest. Suddenly he was seated, naked, at the foot of my bed. I convinced him that since I was lying down, he should do me first. As he leaned forward and took my half-hard cock into his hand, he asked, "How do I do it?" So! He didn't know as much as I had suspected. Using all the logic I could muster, I told Harry Joe to put my prick in his mouth and just blow into it — after all, wasn't that what the term for this sex act told us to do?

I felt his soft, warm lips close around my young, inexperienced dick. He gave a few hard puffs. I was disappointed. Why did the older and wiser guys at school talk about blow jobs as if they were wonderful? This had been a dud, certainly not something I'd soon be lusting after again.

I did the same to Harry Joe, and I found a strange, new pleasure in having his smooth cock in my mouth. Maybe there was something good about a blow job after all. If I'd only had the instinct to suck — but I puffed. The disappointment was evident in his manner. No comments passed between us, and he quickly returned to his bed.

Shortly afterward, I heard him again jacking his prick. He eventually asked if I could get off twice in the same night. To protect my teenage male pride, I lied and added that sometimes even three times. He came again. I pretended to do so too. Shortly after, sleep came for Harry Joe. I lay quietly in my bed in the attic, wondering about the confusion that came with puberty.

The next morning, and for the remaining days of the visit, nothing was mentioned of our foolish attempt at blowing each other. I bragged about my lustful thoughts for the girl down the street. Although no such feelings existed, I had to let Harry Joe know that I was just a typical teenage male.

Over the next several decades, we saw each other less frequently. After high school he had a variety of jobs, married, and raised a family. During my junior year in high school, I fell in love for the first time — with a senior boy. In college I enjoyed catching fleeting glimpses of beautifully formed, naked athletes in the showers and locker room. Somewhere between my time with Harry Joe and the beginning of my teaching career, I learned how to give great head — at least how to do it correctly.

During our brief and infrequent meetings, Harry Joe and I never mentioned that night in the attic. The last time I saw him was at my father's funeral in 1980. He briefly shook my hand and quietly spoke a few awkward phrases of condolence. When our eyes met, I saw nothing in his to indicate that he even remembered that night nearly a quarter of a century earlier when two inexperienced boys played at having sex.

After my father's funeral, I never saw Harry Joe again. He died of stomach cancer two years ago. Our youthful sexual encounter in the attic on Summit Street apparently had had a far greater effect upon the course of my life than upon his.

Seduced by a Younger Boy

Anonymous

1957, age 14

The year must have been 1957. I would have been fourteen and Jim, eleven. He and I were friends by default, because we lived in the country in southern Mississippi and there were few potential playmates.

We got along well despite the age difference, and the fact that there was not much to do. Our principal recreations were long walks and hunting expeditions, the last made possible by my possession of a Benjamin Pump pellet gun. This was no mere BB gun, but an air pistol that shot specially formed lead pellets with considerable force. Our prey included lizards, which could be found anywhere, and the rats that populated my parents' chicken house.

The subject of sex had never arisen. But one afternoon at his house, Jim said he had something to show me. With great secrecy, he lead me into his parents' bedroom and opened a middle drawer in their dresser. Hidden beneath layers of clothing was a paperbound book, perhaps fifteen or twenty pages in length and illustrated with photographs depicting the seduction of an eighteen-year-old man by an older woman. Although several stages of the seduction were shown, and more than one position for intercourse, the photograph that impressed me most was the one that best illustrated the young man: he sat in a chair with his legs spread and held the woman in his lap. This displayed his balls and a considerable length of shaft, upon which his partner was lowering herself. Jim hid the book in his shirt, and we retired to the barn for closer examination.

His next suggestion was that we jerk off. This was something I had never done in the presence of anyone else, although at summer camp, two years earlier, the boys in my cabin had discovered that erect penises made good towel racks. I was especially reluctant to do such a thing in his barn, which was adjacent to the house and hardly private. But Jim was not worried, and proceeded to pull his pants to his knees. He did, as I recall, have a little pubic hair. Although his piece was not full grown, it compensated in enthusiasm for what it lacked in size. We did not touch each other that first time.

For two or three weekends thereafter, we followed that same procedure, borrowing the book as a stimulus, or as a pretext. I can remember some concern that Jim might think me queer because I returned too often to that one photograph, but he said nothing. Soon we left the book in the dresser and began jerking off in the course of our walks through the woods. This was on my parents' property, which was large enough to afford privacy. Sometimes we used an abandoned cabin, but more often we just got off the main paths and stripped naked beside a stream or among the trees.

This went on for almost two years, every time that we got together. I began packing Vaseline in the metal box that was supposed to hold pellets, and we always carried the pistol to keep up the appearance that we were out for the kill. Mutual masturbation became acceptable, yet we never went beyond that. The possibility of rectal penetration crossed my mind, but I never dared mention it to Jim, since nobody in humankind had ever done such a thing — and, besides, it would be dirty. Kissing was unthinkable, and I never considered it. So there was no intimacy, and certainly we wouldn't have acknowledged anything queer about our relationship. In fact we never discussed it, except for my asking Jim how he had learned to jerk off. He told me that one of his cousins had given him a demonstration in the back of the school bus.

Halfway through high school, our relationship ended when my family moved back to town, and into another school district. I never sought out anybody to replace Jim, and his sexual activity from that point on is unknown to me. Soon his family moved to Baton Rouge, and in later years I heard that he played football for Louisiana State University. My guess is that Jim was straight, but my relationship with him helped me to understand that I was not.

White Nights

Bud Berkeley

Suddenly, my eyes popped open and my dick began pumping out load after load. I had been startled out of a deep sleep and a wonderful dream as I felt my penis begin spewing. I sat up in utter disbelief and, in the dim light coming from the hall, I couldn't believe my eyes. My cock was standing straight up, my pajama bottoms were down around my knees, and my sheets were pushed aside. Most puzzling of all, I thought I saw a figure rush out of my room.

What had happened? My mind whirled. I jumped out of bed to inspect the mess I had made of the sheets. I was in a panic to clean the bed before anyone else saw it. I had never wet the bed in all my years of boarding at the school. So often I had heard other cadets getting hell for messing up their sheets. Why did I do it now? Had I had one of those wet dreams that we had been told about?

I was fifteen years old, a cadet in an all-boys school, sleeping alone in my dorm. My roommate was sick at home and I had the dorm to myself. As I frantically scrubbed my "white" off the sheets with a damp washcloth, my mind recalled the darkened figure I thought I saw fleeing my room. "Naw," I figured, "it was my imagination." Crawling back into bed I began to think about my experience, and as my dick stiffened again I began to fantasize: If someone was in my room, who was it? Was it Tim Martin? Yeaah! Or Bill Robertson? Yeaah! I liked him too! The next morning at breakfast, I carefully scanned the eyes of my fellow cadets. Not seeing a guilty look on a single face, I decided it was all my imagination. I'd had a wet dream.

Perhaps, I thought, I had the dream because I didn't jack off enough. Some cadets bragged about beating their meat several times a day. I used to do it more. When I was a year or so younger, I played around a lot with the other cadets, beating dicks, comparing erections, and having "shoot the furthest" contests. I was always the odd man out because I was the only cadet in that school who still had a foreskin. I was more of a curiosity to the other cadets than just another fellow with a dick. I was teased about being uncircumcised but I pretended it didn't bother me.

I felt guilty about my difference, however. Once my age group began to white in earnest and masturbation became more than just a game, I withdrew from gang play in the showers and did my cock beating alone at my parents' home on weekends. After the night before, I decided weekends wasn't often enough.

My roommate was still sick and I was sleeping alone again. I lay awake the next night thinking about my problem. I tossed and turned ... and almost jacked off. But I didn't want to scrub my sheets again.

My mind wandered to my first ejaculation. It was Billy Kenton who made me do it. He lured me into a bathroom at the school, saying, "I want to show you something." He showed me a new way "to go big" and proceeded to jack off right before my eyes. After he popped white he challenged me, "Bet you can't do that?"

"Sure I can," I said, determined once and for all to prove my manhood to this brat whom I never really liked. I didn't know what I was doing but I began pumping my foreskin up and down with as much force as he had used on his skinless dick and, *wow* ... I buckled and heaved and went white!

"Didn't think you were man enough," he chuckled, "with all that baby skin you've still got on your dick!" *Bastard!* He left me alone to stare in wonder at my newly miraculous penis.

I lay awake for several nights, hoping for my nocturnal visitor to return. He didn't. The whole situation became a wonderful fantasy for my next weekend of j/o sessions. I was conjuring up this cadet and that cadet and beating off like crazy ... I think I went through every cadet in the school. "Naw," I again decided, "no one came into my room that night." I returned to school on Monday with a sore foreskin and empty balls.

My roommate was still sick and I was alone in the dorm another week. I was sound asleep one night when I felt a tug on my dick. Instead of being excited, I was frightened. I didn't want to appear awake and frighten the intruder away, yet I wanted to open my eyes and see who he was. Suddenly I felt the most wonderful new sensation on my penis. I squinted my eyelids to see what was happening and, in the dim light, I could see a head bobbing up and down over my dick. Who was it and what was he doing? I couldn't hold back my orgasm and, as I watched in fascination, Joe Scott looked up at my face and my cock popped out of his mouth. He jumped up and ran out of my room. I was in total shock!

Joe Scott? He was an upperclassman! And a football player! He had a great build, and a superlong circumcised dick that other cadets envied. And he had to be at least sixteen or seventeen years old. Joe Scott had *my* cock in his mouth? I was just a punk lowerclassman! Once again my mind twirled! And ... I was in love!

I avoided looking at Joe the next day. How could I let him know I liked what he did to my dick and wanted him to do it again? Besides, I wanted to get my hands on his great cock. My roommate was going to return soon, and Joe and I couldn't be alone after that. I wondered whether Joe even knew I had been awake. Did he know I had watched him swallow my penis? How could I let him know I was thinking about him all day and that I loved him? I wanted his penis in my mouth! I had never before sucked a cock but I sure wanted his. Would I do it right?

Could I swallow his big dick? I lay awake and worried and tossed and turned until Thursday night.

My heart stopped when I heard a noise. A figure entered my room. I could see in the dim light it was Joe. I shut my eyes as he approached my bed. His fingers prodded for my penis, then pulled it out of my pajamas. My dick gave me away as it got rock-stiff immediately. He must have realized I was awake, but I didn't move. He shoved my blankets aside and I felt the tantalizing sensation of my foreskin being pushed back and Joe's lips pressing down on my naked, supersensitive cock head. I moaned and he looked up right into my eyes. Gotcha! I could no longer hide. Now what?

Instinctively, I reached down the side of my bed where Joe was kneeling and I hit the jackpot. I had my fingers wrapped around the biggest, hardest circumcised penis I could ever imagine, and I was feeling the contours of Joe Scott's manhood. I leaned over to look at it, but he quickly jumped on my chest and shoved that football-playing manmeat right into my mouth. I began to choke. He quickly jumped down to my cock and slowly sucked as if to give me instructions. I learned quickly, as he jumped back on my chest and rammed his cock against my tonsils. I was concerned about pleasing him. Suddenly, he jerked his penis out of my mouth and came up to whisper in my ear, "You're doing great, Buddy. Relax and enjoy it." I sucked so long and hard I thought I was rubbing the skin off his wide, flaring glans. Finally, but too soon for me, he exploded in my mouth and I gulped and gulped, determined to swallow everything Joe pumped down my throat. What an honor for an upper-classman have an orgasm in my lowerclassman's mouth!

Joe surprised me by returning to my cock and giving me a slow, caressing blow job, stopping occasionally to observe my foreskin rolling over my cock head. He knew when I was about to shoot and slowed down, seemingly to give me as much pleasure as possible. I was hoping it would last forever but I couldn't hold back and warned him, "Joe, I'm going over the top."

"Give it to me, Buddy," he said as I shot into his head. He was actually swallowing *my* lowerclassman's white! I thought how much I loved this guy as I recovered from my orgasm. He came up to me and gave me a long, deep kiss and whispered, "I dig your dick, Buddy. Thanks." He jumped up and fled the room.

My roommate returned the next week. Joe Scott went on to become the school's champion on the gridiron and I became its best competitive swimmer. The twain never again met. On his graduation day, I sat there conjuring up in my mind his manly contours; that wonderfully long, sculptured circumcised penis. How well I remembered his manhood! No other cadet ever knew of my good luck. Who would believe me that I got my first blow job from the school hero ... who, for a brief moment, was such a caring lover? What a kiss! He said he liked my dick and that meant everything to the lone uncircumcised boy in the school.

Got Paid the First Time and Haven't Been Paid Since

Martin D. Goodkin

1950, age 13

At the age of thirteen the lure of a new Bette Davis movie or jacking off with the guys was strong. This afternoon, when the last period bell rang, Bette Davis won out. Her new movie, *All about Eve,* was opening at the RKO Pelham, in the Bronx, in New York City.

There was a 3:30 showing. Racing from the schoolyard to White Plains Road, where the theater was, ten blocks away, I made it just in time.

Instinctively (my gay brain?), I sat in the last row of the adult smoking section (yes, we had smoking sections then), on the left side, from which the entrance to the men's room was in sight. I would later learn that this location was a great cruising spot.

Two seats away was a guy who occasionally adjusted his fly. I didn't know what groping meant at that age, and I became too involved in the movie to pay attention to him. Soon he got up and I stood to let him pass. His hand brushed against my crotch and I immediately got hard. I had thought it was an accident, but I noticed he lingered at the entrance to the men's room and looked at me. Not knowing what was to happen, I got up and followed him.

The RKO Pelham had the perfect tearoom cruising layout: the door slammed when it closed, then you had to walk down a flight of steps and turn a corner to get to the urinals, which allowed anyone fooling around to get properly arranged if they heard you coming.

When I turned the corner, the man was standing slightly away from the urinal, exposing a big hard-on. Forty-five years ago all adults seemed to have a big cock compared to mine, and as the years have passed his has grown humongous in my mind!

Shaking, not knowing how to cruise, I stepped up to the urinal near him and took out my small but very hard cock. Within seconds he was playing with it and I felt faint. Though my friends and I had jacked off together, we never touched each other's cock.

Just as he was about to bend down — what for?!?! — the door upstairs slammed. I zipped up my trousers and ran up the stairs to my seat.

A few minutes later the man also came back, and instead of sitting two seats away he sat next to me. He asked my name and told me his was Joe. He asked if I would like to have as big a cock as his and I quietly, almost prayerfully, said, "Yes." He suggested that we leave and go over to his place. He got up and I followed.

He lived in a furnished one-room basement apartment. It consisted of a bed, a dresser, and a small washstand.

After entering the apartment he unbuckled my trousers and took my cock out. Saying that it would take a lot of work but that he could really make it big, he put his mouth around it and before he even started sucking, I came. I had never had another person's hand on my cock, let alone a mouth. I was sure I was going to faint, but I didn't.

Joe told me that if I came to see him three or four times a week, not only would it take me longer to come, allowing me to enjoy it more, but also I would see my size increase. He gave me a dollar and told me to come back tomorrow.

I left his apartment, clutching the dollar, and started across Pelham Parkway to go home. I knew that I would be going back to see Joe the next day, but I didn't know what to do about the dollar. It felt wrong carrying it and I thought everyone would know what the bill meant. I buried it in the ground in the Pelham Parkway, a block from Bogart Avenue where I lived.

Over the next two years I went to see Joe at least once a week. As I got used to the good feelings he gave me, I lasted longer before cumming and I reveled in having sex with another man. He taught me sexuality, patience, and reciprocation, and eliminated the fear and nervousness of being gay. I never did take another dollar from him, as I enjoyed him too much to feel I should be paid.

The last time I went to Joe's he wasn't living there anymore and I was afraid to ask his landlady what had happened to him. Had he been arrested for cruising the wrong kid in a theater? Had he just moved on? Had he thought my cock was big enough now and gone to work somewhere else to make another cock grow?

Bette Davis, *All about Eve,* and Joe set me on a path that I have never regretted. My cock did grow bigger, and I do wonder if there is a dollar tree growing in the Bronx in Pelham Parkway.

The Hurly-Burly

Joseph Itiel

As a soldier in the Israeli army, I heard stories about how common it was to meet queers in New York City. Since I was going to study at NYU as soon as I was discharged, I looked forward to meeting some of those queers and, finally, having my first homosexual experience. From my reading, I knew that homosexuals were likely to be blackmailed or to wind up in prison. In New York, I figured, I would not be known by everyone, reducing the likelihood of blackmail.

I was nineteen when I reached New York. On my own, I would never have known where to find a fellow homosexual. It was my former brother-in-law who told me. We were walking along the Hudson, in Riverside Park, when he said to me: "There are many queers in this park at night. I have to come down here and beat them up." To this day I wonder why he felt compelled to say this (though I am pretty sure he never actually did beat anyone up). Did he consider it some sort of civic duty?

It was a cold, clear night in February of 1951 when I finally summoned the courage to go cruising — a word I did not know at the time. Since it would be obvious to any potential partner that I was not an American, and I was not going to reveal that I came from Israel, I decided to say I was Danish. I had spent one month in Copenhagen waiting for my U.S. student visa.

I was scared but also feverishly excited. Somehow, I knew that this would be the night of the Experience I had been yearning for for nineteen long years. I had gotten it on with women, but only to prove to myself that I could do what I thought men needed to do.

Quite a few men were walking aimlessly, to and fro. Intuitively, I knew they were looking for the same thing. But they were so much older than me! Finally, I saw a guy about my own age. He had a friendly face, was slim and of medium height, and had light brown hair. I would have preferred a much darker person. But I was happy that, at last, I saw a suitable partner for the Experience.

I walked toward him, stopped some distance away, and looked out at the river. I had no idea how to start a conversation; neither did he. It was uncomfortably chilly. A cop came to our rescue. As he walked in our direction, I wanted to show him that this guy and I were friends rather

73

than strangers conspiring to engage in a crime against nature. "It's a cold night," I ventured.

His name was Richard, he was a student at Columbia University, and was also nineteen years old. Within minutes we agreed to go to the YMCA. He lived with his parents; I could have taken him to my rooming house but, in spite of my abysmally meager allowance, was still afraid of being blackmailed.

On the subway he asked where I was from. "Denmark," I said.

He considered this for a moment. I was afraid he would speak Danish to me and blow my cover. Instead he said, "I don't believe you. You don't look Danish." This ended our tentative conversation.

I registered at the Y under a false name and address. I considered this a necessary precaution. In our room we undressed immediately, without speaking to each other.

He lay on top of me. Without preliminaries, he inserted his tongue into my mouth. I had never heard of, let alone seen, such an act! It crossed my mind that it was not hygienic. But it excited me so much that I reciprocated.

I wanted, desperately, to go down on him. I was afraid, though, that it would shock him. There was also a language problem. For two boring years I had studied *Macbeth* in my English class in Israel. I could have discussed knowledgeably the witches' hurly-burlies — I suspected that I myself was in the process of committing a hurly-burly — but the word for "blow job" was beyond my ken. With great apprehension, I went down on him.

"Didn't you tell me it was your first time doing homosex?"

"It *is* my first time."

"I don't believe you. You know too much."

I didn't know how to tell him that I had rehearsed this particular act in my mind myriads of times.

We were making love passionately when Richard said, "For full homosex we need to screw each other."

"'Screw'?" I knew the other four-letter word. But it did not take me long to understand his sign language.

"I'll go out and buy some Vaseline," he said.

I would not let him leave. I was too scared. He tried getting into me without lubricant but I howled with pain. Then it was my turn. I did penetrate him a bit but it hurt him too much. When I withdrew, my dick was quite dirty. Strangely, this did not bother me. Richard pointed to the towel and, as if it were the most natural thing to do, I cleaned myself. We resumed our lovemaking and quickly climaxed simultaneously while humping each other.

We dressed in complete silence. I had my Experience and now I needed to go back into the closet, and stay there forever! Richard stuffed the dirty towel under his coat and disposed of it in the street. We took the same train uptown. Finally Richard spoke: "When will I see you again?"

"Never," I said emphatically.

"Why? Didn't you like what we were doing?"

"Yes, I did." I was a pretty honest young man. "I just don't want to be like ... like that."

"Have you heard of the Kinsey report?"

I had not. Even if I had, it would not have made any difference.

"I'll be getting off at Seventy-second Street," Richard said.

I wanted to say to him, "Let's go back to the Y and do it again. We have the room for the night." But, with iron discipline, I repressed the temporary hurly-burly of my mind. "Good-bye," I said.

I never saw Richard again.

Poetry

Craig B. Harris

Never, if I live the remaining sixty years I anticipate, will I hear the name Kevin without a pulsing in every artery leading to a throbbing groin.

Kevin happened to me at nineteen-plus, following a seaspace when — aged about seven to nineteen — family Puritanism controlled, and all my energy went into straight A's and saving money from my paper routes. Poetry, of course, with much mention of "God," none of naked male bodies or of what Kevin would call: S-E-X.

So prim there occurred no introduction to the art of masturbation ... although wet dreams gummed many a sheet in the 1950s, before the years of paper towels, and I'm sure that many of them were difficult to scrunch into the old-time washing machine.

So triggered were my galloping gonads that, getting to a high school class seconds after the second bell rang, I helplessly shot my wad while rushing down the hall.

My first proposed sexual togetherness had come when, age seven, I slept with near-same-age cousin Bill on the clematis-screened front porch of our grandparents' home on their ranch in Washington State. Cowbells of grazing cattle mingled in the night below with "booms" of nighthawks zooming on bugs in upper air.

Now knowing exactly how — or what — to do, but led by an erection, I kept edging upon Cousin Bill (we had both enjoyed the breeding positions of horse-and-mare, bull-and-cow), saying: "Let's be lovers!"

Not a silent enough request, surely, for in the morning, Father (who had been sleeping in the bedroom just inside) gave me a jocular look and said: "'Let's be lovers!' eh?"

Spooked me, it did. That, and a basically puritanical upbringing by parents — both virgins and nearly thirty when they married — who had no remarks regarding sex aside from Dad's telling me, "The man plants a seed in the woman...," which, even at seven, I knew I wasn't going to do.

So I took pause for almost thirteen more years after Bill ... when I *still* didn't know what to do; happily, I was to have a younger, wiser teacher.

As an upperclassman at the University of Washington, set upon a writing life, I'd had feature articles in an off-campus magazine, *Tempest;* poems, too.

Kevin Pocock, another poet published there, seemed a kindred spirit and I wrote to him. It was the first time I'd ever done that, but his poems said something to me. He replied with a phone number. He lived in a former fraternity house converted into a rooming house on Fraternity Row.

Our meeting came when a faculty member who I knew had to go to Los Angeles for a conference. She asked me to stay at her home overnight and, two days later, to drive her car to the airport to pick her up.

I called Kevin and agreed to meet him, after my last class, at his rooming house ... drove up in the professor's classy Nash-Lafayette coupe to see two men, one about my size, five feet nine, the other over six feet, gabbing on the sidewalk; the shorter one waved at me, dashed over as if on springs, and hopped in; "Kevin," he said.

"Wow," I said to myself, speechless, and we drove off, grinning like two apes in a tree, to the house halfway up a green hillside in the Grandview Manors section above Lake Washington, where the Cascade Mountains stretched all across the horizon east and Mount Rainier's fourteen-thousand-plus feet of snow-ice plugged the south.

Talked a streak, we did: how I'd surmised from his poetry his sexual leanings and he, telling me of years in Spokane, across the state, when he'd wondered what he was and found out ... a close group who had a party inviting a friend they "weren't sure of ... but we were in the room when a younger guy came in and this guy we didn't know about took one look, dashed over to him ... picked him up and said: 'O, you beautiful boy!' and carried him off into another room ... *then*, we knew."

"Wish that had happened to me," I said ... "any or all of it."

He laughed: "It very well may. Today."

About my features in *Tempest*, he said: "One about 'Life Alone,' I thought you were one person ... and then one on 'The Pike Place Market,' might have come from a different man altogether; and the poems, different yet, like 'Narcissus to Venus'; I swear, I couldn't tell *who* you'd be when I might meet you, and then, of all things, you wrote to me!"

Almost never had I written to a stranger, but Kevin's poems had touched me at a time when they should have. "Couldn't help writing to a poet like you with a last name ending in *cock,*" I said.

"*You* may be able to write a poem about that, yourself," he said. "Anybody that shows up in a long, new, blue-and-white rig like this ... Answer to a dream I've been having all spring semester. My Spokane man" (he turned an anxious smile) ... "we ... not long together but *deep,* to me ... went away with another guy ... to Chicago. Said they wanted me to come along, too, but threesomes are not my style. Probably as old-fashioned as you, *almost...*"

At the professor's country house, we garaged the Lafayette ... went inside for juice and for me to change out of school clothes. Then Kevin

77

led across the curving lane and into a once-orchard, a few towering trees of which was all that remained of the hillside farm this had been in days when Seattle was a town and this on its northern outskirts. Now, pioneers who had planted the orchard were dead; their children into "U.S.A. Progress"; and developers had the deed.

Up one of the trees he went, agile as Nijinsky.

"Yes," he yelled down ... "I like to dance. *Love it*. Sometimes we have dances in the basement ballroom where I live ... all men, but I'm likely the only one there that *really* likes dancing with another man. Nobody says anything, but they must have a hunch."

Across the road again, after dinner (the professor's casserole), we sat — I on a couch, he on a chair — as twilight fell over Lake Washington and lamplight over Oriental rugs.

We talked of our writing. Talked about my just-finished novel (which, of course, was at hand and I'd loan to him to read).

When I said I'd had no previous experience, he said: "How about what I'm going to read in the book?" I said: "Dreams and wet dreams."

He came across, leaned down, and took me in his arms; we kissed hungrily ... without any of the tongue-thrashing some profess ... until he drew back and said: "That was nice" ... as he walked over and turned off the floor lamp ... and came back to me.

"Hey, Kevin," I said, pointing to my room down the hall beyond the bathroom: "Why don't you just stop off there, if you need to. Go get in my bed and I'll be in."

Big, sweet smile; was that mist of sweat across his forehead from tree climbing? "It's been a l-o-n-g time," he said.

Not long before I had doors locked, lights out, and naked body into bed ... kissing and stroking the desired form and Kevin saying: "You're *very* lovely" as his hands gently slid from nape to ass.

Like my cousin Bill, Kevin was a year younger, but this time he knew what to do. To a degree, anyway. Soon he was undulating in a mild frenzy beneath me. "I don't know what to do!" I whispered.

He held my head; kissed me and said: "It's instinctive!"

Paralyzed in place, I lay ("like a bump on a log," as Father would say); and later Kevin, exhausted, slept with me atop him. I reached down to his male parts; he awoke; stiffened; and *this* time, I moved, too.

No telling what quarts of semen those sheets accepted.

Years later, reading Sam Steward's books, I found what we had done described as frottage: (dictionary) "...the practice of getting sexual stimulation and satisfaction by rubbing something, esp. another person."

Sure enough: nineteen and a half and newly hatched.

We rented ourselves a room on the fourth floor of a Victorian once-family mansion ... loved ourselves raw, while the pocms flew and passions grew.

But one of my former roommates revealed a passion he'd hidden for a year, unknown to me ... and came quickly to lead me away at the end of spring quarter to a love of twenty-four years duration, continuing.

Kevin and another man wrote a play that, after off-Broadway, became a movie ... so he moved forward, too.

I know he set me free.

All Hands on Deck... or Wherever

B.J. Thomas

1954, age 19

Upon graduating from high school I enlisted in the U.S. Navy. At that time I was eighteen and had been going steady with a girl for two years. I didn't know what "gay" meant and I had never had sex with another man. However I do remember that upon seeing Guy Madison in the movies I fantasized in my mind and had wet dreams a few times. I saw every movie he starred in and my hidden desires led to wild jack-off sessions alone in my bedroom. I never questioned this.

After completing boot camp, I was ordered to report to Charleston, South Carolina, to board a minesweeper for a four-month Mediterranean cruise. During this time I recognized that I was turned on by a few of the other sailors' looks, bodies, penis size, or bubble asses.

Just before sailing, the captain summoned "all hands on deck," where he introduced himself and the other officers, charted our voyage, and outlined all rules, procedures, and regulations. At one point (and this has stayed fresh in my mind all these years), he said: "I fully realize that for many of you this is your first cruise and that you will be leaving your wives, sweethearts, and loved ones for four months while we are at sea. I also realize that you are hot red-blooded sailors with natural desires and needs. My only warning is *Do not get caught,* as the Navy will not tolerate any 'conduct unbecoming' — no exceptions will be made." That played in my mind over and over.

Everyone had their duties and chores to attend daily, and standing watch was one of those duties. The officers stood watch during the day and evening but four enlisted men had the watch from 11 p.m. to 6 a.m. Two on the bow and two on the stern. These were at the two main masts, and our duty was to watch for other ships, whales, and anything else we saw, and to report same via radio (which were issued to each of us when reporting aboard) to the steering room.

During these four months I had only three night watches. As luck would have it, my first came when a typhoon warning was on. It was a hot rainy night, so I wore just my white boxer shorts, and put on my bright yellow full-length rubber raincoat, my matching yellow rain boots (no

80

socks), and matching hat, and reported aft. Another sailor arrived. He also wore a full-length raincoat. The storm was getting worse, the wind was howling, and rain was pelting down — we had quite a time trying to stay upright. We looped a rope around the mast, then tied it to both of our waists so we wouldn't be blown overboard. This put us in close proximity to each other.

After an hour or so I heard my mate say, "It's too damn hot for me," and he unbuttoned his raincoat. He was stark naked with a huge hard-on. He grabbed me and pulled me to him, putting his arms around my waist and unbuttoning my raincoat. Was I surprised? Yes. Did I do or say anything? No.

He was quite a few years older than me and he said he was married and "hot." He was extremely good-looking, with a great body. He kept telling me what a great body I had and his hands were all over me. In no time my cock sprang to attention. He came closer, cupped my face, and kissed me — a long, deep French kiss that seemed to go on forever. As he did this, his hands went inside my boxer shorts and he played with my huge uncut cock and balls, moaning.

My innards were churning as I marveled at him, playing with his huge thick cock. He tongued down my body until he reached my shorts. At this point my hand went to his huge meat and balls, and he moaned loudly. He ripped my shorts off me and in a second took my cock down his throat, then sucked on my balls. This continued for a long time, kissing, pawing, moaning, jerking, sucking. The next thing I knew his hands were on my ass, but I shifted, letting him know that this was virgin territory.

He carefully loosened the rope a little so that he could turn his body around. The next thing I knew, his beautiful ass was pressing against my hard cock. He begged me to fuck him. I proceeded slowly. He moaned and grunted but kept pushing his ass toward me. Soon he was lying flat on the deck, legs apart, ass up, raincoat up to his shoulders, and I was fucking away. When I realized that I was going to cum, I pulled out and he reached back and put his hands on my ass and said, "Shoot it." I did. We lay there awhile, catching our breath, and as he turned over I noticed that his stomach and the deck were awash with his cum. He grabbed me, smiled, kissed me, and said, "Remember, this never happened. I'm a married man." We talked for quite a spell until the end of our watch and then proceeded to our separate quarters.

We saw each other a few times after in the mess hall and aboard the ship but nary a glance or a word was ever spoken. It was as if it had never happened.

This experience definitely shaped my future sexual preference. Prior to this I had fantasized, but had no conception of what sex with another man would be like. Afterwards, I knew deep inside that I liked it better than heterosexual sex.

I met other sailors of the same persuasion after this and we went ashore and had encounters in hotel or motel rooms. I had only one other encounter aboard the ship. That was with a high-ranking officer in his stateroom, unbeknown to anyone but the two of us.

Needless to say, I returned to the States and broke up with my girlfriend, fully realizing that I would only be kidding myself to try to play a dual role in life. I have no regrets. I lead a complete (out of the closet) gay lifestyle and reflect back on "my first time" time and time again.

Finding the New World

Anonymous

1953, age 25

The year was 1953 when, as a recently released veteran of the Korean War, I decided to act upon a budding curiosity. At twenty-five, I was absolutely devoid of any sexual experience, other than the usual auto-eroticism. Other men had made passes at me, but I was horrified at the possibility.

In the service, I heard constant stories of sexual advances made at "straight" bars in town or in hitchhiking encounters. I continued to be horrified by some of these accounts, but also felt a certain fascination. One of my best friends in the service portrayed himself as available "trade" with considerable experience, and he slyly hinted that he continued to be thus available. However, as it turned out, and as I somehow comprehended subconsciously, he was embarking on a campaign to prove himself unsuitable for military service by virtue of his sexual appetites. He was obviously willing to take anyone else out of the service along with him through some dramatic revelation "in flagrante delicto." My guardian angel kept me from getting involved.

Numerous men in my basic training company came from the city of Columbus, and several recounted their experiences at a "disgusting" bar there which appears to have been the only gay bar in the city. Being from a small town outside Columbus, I mentally noted the name of this bar.

After release from service, I made it my business to spend an early weekend in Columbus to see what a gay bar was like. It must have taken me two solid hours of walking around the block to find the courage to go through the door. It was an old-fashioned bar, a long one with pivoting seats. Every time the door opened, each seat would pivot in unison to see what or who had come through that door. (It took me two or three visits to the Blue Feather before I realized there never seemed to be anyone there against their will in this "disgusting" bar. I pondered the sexual identities of my service confreres.)

I was ill at ease in this atmosphere, not knowing a soul in the place. My discomfort must have been palpable to the young and attractive bartender. As he prepared to close the bar, he suggested that I come home and spend the night with him. I was grateful for his friendliness, but still frightened out of my wits. He sensed this and went to every length to calm me down.

83

At his home, we proceeded slowly to his bedroom, after some deliberate conversation. He undertook to give me oral attention and explained how I could reciprocate.

It was a good night for me, mostly because I lucked out in being initiated by a man with sensitivity and concern for a first-timer. I shall always be grateful that it was Jon who brought me out. I still was troubled, but I had a friend who wanted to be sure that I received a satisfactory introduction.

We repeated this experience on several other occasions. Obviously Jon, who was several years older than I, had considerable gay experience, but it had not calloused him to the special needs of a first-timer.

We did not develop a permanent relationship. I moved out of the state for thirty years; I have often wondered what became of this gentle man but I've never encountered him since moving to Columbus ten years ago.

For several years thereafter, I could not conceive of any kind of sexual activity other than mutual oral stimulation. Ultimately an older graduate student sought to remedy this defect in my experience. He also was a patient teacher, and initiated me into mutual anal gratification. He always insisted on taking turns, so that I never perceived that the anal recipient was deemed to be in any sense inferior to the "top man." He was fond of saying, "Double your pleasure, double your fun." And obviously he meant it. We also lost track of each other, but a few years ago, I initiated some address inquiries and found him living in San Francisco. We had several years of interesting correspondence until he died of AIDS. I think of both these teachers with some regularity, and always with gratitude for that extra bit of understanding that enabled me ultimately to enjoy fully my sexual status.

3. Countdown to Stonewall (1960-1969)

The title for this section, "Countdown to Stonewall," comes from Michael Lassell's essay. It struck me as an apt phrase — not surprising, given that Lassell is one of our community's most talented poets.

It's easy to see (at least in retrospect) how events of the sixties built up to Stonewall. The election of John Kennedy in 1960 drew many energetic and questioning young people into politics. The civil rights and feminist movements challenged the right of the mainstream to declare an entire group fair game for discrimination. The hippie culture — quaint as it seems today — forced America to rethink certain assumptions about sexual morality. All these events provided a countdown to Stonewall and the modern gay movement. Surely, I thought, as I began compiling this book, these same events would have influenced men who were just coming out.

I was wrong. The turbulence of the sixties went unnoticed by most contributors. All but two of them, in fact, still lived at home when their first experience took place. They were in high school, junior high, or even elementary school, and largely unaffected by the outside world.

This section thus has the highest percentage of first-timers who were under eighteen. That might just be coincidence. But it leads me to wonder if the sixties were a particularly hard time for adults to recognize their homosexuality, living a decade too early to find supportive organizations, a decade too late to pretend that gay sex was just horseplay. There are too few stories here, however, to justify any sweeping generalization.

One thing we *can* say for sure: there were some teenagers who had no name for what they were doing, but were sure having fun back in the sixties!

A Personal Stonewall

Morris Brown Jackson

1969, age 10

The defining events of the summer of '69 were the Apollo moon landing, Woodstock, and my first sexual experience. I had just celebrated my tenth birthday. My mom was out of state attending summer school and my dad traveled a lot for his job, so I was shipped off to my nearest grandparents for the summer.

Summers with them had become an annual pilgrimage while my mom worked on her second master's degree, so I was no stranger to the hot, humid days and balmy nights of South Carolina's low country. Nor was I a stranger to Don and Darryl, the Fulton brothers. You see, my introduction to man-to-man sex was a three-way with two soon-to-be men. Darryl, also age ten, and Don, age twelve, were neighborhood kids who had adopted my grandma as their own, and although it wouldn't be until years later that I would define them as such, they were my first fuck buddies.

At the time, I had only a vague concept of sex — sex, period, not to mention gay sex. Sure, I knew what a faggot was — I'd been called one every day of my life since kindergarten — but I had no technical expertise about what faggots did. To say that I was naive would be a gross understatement: I hadn't a clue that dicks got hard, and trying to imagine what to do with one that was, was beyond me. But all that changed during the summer of 1969.

I have no recollection of any big seduction scene. Don and Darryl were sleeping over and the three of us were piled in the double bed in Grandma's guest room. I was scandalized to learn that they slept not in pajamas, but in their underwear — who knew then that I would one day sleep nude? I seem to remember body contact being initiated with us all tickling each other, all innocent child's play. But the next thing I knew, my dick was in somebody's mouth and it felt good. I wondered if sucking felt as good as being sucked. It did. Then the jar of Vaseline appeared. I intuitively sensed why. It seemed to me that we were just experimenting, that none of us knew what we were doing, although looking back, I suspect that Don really did. He was the one who proposed that we fuck, and since he was the oldest (and hunkiest), I assumed that he knew how. I wasn't disappointed.

Probably because I was the most frail, I was designated a bottom and was the first to be fucked — by Don, whose twelve-year-old dick was already of man-sized proportions. As he entered my virgin asshole, I sucked Darryl. Once the pain of entry subsided and pleasurable sensations dominated, with both digestive orifices filled, I not only knew what faggots did, but also knew for the first time that I was born a faggot and would die a faggot.

I had found nirvana and had become a member of an elite boys' club. Daytime make-believe games of war, Batman and Robin, cops and robbers, all invariably involving boyish roughhousing, then usually gave way to manly passions. It was accepted and understood by my grandparents and Don and Darryl's parents that we spent the night together — every night. So by night, playful tickling gave way to passionate touching, which routinely resulted in three intermeshed bodies, each enjoying the others. Grandma and Grandpa and Mr. and Mrs. Fulton never figured out why we were inseparable.

It was an unusually hot summer, one of humping and pumping, bumping and grinding, moaning and groaning. I may not remember the Stonewall Riots that summer as the defining event in gay history, but in my own personal history, I remember the sultry summer of '69 as the momentous period when I first gleaned the pleasures of gay sex.

The Incredible Lightness of Ejaculation

Brandon Judell

Sex before Robert was books. Imagine the Bronx in the early sixties. My mother borrowed from the Rosenhouses the paperback *Questions Children Ask*. I quickly learned the answers to "Why is Daddy's bigger than mine?" and the inappropriate, for me at least, "How come I don't have one?"

I believe I was eleven, a bit old for such material, but truthfully, although I was near the top of the class in all subjects except gym, sexual matters still descended upon me as a dense fog. My friends also were not the hip, mature ones; not one could be deemed sexually precocious. Open-mouth kissing and breast fondling were way off to the future for my set. Spin the bottle even seemed advanced, and if we could have got a refund in those days, we would have returned the bottle.

Well, anyway, in the Judells' sole bookcase, which was off the bathroom, there on one of its six shelves was Havelock Ellis's *Psychology of Sex*, which I often scanned without much comprehension. Surprisingly, besides *The Carpetbaggers*, which I did comprehend, there was also a book on sexual matters during World War I by a Magnus Hirschfeld. In that one, I just perused the political cartoons of the day: prostitutes beckoning soldiers were depicted as skeletal deaths in bridal gowns — or something like that.

Then there was also the occasional *Playboy* in Dad's night table which I checked out on the rare occasions I was left alone in the apartment. Dad, it should be understood, was extremely Germanic, to the point of caricature. He was of the notion that children should be seen and not heard — and not even seen if copulatory matters were being discussed. I was constantly sentenced to exile whenever the first line of a dirty joke was being let loose by visiting adults.

So Robert was my savior. We had met at a Jewish day camp, and my mother and his grandmother had become friends while waiting for our bus to bring us back from our daily romps in greenness. Soon Robert and I did everything together, which wasn't much. Buying Good Humor ice cream, playing tag, Ping-Pong, Go to the Head of the Class.

On educational matters, we parted ways. I was the bright one who couldn't read enough books. Robert belonged to a record club — or at least his mother did. Once when playing Go to Head of the Class, Robert's question was: Where was Christopher Columbus born? He answered quite seriously, "New York." If you don't believe me, ask Susan Rosenhouse. She was there. But though he wasn't bright, Robert was loyal, funny, attractive to a degree, and dirty blond. What more could one want in a friend? So we were inseparable until his mother remarried, and Robert was taken to Queens.

I was distraught and lonely until Robert came back to visit his grandmother. Did he have stories to tell!!! His first day in his new junior high school was a memorable one. He went into the bathroom and a guy threatened that if Robert didn't go down on him, he'd beat him up. So Robert gave his first blow job. From then on, his sexual expertise grew.

Taking me up to his old bedroom — we were possibly twelve or so by this time — Robert taught me to masturbate. Only clear liquid crawled out of my penis. (I won't even tell you when I started sprouting pubic hair.) I believe Robert showed me how he got hard, and then he touched mine, and I touched his.

Then he told me to lie on his old bed, stomach-down. He pulled my shorts off over my sandals and forced his penis up. It was somewhat painful, but not outrageously so, otherwise I would have yelled, "Stop!"

At that point, after Robert had pumped a bit, he said that he felt like he wanted to kiss me. I'm not sure if I said it was okay to do or if I just thought so, but he didn't.

I don't think we ever kissed but for years we had lots of sex. Much of the time we jerked each other off in Macy's bathrooms in Parkchester. I remember always smelling their terrible liquid soap. Crazed with our sexual discoveries, the two of us constantly invented excuses to get away from our folks or our gang so we could go friction each other off.

One night I let Robert fuck me in my bedroom with just the door closed. It was unlocked and both my folks were home. This was not only playing with fire, it was playing with the Gestapo.

We were daring and carefree, especially during the summers. We shared a locker at the Castle Hill Beach Club, sort of a concrete beach in the Bronx with swimming pools and paddleball courts. When not staring at the showering old men whose balls reached their knees, we used to cum and cum and cum in our shared locker.

It's funny how I can't remember going down on Robert or him on me, but as I force my memories backward, I do get an odoratory sense (is that a word?) of how his youthful balls smelled. So ... it must have happened. And often. But I can't recall. Now thirty years have been masticated. Robert is living in Greenwich Village alone, having been dumped by his lover. The years haven't been kind to him. He has cirrhosis of the liver and is skinny as a rail. It wasn't all the drugs and alcohol and disco that did him in, he insists, it was job stress. I nod. He wants to get together again. He wants to be friends, but I have nothing in common with my first lover, I tell myself. He wants to have sex. I shudder. Two of his teeth are missing. He doesn't read. TV and collecting awful chachkas are how he passes his time.

Robert's favorite phrase now is "to make a long story short," which is something he never does. He drones on and I want to care. I would love to relive that innocence, try to recapture that excitement of my first orgasms when I didn't even know the word "orgasm," but I can't. Robert has become someone who is too needy, an emotional abyss, and I wonder sometimes what saved me from the same outcome? Then I wonder if, other than my good teeth, I was saved at all.

Bodysurfing with Robert

Richard V

Recently, at my twenty-year high school reunion, a grade-school class picture tacked on the bulletin board brought memories of my first sex partner. There he was, as cute as ever, Robert S., sitting at a front desk with his hands crossed on the desk giving me his charming bucktoothed boy-smile.

Later that night I relived the magical summer and fall of '65. Robert was like me — an eleven-year-old wanna-be surfer in Ormond Beach, Florida, yearning to break into the older surfer clan but too small to carry one of the heavy surfboards down to the beach.

In late summer a hurricane reformed the beach, wiping out the outside sandbar and leaving the beach mounded high and steeply sloping down to the water. The waves that used to break on the outside sandbar now swelled up near the shore and crashed down onto the steep slope. The surfers, missing their surfable outside break, all switched to bodysurfing this new "shore pound." Robert and I could do this, and we quickly became their token grimmies.

The rides were short and violent. Young, tanned bodies rode down a wall of frothy water, crashed onto the coarse red coquina sand smarting with sand burns, then jumped up and plunged into the swirling water to do it over and over again. Robert and I tumbled with the coolest and the greatest.

One afternoon all the others quit early, leaving Robert and me alone in the surf. He swam up to me and bluntly asked, "Wanna go to the dunes and suck dick with me?"

My immediate response was positive. I had always wanted to do this but had never figured out who I could approach about it.

Ormond Beach, a suburb north of Daytona Beach, was barely developed at that time. He led me up into the powdery white sand of the first dune line and we followed a path through the palmettos. Only our thin cotton bathing suits separated me and my greatest urge, and my hard-on pushed out in front of me.

Past the palmettos he stopped in a clearing surrounded by ocean-spray-dwarfed oaks and dropped his suit. There it was in front of me, the pink boner I had always wanted.

"It tastes better when it's salty," he said. "Try it."

92

I dropped to my knees in front of him and felt it. Then I smelled it. My first whiff of the musty organ thrilled me so much I felt dizzy.

"Put it in your mouth," he said.

I put it in my mouth and held it there, savoring the sensation of the soft, warm skin.

After a few moments he said, "Don't just sit there, you're supposed to go up and down on it. Let me show you." He removed his member from my mouth, pushed me down into the sand, pulled off my trunks, and gave me head the proper way.

Robert and I became close companions and after school we enjoyed long sixty-nine sessions in the dunes and the woods, never able to complete the act as we weren't mature enough to reach orgasm, but not knowing the difference. When our mouths tired of sucking we relaxed, dicks in mouths. More than once we fell asleep in that position. My most vivid memory is of waking with my face buried in his delicious boy-crotch.

Twenty-nine years later I know something that I did not know then. I loved him.

Where are you Robert?

Freshly Washed Blond Curls

L. Anthony Grubbs

1965, age 13

What is the mystique they have always had? These young rebels, fair of face, pouting in manner, and on a collision course with destiny. They burn beautifully and brightly for a time and then are consumed of their own fire.

I had just such a young man in my life. The year was 1965, the Beatles were storming the country, hair was getting longer, and moral taboos were relaxing. We of that generation were all caught up in the time, except for one guy in my small Oklahoma town. I shall call him DKS. DKS sported the 1950s greaser hair, the t-shirt with the Marlboros rolled in the sleeve. When he ironed his blue jeans he used a whole can of spray starch so the crease would be just right.

He was fifteen and I was thirteen, I had known him all my young years. DKS was the school tough. No one could take him in a fight, yet under all the bravado was the sweetest and kindest person I had ever met. He was my protector from our earliest days in grade school, for I was tall and willowy with a gentle manner. With his muscular body, blond hair, and china blue eyes, he was the secret desire of all the girls, even the ones from the other side of town, the "nice" girls.

We were both from blue-collar families. His father owned a junkyard and mine was a rigger in the oil fields. We were not a part of the social clique, so we spent our time riding bikes, smoking cigarettes behind the Teen Stoppe, and creating as much mischief as we could get away with. We talked about girls (as was required) and fantasized about the dreams our futures would make come true. I was going to be an art teacher and he was going to join the Marines and see the world beyond small-town America. We spent so much time with each other that my stepmother (who had changed his diapers as a baby) used to joke about just adopting him since he was always at our house anyway. D's father drank quite a bit, so we did not spend a lot of time at his house.

D was sleeping several nights a week in my bed, yet I had never touched him. When he came from the shower in his soft white Jockey shorts I always noticed a beautiful bulge in the front, about which I was quite curious. I didn't even know what gay was at that time. Of course we all made jokes about queers, and when we did I felt a slight twinge

94

in my chest. I just didn't see myself as one of those. All I knew was I wanted to see what was hiding in those shorts.

One summer night, with a gentle rain falling and the lightning and thunder in the distance, D and I lay in my bed feeling the cool night air across our faces. Neither of us had said much that night, but I was busy laying plans for a little escapade that evening. Once I heard his breathing deepen and felt his body relax into sleep, I moved closer, cautiously determined to discover by covertness just what was in those shorts. I had decided to do it this way because if he was awake he might think I was a queer and shun me. Just a quick little feel and I would be satisfied.

His hair was freshly washed and the clean smell intoxicated me. The warmth of his body fed me. The closer I got, the bolder I became. Sometimes when I look back and think of that night I see how it formed my sexual likes and fantasy for the rest of my life. Young blonds with curly, fresh-washed hair and firm bodies have driven me nuts ever since. Sex on a rainy night is still highly erotic to me. They say that our first pleasurable experiences set the trends of our sex life for the rest of our lives, and I believe it.

I slowly moved my hand to its intended target. I held my breath lest I betray myself. As I touched the soft cotton something in me changed, something profound. I had made a life choice. Maybe I didn't realize it at the time, but my life would be changed forever from that point. It was all I had ever thought it would be. It was exciting and fulfilling and the feel of his crotch totally aroused me.

He moved with a sigh and I jerked my hand away in guilt. I lay there fearing he had awoken and would be angry with me. I waited, then screwed up my courage for one more quick feel. I was living dangerously tonight. When my hand returned to the same spot I did not encounter the same soft cotton but throbbing young flesh. I had in my hand one quite large, very excited cock. I started to pull my hand away but D put his hand over mine and chuckled, "What took you so long?"

He began to masturbate himself with my hand. Then he took his hand away and I continued on my own. He reached down and finished removing his shorts, then mine. His fingers found my already straining cock and manipulated me in a like manner.

He took his hand away and took me in his arms, kissing me deeply if somewhat awkwardly at first (we got it right real quick). We spent the rest of the night in each other's arms. Both of us felt natural being active and passive in all forms of sex. There was no role-playing, no games, just good, honest, mutual affection. This practice continued for some months till I was farmed out to a "rich" relative because I couldn't get along with my stepmother. After that I ran away and became one of the street kids of the sixties. I never forgot D and how it had been between us. We had never talked about what we did, that might be too "queer." We just did it and enjoyed it.

D was Superman to me; no one could hurt him, he was invincible. When I was fifteen (two years later) I blew back into town and proceeded to ask where I could find D. It seems my young titan had gone the way of those before and after. Having had a fight with a girlfriend, he got drunk and wrapped his car around the front of a semi on a rainy night, our rainy night. I was crushed. I thought no one could ever hurt him and I was right. No one had, he had done it himself. My D, like James Dean before him and River Phoenix after, is somewhere up there combing his blond curls and smiling his crooked smile and I shall never forget him or my first time.

Full House Beats a Pair

Matthew

1969, age about 14

I suppose we all had a crush of some sort or another in eighth grade, even those of us who didn't realize that's what it was. My crush was on John, a handsome boy who had just moved to town a year earlier. We were together in several classes, including English, art, and gym. We became casual friends, going to the movies or riding our bikes together a few times a month. Sometimes his brother Scott, who was a year younger, came with us. They seemed to get along pretty well.

I looked forward to John's calls intensely. I called him, too, but on some level, even then, I realized that it wouldn't look right for me to call him a lot more than he called me.

He had a particularly attractive body, and for some reason, he was always one of the last boys out of the shower after gym. (Not for any of the obvious reasons; I think he just liked long showers.) I slowed down my pace so that I could end up watching him in the shower, then as he dressed. His locker was about fifteen feet down from mine, and I tried to stand so that I could inconspicuously watch as he pulled on his clothes.

One day, when just about everyone else had gone, his dick caught in the elastic band of his Jockey shorts as he pulled them on. He let it ride up so it was poking out the top as he adjusted them around his waist. He caught me watching, gave me a funny look, and only then did he tuck it in place.

My eyes were probably popping out of my head. I knew virtually nothing about sex. I had not learned to masturbate. I knew in a vague way that I wanted this boy, but I had no idea just what I'd do if I had him. Still, the image of him standing there with his dick sticking up out of his underwear replayed itself in my head a dozen times a day for weeks thereafter.

John and I occasionally slept over at each other's houses, as was common for kids in our neighborhood to do in 1969. One Friday night, when I was over at his house, as the evening wore on he suggested that we play strip poker. Sure, I said. His parents' room was at the other end of the house so privacy wasn't much of an issue, but he locked the bedroom door anyway.

He pulled out a deck of cards and we dealt out hands, threw in the cards we didn't want, drew new cards, then compared what we had. The low hand each turn had to take off an item of clothing.

I soon noticed that John was sometimes turning in only one or two cards, then showing a complete bust. It was as if he was keeping his low cards, and trying to lose. Each of us started, of course, by taking off shoes, belts, then t-shirts. Soon John was down to just his white briefs and socks, while I still had on my jeans and both socks. I also had a painfully big boner, so I sat cross-legged with my knees up.

John lost the next hand. I assumed he would take off a sock but without hesitation he peeled out of his underwear, his young cock stiff in the air. My own erection ached harder than ever. After a few more hands, I too was naked and fully exposed.

"I'm really horny," he said. "How about this: whoever loses the next hand gives the other one a blow job." He paused. "And then we'll switch."

I had only the slightest idea what a blow job was, but I was eager to learn more. At that point, however, John's brother Scott burst into the room from the attic door leading under the eaves. "I'm getting in on this too," he announced. He was wearing pajamas, and he, too, had clear evidence of an erection below the loose cloth.

I was mortified. I pulled some loose clothes in front of me, hopped into the bed, and got under the sheets. John seemed more irked than actually embarrassed or mad. He grabbed a pillow and held it in front of his erection, then walked over to Scott. "Get out of here," he said. "You're not supposed to be spying on us." (He later explained that the attic under the eaves connected both bedrooms. They had discovered soon after moving in that they could spy on each other through cracks around the door, but after a dispute, their parents had set a firm rule that they weren't supposed to do so.)

"Let me in on it, or I'm telling." Scott was quite defiant, confident that he could have his way. John tried to push him back toward the attic door, and they ended up wrestling, Scott in his pajamas, John now naked except for his white socks. He quickly pinned his brother, and put one knee on each of Scott's shoulders, his genitals dangling a few inches from his brother's face. It is quite erotic when I think about it now, but at the time, I was too worried to appreciate it all.

"What do you think we should do?" he asked me. I shrugged. This was all too bizarre for me to deal with. Scott was as cute as John, but I had really wanted to mess around just with John. On the other hand, I didn't want any possibility of Scott telling anyone what he had seen. "Maybe we should let him stay. Whatever you think," I said.

"Okay," said John. "You can stay. I'll tell you what. We'll play one hand. The lowest hand has to give blow jobs to the other two, then he beats off himself." Scott was satisfied with that, and John let him up. "But first you have to get undressed, like us." Scott was satisfied with that, too.

A moment later all three of us were sitting in a circle. I was a little uncomfortable with this turn of events, and as I recall, I had gone limp, although both brothers were quite hard. It surprised me that they weren't embarrassed being like this with each other. John dealt the cards, we changed them in, and I looked at what I had. A pair of fives. I remember it quite distinctly. For years I had been hearing about "sex." I looked at those cards and thought, "My first experience with 'sex' is going to be determined by whether that pair of fives is high or low."

My hand turned out to be the middle one. Scott's was best, and John's was worst. I felt a bit of relief that I would be able to watch and see what was expected of me before I had to do anything; I didn't want them to know how inexperienced I was.

It turned out that by blow job, John really just meant a few licks to provide lubrication, then beating the other guy off. That's what he did with his brother and I watched in fascination, my own dick becoming painful with anticipation. Then John turned to me. I lay on the bed, as Scott had done. He took my dick into his mouth, much more fully than he had done with his brother, and sucked briefly, then slid his hand up and down my shaft. Any discomfort I had felt was now long since gone as I focused on the sheer touch of his hand. Soon I had a feeling of impending release that I distantly recognized from my wet dreams, and then I was shooting onto my stomach.

I wanted to give back to John what he had given me. Instead, I had the pleasure of watching him enthusiastically masturbate, his dick soon pumping spurt after spurt of cum. Before Scott went back to his room, John insisted that we all swear never to tell anyone what we'd done.

John and I had sex several times in the year or two that followed. It turned out, as he freely admitted, that he and his brother had often messed around together. In addition, I recognize now that he had what would today be called strong exhibitionistic tendencies. I wonder what he's up to these days?

Genes

Joseph S. Amster

There has been considerable debate recently whether gays are born or if homosexuality is a learned behavior. In my case, I believe I was born this way. I can honestly say I have a natural inclination toward cock sucking. I've always been very oral; I sucked my thumb until I found something better.

I have memories of being attracted to other boys since I was eight. One time I was watching contractors dig the hole for our family swimming pool. I was so excited that I kissed the boy standing next to me. Everyone thought I was weird for doing it, but it felt natural to me.

Over the next few years, I remember playing the usual "nasty" games with other boys in the neighborhood. Nothing out of the ordinary, just the usual things boys do with each other when they're growing up. The summer of 1969 changed all of that.

I was thirteen that summer and had just gone through puberty, so my cock had grown and I had pubic hair. I was the first boy in my group of friends to develop, and I was excited by it. There was one other boy in my group who matured at about the same time, his name was Eddie.

Eddie and I liked to go skinny-dipping in my pool that summer. One day Eddie was feeling particularly daring, so he climbed out of the pool and lay on his back to sun himself. He had a raging hard-on, which lay flat against his stomach. I remember staring at his cock and being turned on by it, but I didn't know why.

A few days later, I locked myself in my bathroom and started playing with my cock. I had always liked the feeling of rubbing my hand over it, but this time it felt especially good. As I continued, I noticed a clear fluid coming out the tip. I had never seen this before, so I kept rubbing the head. Eventually, I felt a tingling sensation in my groin; the more I rubbed the better it felt. Finally, white stuff shot out of my cock and all over my face. It caught me totally off guard.

I was so excited by my discovery that I rushed over to tell Eddie. We locked ourselves in his bedroom, threw off our clothes, and I showed him how to do it. We both came quickly, excited by this new discovery.

As summer progressed, I went to Eddie's house every day so we could beat off together. Eventually we started playing with each other's cocks. One day, as we were lying in the sixty-nine position, I spontaneously started sucking on Eddie's cock. He didn't object, so I kept going. Looking back it seems odd, I had no idea people could do that. I had never seen pictures, read stories, or even heard anyone talk about cock sucking. I feel strongly it was instinct.

I'll never forget that first taste. Soft yet hard, slightly metallic. It was like having a flesh Popsicle and I fully enjoyed it. Licking it all over, moving my mouth up and down. Eventually I used spit to lubricate my hand, which I moved in tandem with my mouth.

I wasn't expecting Eddie to cum; I think it took him by surprise too. Suddenly he shot in my mouth. I didn't like my first taste of cum and withdrew to watch Eddie's orgasm. After it subsided, we decided it was my turn. I lay back and propped my head up on a pillow. Eddie closed his eyes.

Eddie didn't get into it as much as I did, but it was great for me. We had decided to signal each other when we were going to cum, so we didn't have to swallow it. I watched as Eddie sucked my cock and licked my balls. Eventually I gave the signal to Eddie and he withdrew to watch wad after wad of pearly cum shoot from my cock. It was wonderful.

Things went along pretty much the same for the rest of that summer. I would show up at Eddie's, we'd talk for a while, and eventually we had our clothes off and were sucking each other off. One thing I learned early was to have Eddie do me first, because if I did him first he was reluctant to reciprocate. I think he felt guilty afterward.

Eventually, it slowed down and we hardly did it anymore. That fall I moved away and didn't see Eddie until many years later. It was just after high school. Eddie and his brother were renting a summer beach house. I had run into his brother on the beach and he invited me over. When we arrived at their house, Eddie was asleep. We went into his room and his brother woke Eddie up by pulling back the sheets. There was Eddie, naked with a big hard-on. My eyes nearly popped out of my head.

Eddie and I hung out together most of that day. Around sunset we were sitting on the beach when I finally got the nerve up to ask him. "Remember those things we did when we were thirteen?" I asked him. "Did you ever do it again?" "Nope," said Eddie. "Did you ever want to?" I hesitantly asked. "Nope," said Eddie. I left it at that.

I had hoped for more. Actually I was hoping for a repeat performance, since what had happened in my thirteenth summer had fueled masturbation fantasies throughout my teenage years. But it was not to be. What was a life-determining experience for me was no big deal to Eddie.

Gold Rush

Anonymous

I was fourteen when I met Kenneth. I had just begun high school at Ft. Knox, where our family had moved the summer of '69. I don't think I heard anything about Stonewall that summer, or realized what it might mean to me. My mother had married an army sergeant in July after a whirlwind romance of three months, and now I was a brand-new "army brat," with a new dad, in a new town. It was a bit much, so when a guy from my classes and I started getting along well, it helped soothe the transition into my new life.

His dad was a sergeant, like mine, and our families lived in the same housing area. We rode the same bus to school. We had some of the same classes including gym, which neither of us likcd. I gucss I could be described as a nerdish overweight kid and Kenneth was a bit of a Buddy Holly rebel type. He regaled me with tales of his exploits, which included run-ins with bikers and his pursuit of women (not girls), despite his being the same age I was.

Kenneth was no great looker. If he had been, I probably would have been too intimidated to get close to him. I already knew how I felt about men. I think I had known since age six when I visited a public beach and first saw full-grown men and teens with their cocks and hairy nakedness. I found them fascinating. If I could, I would have gone right up to every one of them and investigated thoroughly. I even had a boyfriend a year older when I was eight or nine, with whom I played sex games.

I knew I was attracted to men. I had enjoyed looking at naked boys in the junior high locker room, and had gone through every art book in my hometown library looking at Greek and Roman statues and artwork. I even knew what it was called. Being a bit nerdish, I researched in all the books and magazines I could. But at that time, there was little or no positive information about being "homosexual"; along with the information about homosexuality, I absorbed all the homophobia of the time.

So getting close to guys was not easy for me, especially if I found them attractive or sexy. That's why I say that if he had been really good-looking, we probably would not have become so close.

But we did. We spent a lot of time together, usually just talking or hanging out. He showed me my first pornographic books and magazines I don't know where he got them, maybe from his dad or maybe through some of the exploits he related to me. The pornography was all heterosexual but it added a dimension to my sexual information and fantasies.

One evening, over a weekend or perhaps a school vacation, Kenneth stayed at my house really late. He was tired and I was too. My parents had gone to bed, but I was sure they wouldn't mind if Kenneth spent the night. I knew my mom felt kind of sorry for him, as his mother had left the family not long before that. I asked if he wanted to spend the night and he said sure.

I don't think I had any ulterior motive in issuing my invitation. There would be other times, other friends, when the idea was to get them into bed, but that was all in the future. He said sure, and we undressed and went to bed. Sometime during the night, we ended up laying in the spoon position. Soon Kenneth had his arm around me and I could feel his hard cock in my asscrack. I got awake and excited very quickly.

Nothing happened at first and then Kenneth turned over. I turned over too and assumed the same position he did, but didn't do anything else. After a while I turned over again. So did Kenneth, except this time he reached further over and started rubbing my member through my briefs. Soon he stopped and turned over again. I turned over again and so it went, a sort of follow the leader with Kenneth as the leader.

It wasn't long before we both had our shorts off and Kenneth was pumping his cock in and out of my butt while he was jacking me off. Then we turned over and it was my turn to do the same to him. We continued in this way until we both had "shot our wads" (I think that was the expression we used). We showered together the next morning and I think he would have talked about it, but though I had enjoyed it thoroughly and wanted more, my homophobia rose up. I didn't know how to deal with it and changed the subject. It happened once or twice again after that but it did not seem to have any effect on our relationship or Kenneth's seemingly endless pursuit of women. It would be a long time before my first kiss or my first blow job.

It did affect my sexual style for quite some time. I got stuck trying the same things in the same way with other guys. More often than not it didn't work. It was a long time before I could resolve my internalized homophobia and affirm my gay identity in a positive way. If Kenneth and I had grown up in the eighties instead of the sixties, maybe we would have become lovers, or maybe I would have been more comfortable with the sexual part of our friendship.

As for Kenneth, I don't know how it affected him. We never talked about it and the next summer his dad got transferred to another post. I never heard from him or saw him again. He was my best friend and I often wonder what would have happened if we had had more time together and how he is today. I wonder if he ever thinks of me.

At the Swimming Hole

James Karvonen

1966, age 15

As I grew up during the turbulent sixties, homosexuality was a hush-hush topic. I became sexually active at an early age with several of my childhood friends, but during my preteen years, there never were any real feelings or emotions involved in our joint experimentation. But by the time of my fifteenth summer I realized that I was different from other so-called normal teenagers. In that summer of 1966 I had my first truly homosexual encounter, one that would eventually shape my future preference.

Not far from where I lived, I had a close friend named John. John was three years older than me. As far as I knew, he was strictly heterosexual. We shared the same interest in model trains. About a week before high school let out for summer vacation, I went to John's house to help wire his model train layout. As I went down into the basement I noticed another much younger boy with him. His name was Bobby, and at twelve he was a real heart-throb. I had never seen this boy before but somehow in that first initial eye-to-eye contact, something registered between us. Bobby had dark brown hair, seductive eyes, a smooth, almost perfectly proportioned face, and a smile that could melt even the coldest of hearts.

On that day Bobby and I became good friends. I found out later that he had a paper route and in the days and weeks that followed, when I wasn't with John, I was helping Bobby deliver papers. I never had a interest in girls, but if there is such a thing as love at first sight, that love hit me then, knocking me out for the count.

I had to be careful, because I didn't want to be labeled a queer. But each day I spent with Bobby, my attraction and love for him intensified and finally came to a point where I had to get a grip on myself and face the truth regarding my sexual preference.

It was a hot August day, about two months after I met Bobby. We had become inseparable. I found myself spending more time with him than with anyone else. We were fishing at an isolated fishing hole on the Mohawk River. The fishing was poor and both of us grew bored. Finally Bobby suggested that we find a good place along the stream to go swimming. I thought that it was a great idea, but neither one of us had brought swimming trunks. We were wearing jeans and when wet, jeans could be most uncomfortable, especially when riding a bike.

When I pointed that out to him, Bobby surprised me by saying, "We can go skinny-dipping. You're not shy, are you?"

No, I definitely wasn't shy. As a matter of fact, ever since I had first met Bobby I kept having fantasies about him and what he looked like nude. And now he was suggesting that we go skinny-dipping. What could I say? My fantasy was about to become a reality.

We found a quiet secluded spot about two hundred yards downstream, complete with an old wooden bridge and a weeping willow tree that had a swinging rope attached to an upper limb. The perfect swimming hole. And we had the spot to ourselves.

It didn't take long for us to pull off our clothes. As each article of clothing came off, I could see that Bobby was scoping me, and I naturally scoped him back. Once naked, we faced each other. As I had imagined, Bobby was beautiful in every way. My heart was pounding a mile a minute within the confines of my chest. My eyes explored every inch, nook, and cranny of his lithe boyish body. He had a firm chest that was just broadening around his shoulders. He had a smooth lean stomach, a slightly indented belly button without the slightest hint of any remaining baby fat as he made the transition from child into adolescent. His smooth legs were strong and muscled. But what attracted me most was the medium-sized penis that hung limply between his legs. Like me, Bobby was circumcised. Though not as long nor as thick as mine, nevertheless it was a little larger than I would have imagined on a twelve-year-old boy. His twin orbs were almost adult in size and hung loosely between his legs. He was completely devoid of any pubic hair and that made him even more tantalizing and beautiful to me. My interest in him became evident by the stiffening that was taking place between my legs, to which he giggled and pointed out, "You're getting a boner."

Embarrassed, I turned and dove quickly into the water. He followed, cannonballing right next to me. For the next half hour we frolicked together in the water, having the time of our lives.

We engaged in splash fights against each other, then raced — you name it, we did it. Afterwards, we climbed out of the water and lay down on the mossy ground next to each other to get some sun and dry off. As I was lying there, loving every minute of just being with him, Bobby rolled over on his side to face me, braced himself up, and placed the fingertips of his left hand directly on my chest. He started spidering them over my rigid nipples, down my rib cage, to my stomach. "This is what I do to my little brother and he loves it," Bobby replied.

"So do I," I told him, wanting so much to reach up and embrace him against my nude body. His fingertips danced over the center of my belly then down toward my groin. He then started to giggle. "You're getting a boner again," he informed me, and sure enough I was, but I had no intention of concealing my embarrassment this time. Out of the corner of my eyes I noticed that I wasn't the only one. His penis, thicker now, was also rigid, jutting out from his hairless loins. "Talk about boners, it looks like you have one also."

"So, it happens," he giggled as he danced his fingers down over my lower belly, finally entwining them in my thick thatch of curling pubic hair. By now I was hard as steel.

"You have a lot of hair down here," he said. He played with my bush, smoothing and plucking, then slid his fingers around and under to grasp and cup my orbs.

"Big balls." He smiled as he juggled and caressed them. His fingers inched up to gently wrap around my now-throbbing erection. When he started squeezing and rubbing I almost fainted with ecstasy. I could not believe that he was actually feeling me up. Nor did I ever want to stop him. Making a fist around my erection, he started bending it back and forth, to the left then right. "Stick shift," he shouted, as he continued to play. He then paused then said, "You're leaking." Sure enough, all this play had so stimulated me that I was lubricating. He squeezed, forcing my pre-cum out, then slid his fingers up and down, rubbing my discharge over the length of my member. By now the warm itch had intensified to the point that if he did not stop, it would be all over in a matter of seconds.

"You better stop or you're going to make me shoot off all over the place," I grimaced.

It was as if my plea had fallen on deaf ears. He continued to rub and manipulate my penis with every intention of bringing me to a powerful orgasm. A few seconds later I erupted in thick spurts. My ejaculation didn't seem to faze him, for he continued to masturbate me until I had been totally drained. Finally he removed his semen-coated fingertips. "You made a sticky mess," he informed me, as if I didn't know. He stood up and ran over to the side of the stream to rinse his hand off. When he returned he lay back down beside me and asked, "How did that feel?"

"Tremendous," was all I could say. And it was. I had never shot off with such force and intensity as I did that day Bobby masturbated me.

"John calls it milking the cow." Bobby grinned. "We used to do it all the time until he got a girlfriend. Now he doesn't like fooling around with me anymore. Don't tell him I told you, okay?" He then rolled over on his back. "Would you do me some?" he asked.

I was speechless. First of all, I had never known that John and Bobby used to fool around, for John had never approached me in a sexual manner. And second was that Bobby seemed to take everything in stride, as if it wasn't taboo fooling around with another boy. I knew now that Bobby had prior experience in sexual matters. I was glad that he had now chosen me to have a sexual relationship with. "Are you going to do me or not?" Bobby piped.

"I'll be right there," I told him. "I'm going to rinse off first. I'm pretty gooey." I struggled to my feet, raced to the side of the creek, and dove in. As soon as I climbed out of the water I headed back over to Bobby. I knelt beside him and gently grasped his rigid penis between my thumb and forefingers. He gave me the best hand job that I had ever had, and I planned to do the same to him.

Cupping his orbs with the palm of my hand, I slowly started to stroke him up and down. His legs tightened and he let out a little cry as he succumbed to my gentle and loving strokes. I was in seventh heaven, never dreaming that something like this would ever happen between us. I knew right then where my sexual preferences lay. What happened between us was totally unexpected. I had no idea that such pleasures could be derived between two males. Everything I heard in high school about homosexuality had been said in a mocking tone of voice, joked about as a bad scene. How many teenagers like John were out there, who appeared to be so heterosexual in nature yet have had satisfactory sex with another male, never saying anything about it? John was the last one that I would have expected to have homosexual tendencies, yet that's where Bobby seemed to have derived his education.

By now Bobby's naked body was bathed in a sheen of sweat. He was breathing rapidly and I could tell by his expression that he was enjoying this. As I continued to rub his penis, I decided to do something else I had always fantasized. Pressing my two fingertips up against his frenulum, I leaned over his midsection and making an "O" with my lips, I went down on him, licking his moist glans and taking the entire circumcised knob into my mouth.

He let out a squeal of delight as I bobbed up and down over his swollen knob, using my tongue to explore every indentation and groove that he had displayed before me. As I was giving him the very first blow job that I had given to anyone, I felt his hips start bucking and the tip of his penis thrusting toward the roof of my mouth. I could tell he was on the verge of orgasm and I slid my mouth off his erection to watch as he crested and went over the brink. His thin clear semen bubbled out, dribbling down the sides of his penis to coat my fingertips with his youthful seed. Because of his age he did not have much, but what he did have was more than enough to satisfy me and my love for him.

For the next two years we enjoyed this relationship immensely. We could not wait to get it on with each other. We did everything, including experiments with anal sex. Though we could not express our love openly in school, we continued to satisfy our needs and yearnings for each other in private.

When I turned seventeen, I graduated from high school and took a full-time job. Bobby continued on through high school. Because of our separation, our relationship diminished and eventually ended. But for two years I had the most satisfying and intense sexual relationship that one could have. If only I could somehow turn back the hands of time and repeat those two long, loving years. I could never forget Bobby and I wonder if to this day he still thinks about me.

Show Time

Hyde

Year not given; high school student

I knew him from around. To nod to. I knew his name, knew his parents and two sisters by sight, knew where he lived — in a neighboring enclave slightly more upscale than our own.

I had my eye on him for as long as I can remember; no doubt since before I was even aware I was watching him in particular.

We were of an age but attended different grade schools, due to fickle district boundary lines. I had to content myself with spotting him by chance. In early days I'd see him only rarely, most likely with his mother; at the bank maybe when I was dragged along there by my own mom, or at the office of the pediatrician we shared, the grocery store, in church. Later I could — and did — improve my chances of seeing him by hanging out at the places he frequented. We'd each be with a crowd from our own school, and rarely did the twain fraternize, but I did at least have some opportunity to observe him, to feast my eyes.

I initially had my eye on him simply due to his delightful looks. And he was a beauty — blond, fey, delicately featured, well proportioned ... But later another feature compelled my attention to perhaps a greater extent.

What I noticed about him over time — watching him at the lake, the local movie theater, at the sledding hill — was his exhibitionist tendencies. Only after years of observing him with delicious expectation did I realize that his own obvious pleasure in being admired had, like my pleasure in admiring him, a sexual nature. And still later I learned a vocabulary for it all.

An example of his shameless but subtle ways: at the lake, the typical flooded quarry, he liked to wear his trunks low on his streamlined hips — practically begging to be pantsed. Delight of delights, he was once in my presence obliged. The trunks were only jerked down to his knees rather than properly whipped off altogether; but as I happened to be close by I caught a heaven-sent glimpse before, without haste, he tugged them back up again.

And sledding one morning during Christmas break I followed my idol into the grove of pine trees traditionally used by the males as an outdoor toilet. Standing as close as I dared as I also peed, I watched him sign his initials in the snow with long, elegant, golden letters. Then it just so happened he was facing me as he shook himself, tucked his adorable pink dick away, and zipped up.

A final example from the half dozen such I could relate. I took over a paper route for a sick friend during February and March of the year we were twelve. As luck would have it, the house of my adored show-off was on the route; to be perfectly candid this fact tipped the scales when I was indecisive about filling in as substitute carrier. One Friday evening when I went around collecting, my admired strolled out on the back screened-in porch where his father had kept me waiting. He was dressed only in t-shirt and briefs. White briefs, of course, and a snowy white V-neck undershirt. I think he was wearing white socks as well. My eyes were on his proud little bulge, the red-striped waistband, the place around one thigh where the elastic was stretched and a downy ball was just visible at the right angle. I wanted to fall on my knees and might have, but his mother followed only moments on the heels of his glorious arrival with my $1.40 and a ten-cent tip. She gave him a playful slap on the rump (I thought I might faint) and told him to get inside and get dressed before he froze. There was indeed frost on the ground.

Believe it or not, even after that tantalizing incident he wasn't in my mind officially categorized as an exhibitionist. I must have been slow on the uptake. I just thought of him as knowing himself to be pretty and liking to be appreciated.

He had to like it, the way he encouraged it. The way he'd tuck in his shirt for instance — it defies description. You wouldn't credit it. Or maybe you knew someone like him?

In time we were sent to the same inner-city Jesuit high school, and one afternoon during our sophomore year we found ourselves coming home on the same train late after detention.

I knew I was gay by this point, though I was still working up the nerve to act on it, and I strongly suspected that he — sitting beside me with his shirt half-unbuttoned — was gay too.

We talked en route of nothing consequential and I was cursing myself by the time we pulled up to our station for not being a better conversationalist, for not being more interesting. But outside the turnstiles where we would have parted, he invited me back to his house. His parents both worked, and we'd have the run of the house.

I was game. Nervous, but game.

We had a snack in the kitchen and split a beer. Then we had a beer each. With a grand total of twelve ounces of Rolling Rock in our bellies we weren't drunk, but our virtuous resolve to cram for geometry midterms was undermined.

He offered to show me his room. That took all of two minutes and then he produced a pack of cards. I knew it was coming and was already hard when he mildly suggested strip poker.

He lost, of course — I was probably up against a card sharper. But the game wasn't entirely predictable. I didn't anticipate him taking off his corduroys before removing either his shirt or cardigan, for instance. And I never imagined the extent to which I could get hornier than horny.

Before long he was naked — beautifully so. But, as I still had my pants and underwear on, he insisted we keep playing. It was his house, I thought it only polite to comply. "What if I win the next hand?" I asked, shuffling.

"You decide."

I won.

I had him get up on the bed, on his hands and knees, his butt in the air. With shaking hands I spread his cheeks. I feasted my eyes. I touched him with a forefinger.

That was about as far as we got...

We both came more or less spontaneously.

And then we dressed in silence.

We got together again, three or four times more. And we ran the gamut sexually — both indoors, where I preferred to carry on, and out. In the subsequent years I've enjoyed more than my fair share of encounters; as often as not with men who'd be considered good in bed...

But I've never recaptured the dreamlike, superthrilling, can-this-really-be-happening-to-me, fresh delight of that first time, that first possession.

Barbershop Duet

Michael Nolder Hall

1968, mid- or late teens

I finally swerved into the small shopping center that housed Bill's Barber Shop, cursing the tire squeals that announced my arrival. My father's new 1968 Ford Falcon bounced back from the curb in front of the Mini Mart next door, and I managed to control my shaking hands long enough to turn off the ignition. When I finally looked up, I was grateful that Bill sat motionless in the chair, his face still stuck in the magazine that had kept him from noticing all the times I'd passed by. There would be no explaining what I hoped was about to happen if anyone found out.

He looked up as he saw me come through the door, and got up and out to the side of the chair in one awkward motion, as if he had really hoped to jump behind it. His brown double-knit slacks weren't long enough to hide his green Orlon socks. Tossing the magazine on the counter behind him, he pushed his glasses back up over his eyes.

"Came without your daddy and brother again, huh?"

"Yeah, now that I got my license ... I'm goin' to a dance at school tomorrow night, so I need a haircut again." It startled me that the words came out calmly. I looked away from him to the shelf where he kept the hair tonics and powders.

"Well, guess you better get up here." He turned and reached for the smock as I sat in the chair, and I noticed how old his hands looked. I had always thought of him as old, but I knew from the many conversations he and my father had shared that he had two young children. His family had been in central Florida for generations. The last two times I'd come alone for a haircut, and each time Bill had let his crotch linger for brief moments on the smock where it covered my fingers. This time I hoped to have the courage to touch it, or something. I hadn't allowed myself to think about sex for a long time, not since I was eight or nine, when I used to play "nasty" with the neighbor boys back in Indiana.

"Your hair's hard to cut 'cause of all the cowlicks," he said after a while. He always cut the back of my head first, and now he was slowly making his way around my temples to the front of the chair. Extending my hands to the ends of the chair arms, I felt my sweaty palms slip on the cold vinyl. I knew I would chicken out, but I managed to resume breathing and dug in my fingernails.

Bill made the first clip on my bangs, and the lock fell on my cheek. "Sorry," he said, and as he leaned in close to brush it away with his free hand, his penis fell between my first two fingers. He straightened, but didn't move away. Nothing could have made me move my hand.

He started cutting again, and neither of us spoke while I slowly began slipping my fingers up and down it. The larger it got, the more I wished it were cupped inside my palm instead of hidden in his pants. So my fear was gone, replaced with an excitement that left me shaking just as much.

"Think you can do somethin' with that?" he asked, glancing down to the bulge I had created. Without waiting for an answer I couldn't possibly have forced out, he looked over his shoulder through the shop windows, hesitated, then moved to the folding door behind the chair and motioned me into the room beyond.

There was a toilet and a sink and not much else, but room for the two of us. He peered out through the slit of the door, his hand ready on the handle, and I crouched at his feet. Pulling it out of his pants, I remembered all the times I had rushed into the school bathroom in fourth grade so I could stand at the urinal next to Mr. Seip, my teacher, to watch him pee.

Bill didn't have to tell me to put it in my mouth, but he did finally suggest I suck on it. He could have also suggested what would happen if I did. I knew what cum was, though I didn't have a name for it, but I had never imagined it could end up in my mouth. When that rather quickly came about, I choked and pushed him away, squeezing down on his penis to make it stop. Some of his cum made it into my ear, some onto my shirt, while the stuff in my mouth shot to the floor. I looked up, my mouth still hanging open, but Bill didn't seem concerned with my dumbfoundment; he was gasping and jerking as if he were watching somebody steal his car.

The straightening of clothes and cleaning up took seconds, and I was out the door without even paying for the cut. Driving home, I worried that my mother would see and smell the crustiness of my shirt. But she didn't, and I continued going to Bill to get my hair cut, always driving by until there were no other customers in the shop. We improved our little sessions in his back room over the next few months. But eventually he decided it "wasn't a good idea" anymore, and I had to content myself with just fondling him from the chair. Bill and I never talked about what we were doing, in fact we never really talked about much of anything, but I've told many friends over the years.

Summer of Clumsy Love

Michael Lassell

1967, age 19

My first time was so clumsy, so unromantic, unglamorous, and — I seem to remember — unfulfilling, that I wish it were also unmemorable. For better or worse, it still shows up on the brain screen when I push the "first time" button, and what I recall of that long-awaited first time my genitals touched those of another male ... well, it's surprising that I decided to try it a second time. I was, however, overachiever that I have always been, resolute.

It helped, of course, that I knew I was gay. As early as 1965 (the year I was seventeen) friends wanted to know how I could possibly *know* I was gay if I'd never had sex with anyone, male or female (not uncommon for anyone in those days). I suppose it was a legitimate question, if a bit naive: eroticism, it has been my adult experience, *frequently* raises its engorged head long before the tumescence has a willing target up against or inside of which to test the hypothesis of sexual attraction. In other words, I wanted it a long time before I got it — and I knew who I wanted it with and for and from.

In retrospect I wish I could write that I had sex with the first boy I ever found myself so physically attracted to that my heart nearly stopped every time I saw him. Seeing him naked was too thrilling and too frightening to describe. But we were — what? — thirteen then, and that was a long dry time before I ever got to practice what my body was preaching like some ancient Baptist on Jesus-speed.

I wish I could say that my third or fourth actual sexual experience was my first — with an opera singer who was appearing at the summer theater where I was apprenticing. I made *sure* he knew I was available, and he did, and we did, and it was amazing for me, but I still didn't know how to *give* in a sexual situation. I was still taking, from him, from a girl named Judy down the hall. I was twenty by then. I learned later how to take pleasure from giving it, but there weren't many teachers around, and I had to piece my lessons together from scant empirical research.

Or that my first was the year I turned twenty-two. That was a two-day nonstop affair that began one evening, went all night, moved from adjoining twin beds onto one of them (mine), from the bedroom to the shower, out into the fields of upstate New York at dawn (near the Mohawk River, in the shadow of a ruined nineteenth-century mill), lasted the entire next day, was accompanied by many compliments about technique ("Are you sure you've never done this before?"), came on like a freight train out of a tunnel, and evaporated in the evening air like the last light of a firefly in July.

But, sad, sad to say, my first was — to the best of my fading recollection — in a Colgate University dormitory room in 1967 or so, with a man I did not find particularly attractive, whose name I don't remember, and who not only did not become my lover, but didn't — according to *him* at least — turn out to be gay at all. Which is a crock, or a half-crock, anyway, in case he turned out to be bisexual.

But, a little background: Like many now coeducational schools, Colgate University was an all-boys school at the time, on top of a hill, in a tiny town, miles from anywhere. An ideal place for hard study, but not for sex, which was the idea (sex between the boys not having actually been considered when it was built in 1819). In fact, the straight boys were having sex with each other all the time, it turned out. It was the gay boys who weren't having sex — at least not with each other, which might have been committal. (Men really do hate commitment, don't we?) To be fair, being publicly gay was extremely damaging if not dangerous in 1966 or 1967.

So, it was in the nascent years of the Hippie Era, following hard on the heels of the drug-and-sex revolution which, yes, the Beatles and the Rolling Stones really did instigate in a way, although obviously social conditions were primed. I mean, the Stamp Act would never have caused the American Revolution if the Minutemen weren't already willing and able to fight to the death to get what they wanted, you know?

I was being "an artsy-fartsy malcontent," as I called myself. I wore a navy wool pea jacket, a six-foot-long maroon scarf that I had bought on West Fourth Street in Greenwich Village (at a shop I already knew was geared to gay men), and wire-rimmed glasses that poked out from around a mop of then very thick, quite blond hair.

If I'd known how to play it, and if I'd been in a city, I'd probably be having fabulous, life-affirming sex with gorgeous, intelligent, caring, and socially committed young activists of all the sexual orientations every night of my life. But I was sexually retarded and stuck in the middle of nowhere with my own fourth-generation depression (thanks, Mom) and a bunch of horny postadolescents in the days just long enough before Stonewall that homosexuality was still a horror in all-male communities, but not so much before Stonewall that sensitive men, which is to say the men I was hanging out with, weren't sensitive to the possibilities of experimentation vis-à-vis their private parts.

And so we did. There was a man named Stephen (I remember his full name, but I'll permit him anonymity, should he want it or still be alive to care). He was not gay, I don't think, but he was a pot head. Oh, did I mention how much marijuana inhibits the anti-gay mechanism of young

114

men who aren't getting regularly and righteously laid nearly often enough (which would have to be about every four hours, floods of brand-new hormones being what they are)? Anyway, I was learning how to have mad crushes on unavailable men, a pattern I've made a lifelong pursuit even though I'm supposed to know better, and sort of got it on with people whose major virtue was congenial availability.

Anyway I was occasionally blowing a little weed with Stephen and his buddies, and that occasionally meant a little body action ... like some hugging, lots of lying around wrapped up in each other, lots of slow, sensuous, tentative, and killer-erotic kissing. And here's a wonderful thing about Stephen of the curly blond mop: God he could kiss! And he was not the least bit hypocritical about it either, for which I am eternally grateful.

Stephen, who remained a friend, wasn't prepared to go further than we went, but it wasn't a secret to him, either (I wonder where people get the self-esteem to assume that whatever they are doing is just perfectly all right). We would sometimes hug and kiss and make out in mixed-company situations without giving a rat's nether regions about the reactions of others, and, in fact, most of the people we knew were either delighted, titillated, insecure, accepting, turned on, or too intimidated by middle-class upbringings to object out loud.

There were other men similarly inclined, and I can remember long cold autumn afternoons wrapped in the arms of these boys on the cusp of manhood who were not identifying themselves as homosexual, but who found as much comfort in my arms as I found in theirs — and, yes, there were erections involved in all of this, but there was no ejaculating, at least that I am aware of, and no speaking of it afterward, and no love, no romance, which is, of course, the part I not only desperately wanted then, but want now, too, with — I hope — less desperation, at least less that prospective boyfriends can see.

So, that is who I was in the countdown to Stonewall, and everyone knew it, and I was an actor/writer/artist so what could you expect? And that is how I came to meet — I don't know, let's call him ... Alfred. Alfred was skinny, dark, and Jewish, and he came from a town on Long Island about two shopping centers and a bad restaurant closer to Queens than the one I grew up in.

I don't actually remember if we did the dope/petting routine first at one of these pot parties (Alfred may have been Stephen's roommate, now that I think of it), but he came to my room in the dorm one day (to which I had been condemned by not being rich, cool, worthy, snotty, or ostensibly heterosexual enough to be rushed for a fraternity, although I certainly drank and swore and vomited enough, I promise you). I may have been surprised to see Alfred. I don't remember. He may have told me he was coming over. We might have flirted. Anyway, there he was, and this time there was real-live, honest-to-God contact between my hand and his penis (*under* his white cotton briefs!), and there was contact

115

between his hands and my penis (under my white cotton briefs), and there was a lot of touching and extraordinarily deep kissing (I can remember his hard, dark five-o'clock beard growth grinding into my mouth like sandpaper — a sensation I miss). There was even quite naked contact between his naked dick (skinny) and mine, and quite certainly mutual ejaculation and a lot of noise.

And that's when there was a knock on the door.

Oops!

Now, I should mention that in these pre-enlightened days (and enlightenment came to Colgate far later than to many an institution, all-male or no), a person could be expelled from school for having sex with a woman or just for being *thought* to be homosexual. No proof was necessary, and there was no process of appeal. It was called *in loco parentis*. Legally it meant that the college was acting in place of your parents, but it really meant that the school could be as crazy as your parents, and you had about as much chance of justice as you had at home.

Well, we leapt up, pulled up our clothes the best way we knew how, tried to hide the cum stains, whatever one does in such a situation — hair messed, clothes askew — and I opened the door to greet my good friend Barney (director of the experimental theater group, a close friend then and still, and now an Emmy-winning TV director).

Now, Barney could not have cared less whether I was poking Alfred, a fraternity brother of his at the fraternity you could belong to just by signing up, so it had all the smart kids in the college, and most of the Jewish kids, and a good number of the miniscule number of black students. I, however, felt that an explanation was necessary. Unfortunately, the best I could come up with was: "We were just wrestling." God bless Barney, who restrained himself from cracking up (which he later did, when we were alone and reminiscing), but he pretended, for Alfred's sake if not his own, to believe us.

Alfred, unfortunately, took off for parts unknown to me at the time (female parts), although I tried that, too, in the year or so that followed. None of which I would have minded, had Alfred not simply *denied* that the incident took place not only to my own shocked face but to that of Barney, as well. So I was betrayed by denial, but, you know, shitty as I felt, Alfred was doing what he had to be doing for himself when he thought he had to be doing it, and I was doing the same for myself, poor confused puppies that we all were.

And all of this was in the halcyon days of the Summer of Love and the Summer After the Summer of Love, and the Summer of Stonewall, and my year-long sojourn in London, and British ballet boys and *Hair* and learning how to be gay and a gay drunk at the same time, far from a home to which I would never return again. And I wish my first time had been better, but I guess it was enough, and anyway it was what it was so what can I do about it now?

Frat Brother

Rich Petersen

1963–64, early twenties

His name was Jack. I hadn't known him for long at college, because I had been studying abroad when he joined the fraternity. I returned to campus for my senior year as Jack moved into the house as a sophomore.

Jack was known as the cocksman on campus. He had a reputation for having sex with every girl he dated and was the envy of most everyone in the house. We got to know each other in the usual fraternity-house way. He was fun. We drank beer with the rest of the guys and I helped him type his term papers. He razzed me about my short, curly hair and I razzed him right back about the Elvis ducktail he sported.

Jack wasn't the type of guy I'd grown up with — he wasn't a city boy but was from a small farming town. He had a countryish accent, real tight pants, a swagger ... and a black 1959 Ford hardtop convertible he was very proud of.

It was either late 1963 or early 1964. A bunch of us were at the town's only bar. Jack liked to shoot pool. A couple of our friends lived in the dormitory up the hill, on campus, and Jack offered them a ride at closing time. On the way up the hill the lights went out all over town. This was a frequent occurrence and only heightened our high from drinking. We let our friends off at the dorm and on the way back down to town, Jack reached over and felt my crotch.

It was last thing I would have expected from him. I knew at once what this was all about. No words were spoken for a while, and then he said, "You wanna go play?" I said, "Are you sure? ... Yes, I do."

He drove us to a solitary spot by the river. It was still pitch black. I had fantasized for years about having sex with another man, and was always trying to be in the shower at the same time with other guys. I was a "looker" at the urinals. That something was about to happen with *this* guy, this ladies' man, made it even more exciting.

Remember — it was in the early sixties. I don't think I'd seen but one or two nudie magazines, much less a fuck flick. Nevertheless, my fantasies about men up to that point had been very graphic and sexual, and now this guy was groping me and I knew what was about to happen. It was too good to be true.

He rubbed my cock through my pants until I was hard, then took it out and played with it more. I reached over and felt the erection in his

117

jeans, then unzipped them and took his cock out. It seemed big; I hadn't seen any that close before. I don't really know how big it was, but I knew what to do with it and started to suck it. He loved it and moaned for more. I wanted him to suck mine, of course, but he wouldn't. He kissed and licked around my dick but wouldn't take it in his mouth. I didn't care ... it was all so new and wonderful.

We ended up jacking off together in the backseat of the '59 Ford. At the last minute he grabbed a rag to catch our cum. After settling down, we drove back to the fraternity house and each went to our room. I know we talked on the way back but I don't remember about what. I do remember thinking how good it was that Jack wasn't embarrassed or anything; I hadn't known what his reaction would be.

We had lots more sex during my final year there. I was the one who initiated things now, or so it seemed, because I couldn't get enough. Jack was willing most of the time. I had to urge him a couple of times, but he always went along. Once he put his cock between my legs and rubbed a lot, then said it felt just as good as any girl. I didn't know what that meant at the time, but it sure made me feel good.

At first I worried that our furtive sex would affect our relationship as friends, but he never put me down or shied away from me in a group. I think he really liked me as a friend.

I say this because we kept in touch after I graduated. I went into the Peace Corps and wrote him from South America. He answered. After I married (we didn't know better in the sixties), we continued to keep in touch for a number of years. Since I have now been in a gay relationship for eighteen years, I haven't corresponded with Jack, but I think I'll send him a copy of this story and see what happens. Did this experience shape or influence my sexual preference? I suppose it would have, had I known then it was possible to have a preference. It certainly didn't make me feel bad or anything like that, because I know now I had been gay all along and just didn't know it or have a word for it. Thanks, Jack.

4. Post-Stonewall (1970-1977)

The Stonewall Riots of 1969 are widely credited as the beginning of the gay liberation movement. There were activists and gay organizations before that, but only with Stonewall did the movement mushroom. Within a few months, the American Sociological Association became the first professional organization to take a stand against anti-gay discrimination. By 1972, openly gay delegates were speaking at the Democratic National Convention, and for the first time a gay-positive drama aired on national television.

What effect did all this increased visibility have on gay men who were just becoming sexual?

Not much, it would appear, for those in their midteens and under. They continued to experiment with friends, giving little thought to labels. Many, like their predecessors in the sixties, were cheerfully unaware of any change in the outside world.

But those in their late teens and older were clearly affected by the gay movement. Gayness was in the air — in newspapers, on television, on the student union bulletin board. It was something you were, or could be, or might become if you did it too often. (This last issue was more often a concern for straight-identified partners than for the men who themselves contributed pieces to this book.)

For the first time, it was common to know a happy, healthy, open homosexual. College students, in particular, had many opportunities to see old stereotypes shattered. For some, this made coming out easier. It helped erase the myth that being gay would condemn them to a life of loneliness.

For others, however, the increased visibility brought new difficulties. No longer could you fool around now, and come to terms with your gayness much later. Unless you were quite adept at self-deceit, your first

119

man-to-man sex brought an awareness that you were gay. For some, it was too big a package to swallow all at once.

For each man who had extra difficulty, however, there are wonderful stories about men finding support in unexpected places. Grant Michael Menzies, for example, shows in the lead story that those male apprenticeships of the thirties haven't entirely disappeared.

Several contributors got their start with someone who (to quote a t-shirt I saw at the March on Washington) was "Straight But Not Narrow." I was delighted to get a story from Leigh W. Rutledge, author of the entertaining *Gay Book of Lists,* who showed a straight buddy a pretty fun time back in 1974. Others recount similar experiences. Surely the nascent gay movement had something to do with the fact that so many straight men in the 1970s were willing to experiment a bit. Stonewall's reach extended into many corners.

Cousin

Grant Michael Menzies

1971, age 7

It was not as if I had never seen a naked man before, because I had seen my father. I had watched his slim golden form step from the shower, his brown hands towel off the water spotting his broad, furry shoulders. Nor was it as if I had never touched that body, for in our second-generation American family there was more than a trace of European homoerotic innocence, where boys had played naked in German lakes and walked arm in arm down wet Scottish streets. And how to forget the pleasure, now a quarter century old, of climbing up through the crossed legs of my seated father, shirtless after cutting the grass or working in his shop, smelling of summer, aftershave, and the strangely reassuring aroma of his sweat, to doze on the thick brown mat of his chest?

With a father like this at home, why my cousin John proved so interesting to me is unclear, except the compelling fact that along with having just turned seven — John was nearly ten years older — I was suddenly experiencing constant erections, as if I had been seized by an especially virulent allergy, the primary effect of which was this pleasurable but worrisome physical reaction.

With the erections came thoughts that besieged and overtook my mind, gave everything a sexual tone; and though I loved my father's chest and his arms, I did not want sex with him: but I very much wanted it with John, whom I barely knew. Maybe it was because John and I, though related, were so different. I was small, blond, and quiet; he was tall for his age, dark with the warm, sooty-eyed darkness of his Central American mother. And he seemed worlds away from me in age, experience.

In summer our grandparents' rambling old house normally smelled of nothing but Grandma's cooking, her rose sachets, Grandpa's occasional furtive cigarette, the tang of newly mowed fields next door. But when John was there an electricity was introduced. He was an athlete, so there was always movement in the stillness of the house. He had a loud laugh, so there was always astonishing and joyful noise. And he was "almost a man," as Grandpa put it, so that the room we shared upstairs under the seven-gabled roof smelled rather familiar to me, like my father after he came in from the yard, but far more pungent, enthralling, more like the fresh-cut grass beside the house, like the preserved quince Grandma served at dinner, drawing the mouth like some dark and potent wine.

Once, I had secretly put one of my cousin's t-shirts to my face and breathed his unalloyed maleness, to steal away to the creek afterwards, face hot and penis hard with suffocating consternation.

What I remember of one summer's day: the heat, of course, fruit swinging from the branches outside the dining room windows, striped awnings, some hours playing on the cool clover lawn beside the house, and my grandmother calling me inside, some iced tea in freezing glasses, and then being sent upstairs for the ritual before-dinner nap; and with, joy of joys, my cousin John to accompany me.

We lay there side by side in the big iron bedstead that squeaked when you breathed; and for a time the June warmth, the cool brown gloom of the old furniture and pictures, the confident, quietly busy sounds of the adults below, the excitement of being so close to John, made me drowsy; I slept a little.

Then we were both wide awake; I imagined I had heard summer thunder, but John said no, the sun was out as strong as before. In the shadows my cousin's deep dark eyes stood out with a sort of animal lambency, calm, composed, liquid as the gaze of the mounted stag's head on the wall behind. Somewhat sick with happiness, I wanted to say, "John, John, I love you..." I was only seven, but my feelings were violent, the bed creaked just because my heart was thumping like a crazy drummer out of control, whatever went wrong would be because of me. My mouth opened to say — what? I don't know. What emerged sounded false to me, since I already had some knowledge of what I was asking. I said, "John, what do they mean when they say 'the birds and the bees'?"

John's dark eyes fixed on me; he smiled, he turned toward me. "What men and women do with each other," he murmured with all the *savoir faire* of a grown-up. Blood rushed in my ears. "Didn't anybody ever tell you that?" I shook my head, I was lying, but could he tell? I turned on my stomach because the raging hard-on was forcing itself at right angles from my body.

It seemed as if I watched us from above, or in the reflection of the tilting bureau mirror, because as my cousin told me the forbidden things about what exactly men and women did, I saw him remove his shirt, saw his brown chest and its first wild swirls of black curly hair; and then his pants came off, and then he helped me with mine. "We have to be quiet," he spoke as to the child I was, while his hands touched me as if I were a man like him; I understood this admonition instinctively, listening to our grandmother preparing dinner directly below. Like turning a corner into someplace new, we were both naked — I saw his cock standing up, pulsating, against the sunset-brightened window shades; I watched his face tighten in some strange convulsion, and felt something wet on the bedsheets.

That was all — all I remember. We sat at dinner downstairs an hour later, or was it a few minutes later? It hardly matters; and I found disturbingly that I could not look at anyone at the table. Not from shame, for I could hardly define what that word might mean, but because I felt I had been given a small piece of a huge treasure, one stone from a mountain of diamonds, and I wanted to steal away with it, to watch it sparkle in delicious, holy privacy. When I went outside into the cool evening, I was still not myself, I was different; my body was nothing but a string suspended from an errant balloon, I might fly away to nowhere.

The next time I saw my cousin's body: years later, the morning before his wedding to a rich Jewish girl from San Francisco. John was off, with much laughter, to take a shower, his last as a *free man;* his tight little body whipped about the house in his underwear. Because of his easy laugh I thought it might be okay to slip into the bathroom to take a pretended leak while he walked naked, negligent through the rising steam. No such luck. He smiled a little coldly, he closed the door in my face, he was already unfree. It was a beautiful wedding.

The Ace of Spades

Anonymous

You might think that growing up gay in a rural midwestern town of 950 people would be terrible. But it doesn't have to be. Not if you find the right people to grow up with.

I met Donald in 1964 when my parents were building a house next to his parents' house in the new subdivision. Donald was such a cute kid. He had reddish brown-blond hair, with just enough wave to it to give him a naturally angelic look. He had a few well-placed freckles on his smooth complexion, and everyone adored him. We were only four years old, and had lots of fun playing together. We were glad to find out that we'd be in the same class when we started school.

Our boyhood adventures together were exciting and carefree. We spent summers riding our bikes, wading in the creek, and playing in the mud; in winter we made snow forts. We played cornet duets at music contests, and played billiards in Donald's folks' basement. We had great times together. And as we grew older, we began to think of more interesting things to do.

It is said that adolescent boys often experiment with gay sex, and we were no exception. Sometime in sixth grade, at age eleven, we got the idea to play doctor. We used Donald's toy tool set and my pretend doctor set and operated on each other. Our operating table was an old couch in Donald's parents' basement. We tried such surgical procedures as tourniquets around arms to make veins pop out, then progressed to arm removals using the little saw; and head removals. Quickly we realized that such serious surgery required tying the patient up to keep him in place. This worked great, until the time Donald's mom called down to us that the phone call was for him. I yelled back, "He's all tied up at the moment, but he'll be up in a minute!" Of course, we both thought that was hilarious.

Although it *was* funny, it did scare us into moving our doctor game to the storage closet under the basement stairs at my parents' house. My dad's old Joe Weider weight-lifting bench made an ideal operating table. We called the space "Fort Fantastic," which we wrote on the inside of the door with glow-in-the-dark paint.

By the summer after sixth grade, when we were twelve, the doctor play evolved into a card game. An elaborate list of consequences corresponded to each suit and number. The doctor shuffled the cards, then the victim drew the top card off the deck and checked the list to find out the consequences. Some consequences included the "naked" card, the "dark" card (lights were turned out), the "breather" card (which amounted to a French kiss), the "tie-up" card, the "squish" card (the doctor was to lie on top of the victim), the "torture" card (which meant the victim was tied up and tickled), and the "heat" card (when we turned on a large electric heater and the doctor and victim would play what we called "dying of the heat"). Lastly, the ace of spades. This was the dreaded, yet secretly anticipated "Death Card," as we called it. The victim was stripped naked, tied up in a position chosen by the doctor, and subjected to *all* of the above consequences at the mercy of the administrator, who also had to get naked and squish the victim by lying on top of him. Somehow the ace of spades made its way to the top of the deck quite often!

After several weeks of the Death Card treatments, we didn't bother tying each other up anymore. One day when I was about to be the victim, Donald said, "Julian, can I ask you a funny question?"

"Sure," I said. "What?"

"Can I put my dick in your butt?" Donald asked.

This question shocked the heck out of me. Somewhat confused, and in total wonder as to why he'd want to do such a thing, I said, "That sounds kind of icky. I don't want you to."

"Okay," Donald said, "then let me just lie on top of your back with my dick *on* your butt." I agreed to this, relieved that he didn't insist on doing something bizarre like actual penetration.

Usually we had lain chest-to-chest. But this time I lay down on my stomach, preparing for Donald's touch. Then he lay down softly on top of me, just as he said, and began slow, gentle pelvic rocking motions, giving me pleasure I'd never felt before. The only other time I had thought about feeling Donald's body was when I fantasized about us both getting into a big pair of jeans together naked, chest-to-chest, and thought how good it would feel. I guess that at age twelve your fantasies don't make much sense. But now, here I was, feeling Donald's young, silky-smooth, warm body in real life.

Still, I was scared and tense. I really had no idea that we were having "gay sex." For that matter, I didn't know what gay sex was. Donald did, however, seem to know what was going on; later he said, "Let's trade." So we switched positions, with me on top, and suddenly an uncontrollable urge came over me, and I came on Donald. I truly was naive. I had little idea what had happened.

Donald asked rather sternly, "Did you pee on me?" Bewildered, and defensive, I said no, because it hadn't felt like urination. "Then that was your sperm coming out," Donald said matter-of-factly.

"My what?"

"You know, your sperm!"

"Oh, I guess," I said, still trying to mentally sort out all that had happened.

Donald wiped away the mysterious fluid with his shirt, got dressed, and ran upstairs and back to his house, leaving me alone, confused, and scared.

That was my first time. After that, our meetings grew less frequent. To date, at the age of thirty-five, I have not let any man "put his dick in my butt." I guess I just haven't met the right guy.

I also don't know for sure if Donald is gay or not. He married one of my cousins and they have two cute girls. He lives just outside of town on a couple of acres, and our parents are still neighbors. I see him quite frequently — both around town and at family-related or community functions. We have never mentioned these experiences to each other again.

It wasn't until I was twenty-one that I realized that what I was feeling for men since the age of eleven meant that I am gay.

The Boy in the Red Speedos

Anonymous

Year not given, age 12

It was late November. My parents were eager to have the holiday shopping done, so we drove to Madison for the weekend. My parents loved the malls there. Just across the street from a particularly impressive shopping center was the Madison Holidome. It was an extravagance, but Dad was in the middle of his midlife crisis, so we splurged.

After checking in and tossing the suitcases onto the beds I grabbed my suit and asked if I could go for a swim. They said okay, but hurry. I crossed the lot and bounded down the Astro-Turf steps to the locker rooms below the recreation area.

I stomped into a blue boxer suit. Annoyed. I didn't want to hurry. I didn't want to go shopping. I hated being twelve. It was a borderline age. It was up in the air as to whether they would let me stay alone while they went shopping.

As I emerged from the changing area I saw a teenager swimming laps in the topaz pool. He moved smoothly through the surface like a pulled length of wood. At the next turn I saw he was wearing a Speedo. He was trim and smooth-skinned. Water rippled over him lap after lap.

I felt something as I watched him, something like concentrated bands moving up and down my chest and stomach. It was impossible to turn away. I stood staring from the center step of the three descending to the shallows. After a few more laps he stopped, stood, and lifted his goggles. He rubbed three center fingers over the surface of his closed lids. "Damn chlorine," he said to me with a smile. His eyes were green and bloodshot.

I heard my name. Turning, I saw my parents, parked and ready for shopping. Mom was carrying her big purse. Shit. I asked if I could stay, whining that I wouldn't have the chance to swim again until the coming spring.

At this point the eavesdropping stranger introduced himself as Scott. He was probably fifteen, with dirty blond hair, dimples. He offered to keep an eye on me.

My parents were all smiles, relief, and thankfulness. When they headed for monster mall Scott and I splashed around and bobbed a little bit. We did a couple relays. He kicked my ass and said he was on the swim team back in Milwaukee. He was a sophomore there.

127

Scott said the best thing after a swim was a sauna, makes your muscles feel great, burns all the chlorine off your skin. I tailed him to the locker room. Deserted. I felt a charge just being there; a potency in the air.

He rolled down his red suit. His dick was pale, long, arched over his balls. They hung between his ass cheeks when he bent to grab his white hotel towel. Instead of putting it around his waist he curled it upon his shoulders. I did the same. I watched his butt move down the corridor. It jiggled slightly when he yanked open the heavy wooden door of the sauna. I felt a blast of heat.

Two tiers of wooden benches lined the inside walls. I wrapped my towel around my waist, stepping up and up to the top. Scott spread his towel on the level below me. A low bulb glowed above the caged sauna coils. Silence. I began to sweat almost immediately. The bands about the chest and stomach were tighter now. There was nowhere to flow but with the waves of heat, coaxing, relaxing, and making edges melt and smooth as sweat trickled like fingers down my torso.

Scott ran a hand across his hairless chest and stood, readjusting his towel. His nakedness blasted me. My dick went from puffy to firm to rigid. His dick lolled large and indifferent across his thigh. Still silence, even longer this time, so heavy even the gulp of swallowing interrupted it. Our bodies gleamed in the dim glow, coated in sticky dew.

He touched my ankle, inching upward, hands on my calves, my thighs. "You are so beautiful." Key 712 was corded about the wrist reaching below my towel, wrapping around my erection. "So nice." The smooth movements of his hands jolted me, softer than anything, too soft, just soft enough. I closed my eyes and felt the sensation of his hand swallow me to a blind degree. I was free-falling into something taboo. Something I knew without knowing. I didn't want to resist falling, I wanted to hurl my weight further into it. Take me, gravity.

I heard him shifting on the planks as his mouth kissed my thighs, my inner thighs, finally engulfing me. The picture was clear even with my eyes closed. With toes curled and fists clenched I began rising to meet his mouth. I grabbed his head, wrapping my fingers in that dirty blond hair. In seconds I felt a desperate urge to pee, an out-of-nowhere necessity. God, not down Scott's throat!

I bolted, fleeing the sauna, back to the locker room to the furthest toilet stall. A pearl gleamed at the cap of my penis. I must but couldn't piss!

Scott strummed the metal door. After a moment I let him in. There we were in the furthermost stall of a Holidome locker room and he's giving me a facts-of-life speech. It was sweet and it was crazy. Someone came in the locker room and the fact that other people existed scared us a little bit. After the guy left we went to room 712.

Scott taught me a lot while his parents were at that wedding and mine were at the mall. The next day we drove back home and I never saw him again.

128

Confusion Reigned

L. Prince Heart

1970, teenager

By the summer of 1970, I had grown into a tall, slender though sinewy teenager. Usually I sported a dandelion Afro, a red shirt with sleeves cut off, tight black jeans with white stitching, and black high-top Converse sneakers. I'd suffered little during the upheaval of the sixties, but now came this sexual revolution that was spinning my head as if it were a top. Then, Mickey, my nondescript neighbor across the street, showed up. Many days as I lay on my stomach on the front porch, Mickey would sneak up behind me (I saw him peripherally), mount, and hump me. Though I laughed it off, this planted the seed which bloomed into sexual longing.

That summer I decided to embark on a career as a newspaper boy. It was early-morning delivery, but I enjoyed it. I'd just begun having wet dreams, sparked by dreams of baseball. I discovered nudity in *Penthouse,* and I was shocked. My fantasies, however, remained inexplicably connected to baseball. By the time my birthday rolled around in mid-August, I discovered I could ejaculate. Autoeroticism was ecstasy. I still had no object in mind except gratification when I indulged this urge.

Delivering papers was fun, but getting paid was better. On one sultry late-August evening I went collecting on delinquent accounts. I noticed in my booklet that one Mr. Peter Wilson was some twenty dollars in arrears. He was never home when I collected. Among others, Mr. Wilson was my especial target this hot evening.

By 7:30 I arrived at Mr. Wilson's upstairs apartment. I detected loud music, so I knocked loudly several times before I closed the screen door to leave. Then, the music stopped and the door opened. A youth peered out. He had shiny blond hair and searching blue eyes, and he wanted to know what or whom I wanted.

"I'm lookin' for Mr. Peter Wilson," I informed him, thinking I sought his father. "I'm the paperboy."

"Yes?" he inquired.

"Funny, you don't look like you're old enough to be a mister," I noted with suspicion. He later said he was nineteen.

"Yeah, well, you don't look like you're made of paper, either!" he remarked and laughed lightly.

129

He invited me in. When I mentioned his account was in arrears, he smiled and waved it off. He asked if I wanted something to drink, to which I said no. The smell of alcohol permeated the air. He had been drinking, and he looked younger than I was! He was about my height but more slender. He was wearing a colored t-shirt and tight (tight and revealing) Levi jeans. At that time I wasn't as attuned to physical presence, but in retrospect I know he was an Adonis.

We talked a few minutes — he was a model, he'd just gotten back from California (the *West* Coast), and he had no idea why he'd returned to the *East* Coast. I didn't divulge much about myself. He said he liked my Afro and especially my jeans.

Then he remembered that I was waiting to get paid. Again, he offered me a drink, and I said I'd take a beer, which I didn't drink after I'd opened it. I knew something was different and special about this guy. His jeans revealed he was intriguingly endowed in front, and stacked in the back. I was confused by urges I couldn't comprehend.

Peter said he'd have to look in the bedroom for the money, and then he begged me to help him. That was an unusual request, but despite my reservations about going into anyone's bedroom, I agreed. Peter's walk was graceful and seductive. He gyrated so as to emphasize his eye-catching ass. I was still wondering why I had this stirring sensation in my groin.

The bedroom was dark. Soft music was playing. A candle shone in each corner. About the carpeted floor, magazines were strewn. On the walls were posters of Peter. The poses, in some of which he was scantily clad, were captivating. Peter had a king-size bed. He sat on the bed, and invited me to sit beside him.

When I looked down and inspected the first magazine, I noticed they were porno books. What fascinated and confused me more was that they were *gay* porno books. I asked if I could see one, and Peter placed it into my hands.

A white model in the magazine looked a lot like Peter. Another, a muscular big-dicked dark-skinned black with an Afro, and the blond-haired Peter look-alike were having sex. I became almost apoplectic in sexual desire, though I didn't understand that urge.

Meanwhile, Peter, aware of my deep excitement, was sitting next to me, leaning on my shoulder and blowing on my neck. When I said that what the models were doing wasn't possible, he assured me it was. When I persisted, flipping the pages, he offered to demonstrate for me. I awkwardly acceded. Peter told me to relax and he'd guide me through it.

With a delicate purposeful touch, Peter unzipped my jeans and pulled out my straining dick (which he called a *cock).* He went to get a washcloth and wiped it, for I was uncut. He kissed me on my neck, and blew softly into my ears. Having thus stimulated me to fullness, his head swooped down, and his mouth swathed my cock in euphoric warmth. I closed my eyes in utter satisfaction; nothing equaled this feeling, I thought. Peter continued to suck until he felt I was well primed. Then, he said, he was ready to take me to heaven.

When we were denuded, Peter lay facedown on the bed. He applied some kind of gel to my erect cock and his supple ass. He instructed me to enter him, but I was reluctant. (I *knew* it would hurt him.) Peter told me he'd done it before and that I'd really like it. He was wrong; I *loved* it! He was tight and moved skillfully to excite me to climax.

Momentarily, approaching climax, I panicked. I slowed. Peter asked what was wrong. When I told him, he laughed, realizing I was a virgin. He told me to pump and push as hard as I liked. He got on all fours so I'd have greater access, and he pushed as I pumped. With one hand on each of his hips, I drove myself to climax. Still, confusion reigned.

We cleaned up, and Peter paid me fifty dollars. I asked if I could take the magazine in which the model favored him. He said yes, if I promised to come back. I agreed, but I never returned. It took me a long time to assimilate that experience and its significance into my being.

I had told Peter I wanted to show the magazine to my cousin Ricky, but I never showed Ricky, either. Instead, I showed my mother the book. I told her I'd found it in the cemetery. She laughed at my curiosity and said there were all kinds of people in this world. I asked what would she do if I were like the men in the book. She gave me that disarming matriarchal smile, searched my face, and decided, "Honey, I'll love you no matter what you decide to be."

Teen for the Day

James Russell Mayes

On the bus home I was nervous and my chest felt like someone was squeezing it in his hands because Joseph David Hutting had agreed, after weeks of my manipulations and appeals to "true friendship," to have sex with me. He was curious, he said. Joe was "a good kid," as I was supposed to be. He was in Curriculum One, which was our version of college prep. He was on the varsity golf team, and played trumpet in band. He was shy and childlike, and I liked his wiry, monkey looks.

My family was out of town. Since both Joe and I were "smart," it seemed natural to beg off some family event in order "to study." As soon as we got home, I wanted to go right up to my bedroom. But Joe wanted me to feed him. "I'm too nervous to eat," I said, "aren't you?"

"No. I'm hungry. Let's eat. It'll give us energy."

I watched him eat the peanut butter and jelly sandwich that I had made for him. We were standing in the kitchen, and all I could hear was my heart pumping in my ears. "Aren't you nervous?"

"Yeah, I'm nervous," he said. "Of course I'm nervous."

We sat on the couch. I kissed him. This was the first time I had ever kissed a man, and it was nice. Peanut buttery, but nice. We kissed again, and he put his tongue in my mouth. It was like a silvery minnow, darting over my teeth, not too far in. I felt a great excitement, and pleasure. But Joe's face hadn't changed at all. I asked him, "How was that?"

He shrugged. "It was okay."

I took his hand and led him up the stairs. Even though nobody was home, I locked my bedroom door behind us. We kissed again, and undressed.

As soon as I was naked, everything changed. I lay back on the bed. I wavered. Should we do this? I was the church organist. I was the president of the Bible Club. Only a month before, I had been named "Teen for the Day" on Family Life Radio for my efforts to witness about my faith to others, including Joe. According to the United Brethren Church in Christ, homosexuality was a sin. My mouth went dry. I watched Joe pull down his underpants. He had a boner. "I don't know if I can do this," I said, sitting up. I threw my legs over the side of the bed and was looking down, ashamed of myself, not wanting to look at him.

"Of course you can," Joe said. He pushed me backward onto the bed and kissed me. We rubbed against each other. We ground our hips together, and we rolled back and forth. We had often wrestled before, so there was a bit of that in there. Each of us wanted to be on the bottom, apparently, to feel the weight of the other one on top of him. Joe put his hand down between us and touched the moisture. He looked at his fingers. "You liar," he said. "It's clear. You said it was white."

"Part of it's white, and part of it's clear," I said.

He looked at me, skeptically.

"Really," I said. "I thought you said you jacked off in the bathtub."

"Well, I didn't go all the way."

"You never came before?"

"I have wet dreams."

By this time, I was hungry. We got dressed and went downstairs, and I made myself a scrambled egg sandwich with mustard and mayonnaise. Back then, I was big on scrambled egg sandwiches.

I ate. We were standing in the kitchen. Joe said that he wanted me to fuck him. This was the part about sex that he was curious about. I had read *Everything You Always Wanted to Know about Sex,* and it sounded painful to me. Joe said, "I want to know what it feels like."

We kissed while undressing the second time, and Joe said I tasted like mustard. I climbed into bed on top of his back. He lay flat on his stomach and pulled his cheeks apart with his palms. I pushed so hard that it was hurting me. I felt something give way. It still hurt, but I kept rubbing and rubbing, and then I came.

I had to throw up right away. The idea of my dick up his ass, where shit came out? That was hard to take. I ran into my parents' bathroom and threw up. It was just nerves, and I knew it. But, I thought, it was worth it. This was a kind of discovery for me. I might get sick, but if Joe really liked getting fucked, I could do it for him. With time and practice, eventually I might not get sick at all. I might even start to enjoy it, if he did.

I went back to the bedroom and lay beside him in the dark, telling him these things. "I don't know how to tell you this," Joe said, "but you weren't even *in.* "

"I wasn't?"

"No, it slipped down between my legs."

My eyes were still wet and stinging from the vomit, but Joe had rolled over and I was sitting on top of his softened genitals. I pinned him back against the pillows with his arms out wide like Jesus on the Cross, like wings, and I kissed him. He puckered up his cute monkey lips, and everything was all right. In fact, it was quite nice.

When I pulled away, Joe said, "Do this." He flattened both of his palms against mine and moved them around in the air pressed like an image in a mirror against itself. Only this was three-dimensional, and moving.

I asked, "Why?"

"I don't know. It feels neat."

"It feels weird." I rolled off of him and put a song on: the theme from *Rocky*.

It was Joe's favorite song. He was a trumpet player.

We had sex once or twice more, I think, I can't remember exactly. We measured our cocks and found them equal in length. I asked if he liked my butt, and he did. "It's soft," he said. But we fell asleep on different sides of the bed. A few years later, Joe decided he was straight.

How could I deny him the right to be straight if he allowed me the right to be gay? After all, he helped me through the whole coming-out process, took me to my first gay bar, even stayed up late reading *Another Mother Tongue* by Judy Grahn to me. We were roommates for years until I moved in with my lover Ed. But Joe and I are still best friends. It's not just that we believe in each other. We believe in whomever it is that each of us is trying to become.

Moment of a Lifetime

Esteban E.

As high school seniors in 1975, my best friend Steve D. and I spent a great deal of time together. We had known each other since grammar school but didn't become tight until turning seventeen, partly because our girlfriends were close. This meant a lot of convenient double-dating, comparing notes, and sharing confidential information.

Gradually, Steve made mine his second home. On weekends when our sweeties were otherwise engaged, Steve and I went to movies, the beach, or smoked pot and watched TV in my bedroom. Increasingly, I started becoming aware of why so many chicks had crushes on him. He was buffed and gorgeous, a blond, green-eyed Dennis Wilson type. Before, though I admired the physiques of the jocks during shower time, I had never consciously felt any sexual arousal. But as sex with Susan seemed to taper off, beating off became chronic. I didn't care if Steve was there, since getting stoned on pot just intensified my horniness. Pretty soon he took to similar self-service. Watching his thick red cock squirt come into a paper cup, I surrendered to boy-craziness. I cajoled him incessantly to get down with me or at least let me suck and lick his meat. At first he just laughed and called me a "horny pervert."

I got bolder, rubbing his butt, smacking my lips over his bod, and insisting I could give him the pleasure his Lenny was denying him. He'd get pissed and threaten to tell the guys I was turning fag. Hurt by his refusal to at least try one-on-one friendship sex, I stopped with no explanation. His funny looks at me and nervous silence showed he wondered what was up.

One night after discovering our "nice" Catholic girls were moonlighting with other dudes, he came over slightly drunk. We got high watching TV cartoons, and then he called my name. I turned around and his cutoffs were dropped below his knees with a lovely, hard bone jutting out directly at me. I stared at the penis head and imagined it beckoning.

"C'mon, suck me," he said in a low, slurred growl. I was helpless when he drew closer to my face. He kept saying, "It's your wish come true," and I pressed my flushed face against his oily, pungent nut sac. I grabbed his cock with one tight grip and licked up from his belly button, chest, neck, ears, and mouth. We soul-kissed for a long time before I lay back and he lowered his beautiful genitals and ass over my face as he orally took me. We sucked, slurped, and probed our hot spots for what seemed like hours when he greased my butt with hand lotion, lifted my legs up, and worked his way inside me. I humped like a bitch in heat.

After coming he lowered his ass onto my mouth as he lubed his butthole, which eventually was fitted to my prick. When it was over, we fell asleep, knowing our homofuck was likely to be an indelible moment of a lifetime.

We carried on like the world's first lovers for about a month after that. Then, for reasons he would not explain, he said it was over. Eventually, he drifted away and his guilt infected me, too. Although I yearned for another sexcapade with a man, it has only been in the last year that I found the fortitude to gird my loins and initiate something: I have a date this weekend and I can only hope it is fractionally as magical as what I had with Steve so long ago.

I still love women, but sex with a man is a rocket ride to paradise. It will be safe, of course, a responsibility that makes me a homoerotic cherry for a second time.

Gay Bedside Companion

Leigh W. Rutledge

1974, age 18

I was eighteen. Matt and I had been buddies for about six months, ever since he'd applied for an after-school job at the motel my parents owned. He was a year younger than I was. We went jeeping and rock climbing a lot together. He was blond, short, and muscular. He was a competitive pole-vaulter on his high school's track and field team. He had high, well-developed pecs with large, flat nipples; his waist was thin; he had a high, small, totally hairless butt. I got a couple of chances to see it when we'd go skinny-dipping in his parents' pool.

It was the summer before I went away to college in 1974. Matt introduced me to pot. I'd always been leery of smoking it. I'd gotten drunk a few times in high school (and had almost had sex drunk one night with a wrestler I knew — but I chickened out at the last minute), but I'd never tried marijuana or anything heavier. I was also still a virgin, not counting a couple of typical "Let's play doctor" adventures in elementary school. I had never sucked cock before or gotten fucked up the ass. I'd never even really *touched* another guy's hard-on (except for those few boys back in fourth and fifth grades).

Whenever Matt got stoned, he talked about sex. Once, he told me, he'd rubbed butter all over his ass when he was twelve and let the family dog lick it off. Another time he'd tasted his own cum, just out of curiosity. But mostly he talked about chicks. Hearing the words "blow job" and "head" coming out of his mouth always gave me a hard-on, and whenever I went home after seeing him I'd masturbate almost immediately.

I slept over at his house one night that August. We weren't stoned that night, but we were in a rowdy mood. We were lying in bed and still talking at two in the morning. We shared a big double bed. Neither one of us wore underwear to bed, let alone pajamas, and we were both naked under the sheets. I kept finding reasons to brush my hand against his bare thigh (I thought I was being clever and inconspicuous about it). I'd had a hard-on for about an hour. I guess I had touched Matt one too many times, because he suddenly propped himself up on an elbow and looked over at me with a steady gaze and asked, "You trying to start something with me?"

My entire body froze in panic. I broke into an instant cold sweat.

There was a long, long silence. Matt flopped his head back down on his pillow again. "It's okay," he suddenly told me in a whisper. "I fooled around with Kenny, my best friend, in our swimming pool last summer. I let him play around with me underwater. It felt kind of good."

A mixture of adrenaline, horniness, fear, guilt, and anticipation gave me a feeling like vertigo. It was like standing on a high-dive for the first time — and watching one's self with a kind of cold detachment, wondering if one was *really* going to make the jump or crawl back down the ladder like a coward.

Suddenly Matt jumped up impulsively and tossed back the sheets. He crouched next to me on the bed. "Well, if you aren't going to make the first move," he said with amiable impatience, "then I am." Then he flopped himself rather matter-of-factly facedown on top of me. His hard-on rubbed against mine. "Just don't try and kiss me," he whispered. "I don't think I could handle another guy *kissing* me."

He rubbed himself against me for maybe five minutes. At first, he looked me right in the eye as he did it — his eyes seemed full of curiosity — but then he buried his face in the pillow behind me. We were soon bucking and thrusting and squirming together. I could smell his fresh sweat. I reached around and touched his ass. I'd never touched a naked male ass before. The skin was soft and warm, unlike the skin on any other part of the body. It had a feeling all its own, and I'll never forget the surge of intoxication I experienced feeling it move and tense and buck beneath my hand.

"You ever been fucked in the ass?" Matt asked me.

"No," I said.

"Turn over," he said coaxingly.

I hesitated.

"Turn over," he said, more firmly. "Let's do it. If it feels good, do it — that's what I always say."

I'd fantasized about this moment — getting butt-fucked — at least since I was fourteen; I'd sometimes masturbated sticking a finger up my butt. But now that the reality was here, I felt scared and indecisive. Nor was I entirely free of guilt.

I slowly turned over on my belly. Matt got into position behind me. I could feel him trembling a little. His breathing seemed to change.

"I don't care what kind of hole I fuck," he said, his voice more agitated than before, "just so long as it feels good."

He tried several times to get the head of his dick up into my rectum, and when he finally succeeded it hurt so violently I started to pass out. "Relax, relax," he whispered frantically. "Play with yourself, do whatever you need to do. Relax. One way or another, I'm going to fuck you..."

But it was no good. I couldn't take it.

He finally settled on jacking off while I crawled down between his thighs and licked his balls. Meanwhile, I was rubbing my cock against the mattress. After we both ejaculated, we went right to sleep.

He never tried to fuck me in the ass again, but I gave him head four or five times in the weeks after that. His dick wasn't particularly long but it was enormously fat. To this day, every time I read a porno story in which someone has a "beer-can dick" I think, with a laugh, of Matt.

Sometimes he liked to look at *Playboy* while I sucked his cock. Other times he'd just lie back on the carpet, his jeans down around his thighs, and he'd watch, mesmerized, as his cock went in and out of my mouth. The feeling of his hard-on was a continuing revelation to me — I couldn't get over how good and mysterious and exciting it felt in my hand or moving between my lips. I got my first taste of semen with him. I loved the way it smelled, but I probably enjoyed the *thought* of swallowing a guy's load more than I actually enjoyed the taste.

Sometimes Matt seemed completely at ease with our sexual relationship. He called his dick "Herbie," and as he was undoing his jeans and pushing his underwear down, he'd say things like, "Herbie likes you," or "Herbie wants to keep your mouth company." Other times, he seemed abruptly uncomfortable with the whole situation. "I'm not sure we should be doing this," he'd say. "I'm not sure it's right. You can wind up queer if you do too much of this."

I went away to college in early September, and that was the end of our friendship, despite half a dozen halfhearted attempts to stay in touch.

About three or four years after that summer, I called his parents one night, out of curiosity, to see what Matt was doing with his life. They told me he'd gotten married and was living in Hawaii. He worked for a scuba-diving company in Honolulu. They gave me his address so I could write to him — "Oh, he'd *love* to hear from you," his mother said, with obligatory enthusiasm — but I never did.

I sometimes wonder if, when he's fucking his wife, he ever thinks of me. I also wonder how he feels about it all looking back now — if, indeed, he ever allows himself to look back on what we did. I sincerely hope he hasn't become one of those bewildered and slightly haggard married men who cruise the local park looking for head a couple of times a year, always with a tight expression of uneasiness and misery on their faces.

Eighteen

Alex

1974, age 18

My first experience with gay sex (or any sex, for that matter) coincided with my eighteenth birthday. My best friend from high school, Gary, had turned eighteen a few months earlier. Two weeks before my own birthday, much to my delight, he had admitted his attraction to me. I had been in love with Gary for a long time and was relieved that my feelings were reciprocated. We were both pretty naive and had never talked about being gay before. We had hugged and kissed, but there was never the time or opportunity to get into anything heavier.

It was September of 1974. I had come home from college to celebrate my eighteenth birthday with Gary and his sister. I had already arranged with my parents to let Gary spend the night at our house, since I assumed we would be getting home from the bar rather late. For several days beforehand I fantasized about that night and what I imagined would happen when Gary and I finally ended up in bed together and alone. I had to jerk off every time I thought about it. For years I had lusted after other boys in the showers after gym; now I was finally going to act on those desires!

The three of us hit a couple of bars, where Gary's sister gave me advice on what drinks to order, now that I was of legal age. Gary and I both settled on vodka collinses that evening. But our minds were not on the music or our drinks; we were eager to get back home and into bed. Finally we told Gary's sister that we were really tired and we left the bar.

When we got back to my room, Gary and I became suddenly modest. We had never even seen each other undressed before. We changed into our pajamas separately in the bathroom, then tentatively got into bed together. I turned out the light and turned toward Gary, taking him into my arms. Our hands found their way underneath our pajama tops. We caressed each other's back and chest, the whole time rubbing our bodies together with my mouth pressed tightly to his. I could feel Gary's hard-on rubbing against my own through the layers of pajama and Jockey shorts. Our tongues found one another and we began kissing passionately, working ourselves up to a sexual frenzy that neither of us had ever experienced. I felt hot and flushed.

"Hold on," I said. "I've got to take this off." I hurriedly removed my pajama top. I turned back to Gary and discovered that he had done the same.

140

"One down and two to go," Gary murmured. I didn't know at first what he was talking about, then realized he was referring to our clothing. I hesitated, then pulled down my pajama bottoms and shorts all at once and tossed them onto the floor. I couldn't see much in the dark, but my right hand grazed against Gary's bare leg, which indicated that he had done the same. At long last, I thought, I'm in bed naked with another man.

I was so excited that for a few seconds I did nothing, wanting only to savor this moment. Then, slowly, I reached out toward his crotch, until my hand came in contact with a thick, full patch of pubic hair and a hard cock. Instinctively I wrapped my fingers around it and squeezed lightly. It was big and felt wonderful in my hand.

"What do you think you're doing?!" Gary exclaimed in alarm, pushing my hand away. I was taken aback, since I assumed that I was doing just what we both wanted. So we just cuddled and hugged for a while, but the memory of Gary's hard cock in my hand made me so horny that I just had to cum. After much pleading and cajoling, I convinced him to put his hand on my cock and jerk me off. It took a long time, but I was so turned on that when I finally did have an orgasm, I sprayed my entire (then hairless) chest with semen. Gary still didn't want me to touch his cock, so we went to sleep.

In the morning, Gary wanted to get out of there as quickly as possible. I messed up the other bed in the room so my parents would think that we had slept in separate beds. Later Gary told me that he wasn't as ready for sex as he thought he was; our night together didn't live up to his expectations either. "I thought we'd both be cumming like crazy all night long," he told me.

In the months that followed, I began a serious relationship with Gary. He loosened up and we took our sexual experimentation further. He had a beautiful cock which I loved to suck whenever he would let me (though he never reciprocated). I loved him very much, although in less than a year he broke up with me because he couldn't deal with being gay. But I'm glad I still have such vivid memories of my first sexual experience.

Brad

Donald M. Reynolds

1975, college freshman

I first laid eyes on Brad after moving to Susanville, California, in February 1970. We were in seventh grade, both running errands during class for our teachers. I was with another boy who disliked Brad and, to prove it, called him a fairy. I told the guy to never say that again, and surprisingly he never did. It was my first real act of compassion. I realized Brad was marked because he was effeminate, but I was attracted to his dark, Latino looks and to the fact that he survived despite the hostility from his peers.

We didn't become friends until our freshman year in high school, when we became a feared entity. We had brains and caustic tongues, reason for the guys to hate us and the girls to relate. We were popular, but each of us felt the isolation of being different, if not just gay. I was artistic, a freak of nature in a logging community. Brad was an abused child from a large family who got the fist from his father at every turn. We were both at odds, and dodging the punch became something of a habit.

Ours was a casual bonding at first, but I realized early on that I loved him. At the end of our sophomore year I told him this. He didn't respond. Later he used it against me, more because I had had the strength to announce how I felt. Never at ease with his feelings, it made him uncomfortable, but our friendship grew nevertheless.

Everyone thought we were lovers, but that gentile notion was met with resistance on both fronts. Our peers called us faggots and queers, and we denied both the fact and the act. The pressure of living in a small town galvanized our stubbornness to not prove them right. After we graduated the pressure was off, however, and things happened rapidly.

In the fall of 1975, Brad lived in Sparks, Nevada, with his grandmother. He attended beauty school there. I had moved to Redding to attend junior college. On a visit home, I went to a party where I met my first openly gay man. He was drunk, had just broken up with his lover, and asked me to sleep with him that night. I said no, but the attraction was strong. Something of a brief, nonsexual romance developed and Brad became angry, though he never admitted jealousy. Yet it was obvious he felt a competition he didn't want to deal with. A month later we had sex for the first time.

I was visiting him in Sparks and we had come back to his grandmother's house after a night out in early December 1975. Brad took a shower and I lay on the sofa bed made up for me by his grandmother. I was watching TV when he came out, dressed in a robe, and sat down next to me. We made small talk, watched the tube.

He started nudging my hipbone with his foot, tickling me and digging into the space between the mattress and my crotch. It was clear what he wanted, so I reached up underneath his robe and started stroking his cock. He was hard and the feel of his muscle nearly made me cum with my first touch. I pulled back his robe to get a good look, then moved closer to start giving him head. His groin smelled fresh from the shower, yet earthy, warm. As I put his cock in my mouth a flood of sensations came over me. It was like I felt my body for the first time.

After only five minutes I came in a frenzy, still fully dressed and horny as hell. We laughed at my awkwardness, trying to be quiet, then rushed into the bathroom for privacy. I took my clothes off; he kept his robe on. He stood in front of the bathroom sink and grabbed his grandmother's Vaseline. I was still fully erect when he took the grease, lubed my cock, and moved me inside him. I started fucking him, slowly and off kilter at first, amazed at the sensation of being inside another man. Once I got my balance and rhythm I fucked him faster and deeper, awed by the new instinct. For all the fantasizing and jacking off I'd done, I was amazed at how much more exciting the actual act was.

I fucked and sucked him for about an hour and a half. He wouldn't kiss, nor would he suck me, but I didn't care. I got off four times, he three, and then we just stopped. We were both surprised and turned oddly shy as we cleaned ourselves up. We didn't say a word about it. We simply went to bed. The next morning we gave each other a knowing smile, nothing more.

I'm certain it hadn't been his first time, but we never discussed it. We continued to have sex for about three years. Once he overcame his resistance to being kissed, it got better. We never talked of a relationship, never defined ourselves as gay, but sex with him was so intense it seemed to transcend words.

I've always felt deeply affected by our bond. Because I had accepted being gay early on, and expressed what I felt, my sense of empathy and my patience grew strong. I went through a period of denial in my late teens, but finally came out at twenty-one after disastrous attempts to play it straight. Brad never really came out except later, in drag. I always felt it was something for him to hide behind, a way to express what he couldn't say.

I moved to San Francisco in 1983 and contact became sporadic, information sketchy. He started performing in clubs as "Brandy" and was later crowned Miss Gay Reno. I saw him in 1987 and was amazed at his beauty and wit. He used that caustic tongue, honed back in high school, to great effect.

Later he became infected with HIV, developed AIDS, and struggled to get good medical care. I learned this in 1991 during a chance call. He was elated to hear my voice. There was such a longing in his. We talked and laughed. There were attempts to console, dissuade the fear. It was the first time we really talked to each other. After we hung up he called back to tell me he loved me. I told him I loved him too. Then I cried. Months later I learned he died on October 11, 1991. I felt a despair I hadn't anticipated, of my history being ripped by its root. I've been haunted by him since, by his taste, smell, the feel of his skin. And by a fact I never fully acknowledged when he was alive: he was my first love.

Clocks & Cocks

D.D. Chapman

1975, age 19

When I was nineteen, and already had some suspicions about my attraction to other guys, I was also studying some areas in metaphysics. From the Rosicrucians, I had learned a cute little trick for telling time without looking at a clock. I simply closed my eyes, cleared my mind, took a deep breath, exhaled, asked mentally, "What time is it now?" and accepted the first thing that popped into my head. The trick is to not stop and think, "Well I just had lunch about an hour ago, and it was 12:30 then..." To successfully develop this hidden talent that we all have, one must learn to be completely spontaneous.

After two weeks, I got so good at this, I stopped wearing my watch. Soon I applied the same trick to other things, like when the phone rang: "Who is calling me?" I had an older female friend, who was taking classes in metaphysics to develop her ESP.

I was still living at home, working at my father's restaurant. One day I saw a man walking his Irish setter in the parking lot. He was about five feet eleven, with a lean, well-defined muscular build. His medium brown hair had been lightened by the sun, he had a deep tan, warm brown eyes, and a trimmed beard and mustache.

It was early evening and I started a conversation, asking all sorts of questions about his dog. We talked in the parking lot for three hours. He told me that he was twenty-seven and worked for the post office. Then he told me about his wife. He also raised two subjects that struck me as odd. He said that he had some gay friends in a nearby large city, and somehow we got on the subject of dick size.

"You know the old wives' tale, don't you?" he asked.

"No, what old wives' tale?"

"Well, mothers used to tell their daughters that they could tell how big a man's dick is by doing this with the man's hand," he explained. He held up his largish hand and bent the middle finger down to the lower palm, then stretched it out again. He pointed to distance from the spot on his palm where his middle fingertip had been, to the tip of his extended finger. "That's how long it's supposed to be when he's hard." Then he looked at his hand and said, "But I'm much bigger than that!"

I stood there thinking to myself, "Gee, that's a strange thing for a supposedly straight guy to say!"

Over the next two weeks, we got to be good friends. He and his wife had me over for dinner a couple of times. He finished his work in the early afternoon, and got home right after I finished working the lunch rush. His wife worked until 6:00. I'd go over to his house and we'd relax in the sun together and talk. He dropped so many hints that I finally asked if he was gay. Instead of answering, he asked, "Are you?"

"No, but I thought that I'd try it once before I settled down and got married," I replied.

Then it all came out. Yes, he was gay, his wife had no idea, *and* he had a lover in the nearby big city.

During the following week, I felt myself receiving "messages" from various inner sources. I had a feeling that I was going to have sex with this guy. I did my little ESP trick and asked, "When?"

The answer was clear. "July 7th, in the afternoon." Over the next several days I was in a panic. Part of me wanted to try it, part of me was scared. An astrology forecast announced that July 7, 1975, would be an important turning point in my life. I went to my friend in the ESP class, and asked her what was going on.

She tuned in and said, "You are about to learn something important about yourself, something that is going to affect the rest of your life. It is important for you to relax and go with the flow. Do not build a wall around yourself. Do not put yourself on a pedestal. Just let things flow naturally." (I found out weeks later that she had no idea what this message was about.)

So I relaxed, and decided to let things unfold. The day came, I worked lunch, rushed home to take a shower, and rushed back to my bearded friend's house. He got home and immediately jumped into the shower.

As I sat on his sofa, listening to the water run in the bathroom, I thought to myself, "Oh, jeez, I know what's going to happen now. He's going to come out and want to have sex with me, I'll be too scared to even get hard. I'll be so embarrassed that I'll never be curious about having sex with a guy, ever again! I'll be 'cured'!"

Well ... that's not what happened. He did come out of the bathroom, with his towel around his waist. He sat on the sofa next to me. The next thing I knew, we were kissing and hugging passionately. My fears dissolved. It was like discovering the missing puzzle piece. My young, inexperienced dick was so hard, it felt brittle. Slowly, as we continued to kiss, I started pulling off my clothes, with his assistance. We stretched out on the sofa, our naked bodies pressed together, as his tongue searched out every part of my mouth. Then he suggested that we might be more comfortable in the bedroom.

As we got up, I discovered the source of his pride. It was *huge*. I later learned that he was called "Horse" in the gay bars around the city. On his bed, we assumed the sixty-nine position. It was an effort to get just the head of his cock inside my mouth. I did the best I could with my tongue

146

and hand. Soon he was cumming and I eagerly drank his hot love juices. Yes, I had already developed a passionate crush on him. I came right after him as he jacked my dick.

"You swallowed it?" he asked in disbelief.

"Yeah," I answered cautiously. "Why? Wasn't I supposed to?"

"Well, it's okay, it's not going to hurt you or anything."

When he had caught his breath, he looked at me with a scowl. "This isn't your first time!" he accused.

I was puzzled. "Yes, it is."

"I've been doing this with Joe for six months and I still can't swallow it!" he admitted.

"Well, I've tasted my own before, and it's no big deal."

After we had dressed, he suggested that "maybe next time I could screw you."

I said, "With *that* thing?! I don't think it would fit!"

"Oh, sure it will," he assured me. "I've screwed smaller guys than you!"

It didn't happen. We remained friends, but we had no more encounters. He did, however, introduce me to a friend of his, who was average size, and had the art of screwing down to a science. For some time after that, I continued to correctly predict the dates of my sexual encounters, usually weeks in advance.

Tour of Duty

Len

I went through the usual stages of growing up and slowly discovering my attraction to men: inexplicable excitement while looking at Charles Atlas ads or enjoying sneak glances at my schoolmates' hairy legs and crotches in the high school locker room. By the time I was eighteen I knew I was attracted to men but, determined to live a "normal" life, decided to force myself to be exclusively straight. I enlisted in the air force and, six months later, married my high school sweetheart.

The year was 1972. At first I was able to perform so well with my wife that I actually thought I had overcome my "problem." By the end of our first year, however, those visions of men's hairy legs and crotches slowly returned, especially in the heat of lovemaking. The more I tried to ignore them, the more vividly and frequently they appeared. I eventually found myself groping my wife's crotch in my sleep, longing to find something solid to grab. I grew more and more frustrated.

With the sexual revolution of the sixties still in the air, my wife and I frequently had open discussions about sex. One time I asked if she would ever fool around with a woman. She didn't think so, but then she had never tried it. As I had hoped, she asked the same question of me with a man. I explained that I was curious what it was like and might even try it if the situation presented itself. I downplayed it so much, though, that it actually sounded pretty casual and cool.

Toward the end of 1973 we were shipped to Okinawa for a two-and-a-half-year tour. Life on the island was pretty boring. To break the monotony, we frequently got together with other military personnel and their wives for baby showers, parties, and card games. It was at one of these card parties that it happened.

Larry and Sue lived a couple of houses away. Sue, at nineteen, was a proud Texas girl whom Larry had met and married when he was stationed there. She amused everyone with her small-town naivete. Larry was the same age as me, about twenty, and from Queens, New York. He was street-smart and struck me as the type who had seen and done just about everything.

We often got together with Larry and Sue for card games. One night, I brought out some vodka and we spent the early part of the night playing canasta and sipping screwdrivers. After a couple of hours, I jokingly suggested a game of strip poker. To my delight Larry was all for it, and after another drink or two, the girls decided, "What the hell." An hour or so of laughing, teasing, and stripping later, we found ourselves sitting around the table buck naked.

During the course of the game, I couldn't help but notice that every once in a while Larry's foot brushed up against my leg. Was it my imagination? Was it an accident? Just the possibility that it was intentional sent the blood racing through my veins. It was a thrill just to watch him remove his clothes piece by piece. He was as tall and tight as a statue: six feet of lean muscle with perfectly defined pecs and biceps, and abs you could do your laundry on. His legs were covered with wiry hair, and oh, that crotch! His dick was long and thick; I couldn't have imagined a more beautiful sight in my dreams!

By the game's end, everyone was feeling the booze and his and her own oats. We slipped to the living room floor, where Larry proceeded to pump his wife and I mine, side by side. It was hot as hell watching his swollen rod slide in and out. After about ten minutes of that, I suddenly felt a hand slip between my wife's and my crotch as I continued my own fucking. Was that *his* hand? Was that *my* cock it was wrapped around? I thought for sure I was going to blow on the spot, but then Sue interrupted it all with a whining drawl. "Larrrry, Ah'm sick ... take me home!" Apparently she'd had a bit more vodka than she could handle.

I figured the party was over. We dismounted and I watched Larry dress Sue as well as himself. She staggered as he helped her to the door. His parting words were "I'll be back in a minute."

My wife and I sat on the sofa, still naked, discussing what had happened. "Did you notice that Larry was groping *you?*" she asked.

"I guess so," I replied, trying desperately not to show my excitement.

"Well, you did say you were curious. If he comes back, now's your chance."

I couldn't believe what I was hearing. What if he did come back?

Ten minutes later Larry returned; he had put Sue to bed in record time. Without the slightest hint of pretense, he grabbed my cock with one hand and started moving up and down its length. I lightly placed my hand across his still-clothed crotch. This was all the encouragement he needed.

Within seconds, Larry had his clothes off again and pulled me to the floor. My wife, still naked, sat on the sofa watching. She must have sensed that this was going to be the men's night, for she made no attempt to join us.

The way Larry explored and felt my body, it seemed obvious I wasn't the first man he had enjoyed this way. At first I just lay there on my back, letting him touch, fondle, and lick whatever he wanted. I had no idea what was fair game between two men; with him leading the way, I reasoned, and with my wife "judging" from the grandstand, I would learn what was acceptable.

149

From the second he started touching me, each cell of my body came alive with its own individual sensations, almost as if they weren't connected in any way but rather were separate units dancing unto themselves. Each time the hair from his chest or legs brushed against my naked skin, it was like wires connecting in an explosion of sparks. He massaged me from head to toe and licked me from top to bottom, then settled in my groin, grabbing my eight-inch cock with both hands and stroking it up and down. He sat between my legs, head bent over, studying the clear droplets of sticky fluid oozing from the hole of my cock head. He reminded me of a child studying a snowflake.

Then, like the child, he proceeded to slowly snake his tongue out to lick, taste, and further analyze it. Having satisfied his taste buds, he removed one hand and engulfed the cock head entirely with his mouth, circling the glans over and over with his tongue while gently working the base of my shaft up and down with his hand. I was surely in heaven!

At this time I looked up at my wife. I was searching for a sign, some sort of signal that perhaps we had crossed her line of disapproval. Instead she sat motionless with a look of intrigue and, yes, excitement. She was turned on! This was my chance to finally live some of my lifelong fantasies.

I sat up and rolled Larry onto his back, then ran my tongue along his neck, chest, and armpits while my hands stroked his calves, thighs, and stomach. It was so different from touching a woman; it was rough and bristly, yet it felt natural. If I could have combined all the excitement I had felt from every time I'd had sex with my wife into one moment, it wouldn't come close to what I was experiencing now. I spent ten minutes feeling and tasting his body, wanting to save his crotch for last. Finally I worked my way to his midsection and felt his stiffness.

He was hard as a steel pole. I grabbed with one hand and explored, pulling up and down shyly at first, then with more confidence. Another glance at my wife reassured me that all was okay and I moved my face closer. I lay my head in his lap and buried my nose in his jungle of wiry hair, smelling for the first time the musky, captivating aroma of male crotch-sweat. My hand, wrapped around his shaft, journeyed its way up and down its full length. I licked the base and slowly worked my way up until I reached its crowning glory. I plunged my mouth down on his cock as far as it would go and gagged, untrained as I was at this. I started fucking his dick with my mouth, trying to learn the art as fast as I could. My tongue darted out and found his piss-hole. It was large; I could fit the tip of my tongue about a quarter of an inch in. I was ecstatic.

Larry was not content to just lie there. After a short while he guided our bodies into position and soon we were sucking each other off simultaneously. It quickly became a feeding frenzy; two men hungrily devouring each other's cocks and balls. We became a machine, heads and crotches bending and grinding in unison. The pace quickened, faster and faster, until I could feel his balls tighten and nearly disappear. I knew what was coming but had no idea what to do. I wanted to taste him, but would it be acceptable? The thought of the impending explosion excited me to the point of no return and I announced that I was about to pop. I expected him to release my cock so I could shoot my load into the air; instead his mouth adhered even more hungrily, even as he screwed my face furiously with his own dick.

The message was clear. I started bucking, my cock pulsing wads of hot jism into his mouth. At the same time, I felt the first splash of his sizzling cum hit the back of my throat. I didn't know if I should swallow, so I just let my mouth fill with the hot liquid. We seemed to cum forever, almost as if we were having two orgasms each instead of just one. When both of us had ceased our spasms, with cum running out at the corners of our mouths, we went into the bathroom and spit it out.

Larry dressed and went home as matter-of-factly as he had arrived. My wife asked if I had enjoyed it, and naturally I played it down by saying that it was okay; my curiosity had been satisfied and I was "certain I would never try it again."

I saw Larry the next day; I was anxious to talk about what had happened. I wanted to tell him how I had craved that kind of sex for years and that I had enjoyed it. I was certain that he was no novice at it, and hoped he could explain it all to me. To break the ice I asked if he had enjoyed it and his reply was "It was okay." I then asked if it was his first time, not wanting to insult him by assuming that it wasn't. I was sure he was lying when he replied that it was indeed his first. After his response, I couldn't bring myself to talk about it any further. I suddenly felt ashamed and dirty.

We shared three more clandestine sexual encounters (no wives included) before shipping out at the end of our tour. We never discussed any of them. He went back to Texas with his wife and I to Connecticut with mine. It was an exciting first-time experience, but in many ways disappointing. There never was any emotion or intimacy between us; we were just two men taking care of an instinctive need that at the time I didn't quite understand.

Directions Out

Frank Vlastnik

1971, age 20

"Frankie!"

It was my father again. All I wanted to do today was read my book in peace, and I kept getting interrupted.

"The guy's coming to fix the burner today, and I'm going to be downstairs with him, so please answer the phone if anyone calls."

"Yes, Dad." I shuffled back into my room and closed the door, so I wouldn't be interrupted by the repairman. A short time later I heard him arrive.

"Peace at last," I thought.

Immersed in my book, I lost track of the time until nature called. I had to pass through the kitchen, where I discovered my father and the repairman having a beer, discussing tools and other handyman subjects.

"Frankie, this is Rafael," he introduced us.

I shook the still somewhat dirty hand of a short, dark man, with closely cut jet black hair and a receding hairline. I guessed him to be in his late twenties. I went to the bathroom and returned to my room, again closing the door behind me.

Five minutes later, my father called again.

"Frankie," my father explained, "Rafael needs some help to find his way out of here. I tried to explain it to him, but he suggested it would be easier if you go in the van to show him."

We lived in a private community, with only one entrance leading to a series of winding roads, spreading in every direction. It was possible that someone could lose his way once inside. However, our house happened to be on the main thoroughfare, and you could practically see the main entrance from our front door. Was this guy that dim-witted?

I became suspicious of Rafael's odd request, but agreed to go with him in the van. He made small talk as I tried to explain which way to go. But he didn't seem all that interested in my instructions. He suddenly changed the subject: "Are you gay?"

Whoa! That's what all this was leading up to! Now it all made sense. My rank inexperience with cruising techniques prevented me from realizing that this was all a ruse to get into my pants!

I answered him truthfully, "I ,.. I don't know."

I was twenty years old and still a virgin. I really didn't know if I was gay or not. Sure, all my sexual fantasies were about men, I jerked off to pictures of men in underwear in the Sears catalog, and I couldn't keep my eyes off my classmates' baskets back in my all-boys high school. Yet — I wasn't *sure.*

He was impatient with my indecision. "Do you like this?" He stopped the van, reached over, and put his hand on my crotch.

"Well ... yes," I mumbled. Liking a hand on one's crotch is not exactly a litmus test to determine homosexuality, but it was good enough proof for him. It also helped me resolve my own conflicts and indecisiveness. Yes! I *was* gay!

My mind raced with thoughts of what was about to happen, at once fearful of getting myself into a precarious situation, and excited by the imminent possibility of my first sexual experience with a man.

One of my most persistent sexual fantasies was to suck cock. I had always wondered what it would be like to hold a dick in my mouth, to let my tongue swirl around its head, to try to swallow it all down to the root. I didn't even know if I'd even like it, but I knew I had to try. Now, here, with no effort on my part, I would have this opportunity.

Rafael pulled down a side street and parked at the edge of an empty ballfield. It was broad daylight on a Saturday afternoon, and we were within thirty feet of the closest house. Anyone could have walked by at any time — and it could easily be someone I knew. Yet my cautionary instincts were suppressed. A more powerful, thrilling, testosterone-fed instinct was controlling me now.

He undid his zipper and took out the object of my desires. It was already hard and looked about the same size as mine. "Take yours out," he cajoled.

I did. He reached over and stroked my dick. He seemed to like the look of it, and leaned over, put his lips over the head, and began to suck. He stopped after several seconds, and with a hand on my neck, slowly pushed my head into his lap.

I could taste the piss and salt and sweat, but these didn't bother me at all. The feel of that warm rod in my mouth was my nirvana. I slurped up and down his cock like I had been doing it all my life.

His words as he gently pulled my eager lips away have always stayed with me: "You blow like a pro." For someone who had just given his first blow job, this was accolade indeed! It pleased me immensely to learn that I was so good at something I had never done before, and something I liked so much.

I wasn't prepared for his next request.

"Do you want to get fucked?"

"How? Where?" I almost stuttered. He nodded toward the back of the van.

I turned to look in the back. I don't know why I even bothered to look. If I had seen the inside of a van with wall-to-wall carpet, a comfy sofa, and lace doilies — well *maybe* I'd consider it. But all I saw was a hard metal floor strewn with dirty, greasy tools. Even if I *was* ready to give up my cherry to him, it wouldn't happen in a place like that. I realized I had reached the bounds of my initial foray into the world of gay sex.

"I have to get back. My father will wonder what's taking so long," I said as I zipped up.

Rafael was not pleased with this turn of events. "Get back here!" he yelled. "I'll tell your father you came on to me!"

His little threat aside, I understood his upset. He didn't get what he was after. But *I* did — an official entree to the ranks of cocksuckers. I was no longer uncertain about my sexuality. I knew who I was and what I liked.

And I got even more: a great story to tell at parties. How many gay men have had fantasies about doing it with a repairman? I can say I did, and moreover, it was my first time.

A Tactile Experience

Will Dixon-Gray

1972, age 19

All the happy memories from my early adult years are tinged with doubt now; I rarely reminisce. I have learned that the deceit that was the bedrock of my first relationship began early on in our twelve years together. Now, however, ten years after the tumultuous end of our love and friendship, I am beginning to accept the past. My emotions, I know, were real; my trust, sincere; my innocence genuine.

We met the day I was hired at a small accounting firm, in the spring of 1971. I was nineteen, he was thirty. I was planning to attempt college in a half year. We became casual friends and ate lunch together regularly. In the fall he invited me to dinner at his place with his roommate. I slept on the couch; they slept in their rooms. The next morning, driving to work, he told me he was gay. The structure of my emotional being, never clear, suddenly came into focus.

Perhaps if he had been clear that he had more than a roommate, we would not have become the couple we did, but that was not in his nature. For my part, I had never been in love. I accepted everything without doubt and took my cues from him, including in matters of sex.

It's funny, considering that our sexual relationship was based so strongly on intercourse, that my first time should be so similar to the sex I experience today. Only, then, I was in love. That gave the mundane meaning.

We were in my dorm room, listening to the stereo and drinking wine, something I was just learning about. We were both sitting on my bed and we kissed. I turned off the light, then we lay down and made out. I loved feeling our tongues exploring each other's mouths and the weight of his body pressed against mine. My penis was folded down within my briefs and ached from being bent as it got hard. I tried to ignore it and enjoy the sensations of the kiss. I didn't know what gay men could do sexually. At the time, I didn't even know there was more than one way they could have sex; it was just a question of "what they did."

I get stimulated easily. I can get excited just by having a man I find attractive stroke the inside of my forearm. So when he pulled my flannel shirt out of my jeans and reached up to stroke my chest underneath it, I trembled from arousal. He paused and asked if I was cold, and I assured him that I was simply excited. Then he unclasped my belt, opened the top of my jeans, and reached down outside of my briefs.

It seems, looking back, as though my senses mixed then. There were moments when I heard parts of songs on the stereo and the music sounded so new, I could have been hearing it for the first time. And I remember flashes of sight, as we were lit by the lights of the amplifier. But the underlying memory is tactile. Through the snug cotton of my briefs he inched my penis around until it was pointing up, with the head sticking above the band and his hand stroking it as we lay alongside each other in a kiss that seemed to stretch backward in time.

I felt myself tightening up inside and didn't know what to do. I was afraid to come, but trusted him to know what was happening to me. He stopped stroking for a second to reach under my briefs and cup his fingers around my cock and speed up the movement. It was only moments before I came. My cry was muffled by our mouths still pressed together. He continued to pump me as I came in pulses, the spasms continuing after any fluid was spent.

After I had finished we lay together for a while. Then he looked at the alarm clock and, surprised at how late it was, lamented that he had to go. He turned the light on and began to fix his clothes. I was confused, since I thought I should reciprocate the pleasure he had given me, but he assured me there would be time. In moments he had left.

I took off my shirt, which had been the target of my orgasm, and wiped myself off with the dry part, then stuffed it into my laundry bag. I pulled on a t-shirt, pushed my hair around with my hands, and went out the door and down the hallway to the communal bathroom to pee and wash my hands, with no conscious thoughts as my mind, perhaps, tried to scribe the experience before it was lost forever.

Seminary

Michael Austin Shell

I'm only half joking when I say God called me to seminary in order to bring me out and to bless my gayness.

As a beginning Cornell freshman in 1968, I was a Lutheran preacher's kid so deeply closeted I had never jerked off to orgasm, didn't know the word "homosexual," and had no sense of what my longing for boys was about. That winter I stumbled onto a porno story about a teenager being "forcibly" seduced by two camp counselors. It was at once horrifying and fascinating to recognize that this was what I wanted.

Though I jerked off almost obsessively after that, I stayed closeted. I fantasized about dorm mates, but I couldn't admit what was happening. By my senior year, Cornell had an active gay and lesbian student group. Before one showing of *The Boys in the Band*, its members stood up to say they would tell the real story of gay people after the movie. I got out fast.

That year I fell in love with my best friend Mike, a cheery, sexy pixie of an artist and tenor. We were both active in campus ministry. When he decided to go to seminary in Chicago, I convinced myself to go along. To my dismay he backed out at the last moment. Left on my own, I plunged into a high-caliber preministerial program that I thoroughly enjoyed — except that emotionally I was coming apart.

My main torment was the crush I immediately developed for an apartment mate. Rick was a slender, unpretentious Michigan farmboy. We didn't share the close friendship Mike and I had, but his body drove me crazy. For the first time I found myself creating explicit fantasies about a real person. They were usually long scenes of affectionate foreplay that ended with me sucking or jerking him off.

Following a classic seminary drinking bash early in 1973, I was sitting on our couch, feeling gloomy. Rick sat down beside me and asked what was wrong. Without even thinking I said, "I've got a crush on you." I don't remember what he said, but his response was totally surprising.

In a matter-of-fact way, he took me into his room, got us both naked and into bed, and began jerking me off with spit on his hand. I started pumping his hard-on, thinking how strange it was to hold another man's dick. He came pretty quickly. Without the foreplay I'd imagined, though, I couldn't get off, despite Rick's persistent efforts. I finally had to stop him, and I had a sore dick for a couple of days.

We never talked about this afterwards. The next month I left seminary and got a library job back at Cornell. I knew I had to come out for real. Fortunately, in the early seventies, Ithaca, New York, was an almost utopian place to do so.

An ironic postscript: Mike was still in Ithaca and had come out as well. He cooked me a Chinese dinner one evening that summer. We spent an affectionate night cuddling and jerking each other off with baby oil. Mike didn't want a sexual relationship, though. That really hurt, because I hadn't yet learned that "falling in love" doesn't always go both ways. He moved to Greenwich Village later that year.

I've never assumed Rick was gay, though he'd obviously had jerk-off sessions before — all the old farmboy myths come to mind. In any case, I'm grateful to him for his unaffected kindness and his total lack of shame or condescension about our experience. Though for me it was erotically disappointing, it confirmed my gay desires. More important: Rick helped me begin to accept that love and desire for other men can be God's blessing, rather than God's curse.

Risen Indeed

Anonymous

1970s, age not given

Washington in the 1970s was filled with beautiful men, but I could not ultimately admit I was gay. Not yet.

The first time I saw the clerk in that Georgetown bookstore my hormones went off like popcorn. Daniel was slim and dark-haired, with bright, black, foxlike eyes. I returned frequently, engaging in book chat, but always unsure how to introduce The Topic. Finally something he said revealed that he was gay, as I'd hoped. I ached to offer him the gift of my virginity, but something held me back.

Saturday afternoon of the Easter weekend, I saw a movie, one of those sexual roundelays in which *everybody* in the world seemed to be having sex. Leaving the movie, a profound depression settled over me. I longed for something. Someone. *Him.*

I drove into Georgetown just before the bookstore closed. My clerk smiled at me and said, "Well, I've been expecting you."

"What?" How did he know?

He laughed and squeezed my shoulder. "I have to close up the store. Do you want a cup of coffee?" He showed me to the office and went to lock up. This was it! I was instantly erect.

While making the coffee he smiled and said, "I can tell you're interested in me. You're gay, right?" And for the first time, I admitted that I was. Even if I wasn't *completely* sure I was gay, I knew I desired this man.

"Well, I'd like to have sex with you," he said. "But I can't. I'm a Buddhist. One thing I'm striving for is the negation of all desires." My expectations crumbled as he described his spiritual aims. I suggested that he could do it *without* desire, then. Simply have sex, just *do* it. *I* was the one with the desires. He laughed. "Hey, Georgetown is full of men."

"But I want *you*," I said, with simple logic.

None of my arguments worked; he would not yield. I left with one small hope: his insistence that I could find somebody else.

I knew of a bar on Wisconsin Avenue, a tiny spot. It was a gay bar, I'd heard at least that much, but my timidity had kept me outside. I went in. It was dark and smoky, of course, and filled with people just like me.

Just like me.

159

Suddenly it seemed right; I belonged here. I introduced myself to the first man I saw. His name was Bob. He was pleasant-looking, about my height, burly, with soft brown eyes and a mustache. He stood with feet apart, leaning forward, like a boxer.

I bought him a beer. We talked briefly, but I quickly decided I wanted him. Cutting to the chase, I came out with the corniest line I have ever used: "Would you like someplace to rise on Easter morning?" He nodded and drained his beer. I was astonished. It was so easy!

Bob followed me out to my apartment in his car, a bright red-orange Volkswagen Beetle. The ride seemed to take hours. I kept glancing in the rearview mirror, terrified he might change his mind. But we finally arrived.

In the apartment he undressed me slowly, and I undressed him. He wasn't perfect, but to me he was beautiful: muscular body, running slightly to seed; small brown nipples winking through thick chest hair; a modest cock growing less modest every second. I sank to my knees and nibbled him. He pulled me to my feet.

"Your first time, right?"

I nodded. "How did you know?"

"Well, to begin with, your eyes are big as saucers. Let's not *start* sucking cock, okay? Leave it for later."

Bob took me by the shoulders. He parted my lips with his tongue and I accepted it eagerly. He tasted faintly of peppermint, the bristle of his mustache an added pleasure. He guided me to the bed. Bob's scent was gamey, dark and steamy and rich, altogether intoxicating. Astride me, he lifted my arms, kissing my armpits, moving down to my nipples. In the pale lamplight the sight of Bob exploring my body was the most thrilling thing I'd ever seen. He nibbled the hair below my navel, working lower and lower, finally running his tongue along the length of my penis. "No ... not yet," I moaned. He brought his mouth back to mine and plunged his tongue deep into my throat. My skin never felt so alive, my cock so hard it hurt.

"Let's sixty-nine," I said.

Bob's eyes widened with amused surprise. "Well, you *are* eager, aren't you?" He turned around above me, and took me into his mouth. The scent of musk intensified dramatically. I closed my lips around his cock. It was hard and soft at the same time, a revelation. Our gentle thrusting settled into an easy rhythm, then accelerated. I quickly exploded into his mouth and he gulped it down. After a while, Bob came, even more deeply, his ass shuddering in my hands. I was surprised at the ashy flavor of his come. Did all semen taste like this? It was all over soon, too soon, and he cupped himself around my body, preparing for sleep.

My exhilaration at his closeness kept me from falling asleep. My restlessness wakened Bob. He offered to leave. I protested but when he left, I felt oddly relieved. Yet I still couldn't sleep. I wanted him back.

The next day I was a battleground of conflicting feelings: elation, guilt, sexual excitement, and longing for Bob's return. My experience with him was the beginning of a period of intense sexual activity, and other partners initiated me into other pleasures. Still, I looked for Bob for a long time, but never saw him again. And for years, every time I saw a bright red-orange Volkswagen I looked to see if it was him. I'd never noticed there were so many of them on the street.

Stubble

Stephen Lane

It was the feel of stubble when he kissed me. The kiss was deep and electrifying, the sex we had later, my first ever with a man, was emancipating. But I will always remember the first, knee-buckling sensation of a man's sandpaper face against mine.

▼

Johnny had befriended me out of pity, no doubt. I was a rock singer hired to sing and dance in a theatrical production at Opryland, U.S.A., and was completely out of my element. Johnny was totally in his. He was the proverbial triple threat, a singer who could dance and act. The entire cast of fourteen were as talented as they were strikingly attractive. I was insecure ... and broke. Quitting was simply out of the question.

I had heard through the rehearsal grapevine that Johnny was also gay. I prided myself on my open, "1970s kind of mind," and felt no threat when he asked if I needed any help. I was, in fact, relieved and somewhat flattered.

The cast rehearsed at the park on weekends, and Johnny and I talked on the sidewalk by his apartment building during the first sunny weekdays of spring. Johnny was a handsome man that many thought might have been part African-American, though no one really cared. He was friendly, immensely popular, and with me, as patient as Job. Johnny exhibited no signs of what I had been schooled to believe were stereotypical homosexual behaviors, no lisping, no flamboyance, no Bette Davis impressions. And he never made what could be remotely considered a pass at me.

On one Tuesday afternoon I cried uncle after a frustrating day of rehearsal, and we broke to Johnny's apartment for lunch. While Johnny made the sandwiches, I admired the wall of photos in the hallway.

"So how long have you and Lloyd been together?"

"Almost seven years," Johnny yelled from the kitchen.

"That's great," I figured was the appropriate response. It did seem a great accomplishment for someone who, like myself, was only in his midtwenties.

"Yeah, well, it's kinda rocky right now," Johnny said, carrying two loaded plates from the kitchen. "But we'll work it out ... or we won't."

We ate our lunch in an awkward silence.

162

The four weeks of rehearsal flew by, and I was making my mentor proud. One day Johnny suggested we meet at an old downtown department store where a friend of his was giving a puppet show for kids. The morning arrived and, as show time approached, I anxiously waited for Johnny near the tiny stage.

"Wasn't Johnny supposed to come?" lamented the puppeteer.

"I guess he meant the next show," I offered, placating both the puppeteer and myself. "We were supposed to meet here."

The miniature curtain rose on schedule in front of its miniature audience. Though three screaming toddlers had to be hustled away prematurely by embarrassed mothers, the show was otherwise a resounding success. After the second show I phoned Johnny's apartment. No answer. I sat through the third show, impatiently mouthing the puppet's dialogue while I obsessively checked my watch ... no Johnny. With the ending of the fourth and final show, the puppeteer effusively thanked me for staying, mistaking my presence for fanaticism. It was fanaticism of another sort altogether. I responded politely and left in a funk. I had stood through four puppet shows in as many hours thinking, among other things, that if there's one thing I hate worse than mimes and late ex-friends, it's puppets. It never occurred to me not to wait.

"What a jerk," I fumed to myself "He's in deep shit. When I get home, I'll call his ass all night ... He fuckin' stood me up!"

I sped home to my apartment, slammed in the door, and angrily punched out the offender's phone number. Johnny answered.

"Where the hell were you?!" he shouted.

"Me? Where the hell were you?!"

"Waiting for you to pick me up."

"What?"

"You know my car's in the shop."

"I don't remember ... Then why weren't you home when I called?" I had him there.

"I got pissed and *walked* to the gym. And did I have a *goood workout.*"

"I'm sorry, I..."

"Hey, forget it." Johnny was beginning to sound amused and suddenly I realized how totally disappointed and lonely I felt.

"Well, I'm really sorry I blew it ... maybe ... well, I ... I guess I'll see you tomorrow."

"Hey, why don't I buy some groceries, come over, and fix you dinner?"

"What about Lloyd?"

"Lloyd hasn't come home for two nights ... I'll explain it all later."

"Are you okay?" I said, not able to suppress the excitement in my voice.

"I'll be great when I get there. See ya in a few."

Johnny hung up and my mind was racing. I tried to tidy up my one-room efficiency, but was too distracted. I was shoving dirty clothes

163

under the couch when Johnny banged on my door. He burst through, his arms loaded with grocery bags that he dumped onto the kitchen counter. Turning, he sighed, smiled, then looked at the floor pensively.

"You okay, Johnny?"

He looked up, directly into my eyes. It was my turn to look at the floor. Johnny slowly came over to me, lifted my chin with his hand, and smiled sympathetically.

"I guess we better get this out of the way before dinner," he whispered.

He leaned over and kissed me gently on the mouth. There was a rushing sound like a tornado that sucked the doors off my sexual closet and out of my life forever.

As I floated back down to earth, I fought to find the source of this overwhelming and conclusive reaction. What was it about this simple kiss that had nailed my deepest, most suppressed longings? We kissed again, more passionately, and then I knew.

"It's a man's face against mine. It's the stubble."

5. We Are Everywhere (1978-1985)

Let's briefly look back half a century. In the first story of this book, K.R.B. recalls that in the 1930s, "being 'queer' simply meant you actively sucked cock or you passively let someone fuck your butt. Since Harley and I neither sucked nor fucked, we had no occasion to think what we did was homosexual. In those days, in my part of the country at least, mutual masturbation between men was okay for heterosexual enjoyment."

Well, not anymore.

As we hit the 1980s, everybody was more aware of homosexuality. Mutual masturbation could no longer pass as standard heterosexual behavior. If you had sex with another guy you were gay — in your mind, in his mind, in the mind of anyone who knew. As the opening story shows, some men paid a heavy price for having this realization forced on them before they were prepared to accept it.

Others did a bit of mental fudging about exactly what constituted sex. Kevin Curry, for example, tells about his friend Daniel, who was eager to suck dick and be sucked, but didn't want to come. That would have meant he was gay! In the nineties, we'll see a man who could rationalize allowing his nipples to be sucked, but didn't want that mouth moving below his waist. No one in our earlier stories is driven to such convoluted rationalizations.

▼

Another new pattern emerges here. In the past, men had gay sex, then sooner or later came to realize they were gay. Here, we increasingly find men who intellectually realized they were gay, and *then* did something about it.

The section ends in 1985, as AIDS reached the national consciousness. The gay world was very aware of AIDS during the first half of the decade. But it was generally ignored by the population at large until Rock Hudson's 1985 illness and death. Only a few fleeting references to AIDS appear here, always as something distant, foreign, frightening, and unknown.

▼

On a lighter side, underwear becomes more varied in this period. No longer are white cotton Jockey shorts, or the occasional boxers, *de rigueur*. Colored and bikini underwear makes an appearance. Some will consider this progress, others a great loss. Surely no one will be neutral.

Luke

Bud C. (for L.C.)

My first queer sex was my first orgasm. I grew up in a good-sized southern city but spent lots of time on the farm where my dad was born. I knew I liked guys the summer before my farm cousin and I turned fourteen, but I had not yet grasped the possibilities.

Since childhood Luke and I had shared "our" spot in the hayloft where we pissed down into a stall below. It made great splashes, and entertained us to no end. One afternoon Luke said, "Come on! Let's take a leak!" We raced to the barn, clambered up, then let 'er flow, laughing, giggling, sword-fighting piss in air. About peed out, Luke milked himself and asked, "Ever get it hard?"

Caught me off guard. I knew it *got* hard, but I thought "hard" was something it did *all by itself*. I gawked as Luke made his dick bigger and bigger. "Here, let me show you," and he started on mine. With no prompting I took over his. Microseconds later clothes were trampled into hay. Luke knew his way around a male body even at thirteen — don't ask me how. We fell over each other yanking pulling stroking tasting. His tongue made hard rocks of my nipples and mine did his. By the time his mouth wrapped around my dick, the proverbial stars broadsided me.

I watched, hypnotized, as most of my dick disappeared into Luke's face. The realization gripped me that *something* was going to happen — though I didn't know the foggiest what. I jerked from his mouth, jumped up, leaned *way* over the stall, and shouted, "I gotta piss! Gotta piss real bad!" It wasn't urine but ropy glops that drifted down and splattered below. Luke stood next to me pumping and more goop glided down next to mine. Luke reached over, pulled on my dick, and said, "That's not piss." I felt stupid but good.

Luke and I continued our explorations: in the barn, fields, camping, up trees on our dads' deer stands. He was fascinated with my shiny circumcised dick head and I envied his huge uncut country cock, foreskin trapping mystery inside. Luke resolved to see the head of *his* dick. We eagerly took on the project of stretching foreskin. Gradually we worked bigger and bigger stuff under the sheath, finally fingertips. The project took months but occupied young minds and summer afternoons — it hurt but it was what Luke wanted. Eventually the opening was big enough for a tongue: mine. Swirling around inside tasted incredible. Salty. Funky.

Well, Vegemite-like. (Those Aussies *know* what to spread on toast.) The licking drove Luke crazy and made him more determined.

After a couple of weeks, Luke greeted me, "Come on! Somethin' I gotta show you!" We raced to the barn. Sure enough, out of all that loose skin popped the head of Luke's dick. It was gorgeous. I touched it but he jerked back yelping, "Too sensitive!" so I carefully stroked just the shaft. It got big and hard, but then all those loops of foreskin bunched up and lodged behind the rosy bulb. The head slowly swelled up and turned purple. We panicked and Luke started whimpering. Quick thinking, saliva, and surgical use of teeth made Luke holler but saved his dick. Or so we thought.

Luke's foreskin got looser with time. He could bury a third of my dick up in its folds to let me experience what having one was like. Everything was perfectly queer and innocent for years. Then Luke tried to initiate another boy cousin into our games and things got rough. The cousin told all our folks. Luke was taken aback. He couldn't imagine the fuss or why any guy wouldn't want to be part of anything so good. I knew Luke was naive but that episode changed him. Later, though, it seemed like everyone else forgot.

Luke and I had little in common apart from kinship and good sex. He was an athlete, football, baseball, incredible hands. His body matured better and better. Me, I was the brainiac. I started meeting other guys and realized potential in queerness. Luke got into scrapes. When we were sixteen or seventeen, we'd do great sex, blow big wads, then Luke would start calling one or both of us faggots, saying we were gonna burn in hell, or that we were sick and "somebody oughta put us outta our misery." And there was that camping trip where he put a loaded sixteen-gauge shotgun to his eye, looked down the barrel, wrapped his big toe around the trigger, and said, "I wonder what it looks like coming at you?"

We graduated high school, went to college. Luke tried dating girls but was too big. Well, Luke *could* piss out the side vent of overalls without taking down the bib. So the girls gossiped and giggled. Tore Luke up. At least a man, gay or straight, pays proper respect to endowment.

When we were eighteen, Luke's prize possession, a mint-condition white Ford Fairlane, wrapped around an old oak at sixty miles an hour with Luke at the wheel. Luke had to be cut out of the wreckage but was wearing a seat belt and was not badly hurt. In the hospital he wouldn't look at me. The sheriff displayed the wreck at the courthouse as a teaching tool for teenage drivers.

A couple of months after we turned nineteen, again at the hospital, Luke had a flesh wound. When we were alone, Luke said, "I chickened out. So I shot my fucking leg. Shot my fucking leg for being such a faggot chicken-shit." What could I say? What could I do? We never had sex after that. The family labeled Luke "accident-prone." I knew the truth. He quit school and took a job at the county hospital.

Six months to the day after my nineteenth birthday, I stumbled going into the farm's old sharecropper house. My feet weren't working. I put off going in until after they'd taken Luke's body away. His dad showed me how Luke was on his side lying on the floor with a death grip on the edge of an old wooden table, as if he was trying to hold on. On the table were an empty fifth of Jim Beam, amber-colored medicine bottles, and neat rows of colorful pills and capsules. Our uncle, the county coroner, put down "accidental ingestion of pills and ethanol."

▼

My butt was virgin until I was nineteen — but I guess that's another "First Time" story, huh? Goes something like this: It must have been a couple of weeks after Luke's funeral. I met an older guy in the park. Back at his place, his magnum dick reminded me of Luke's. He wanted head but on impulse I asked to be screwed. The guy rode me hard, condom confettied, hurt like hell from poke one to pop, I ended up sobbing. Uncontrollably. He apologized for causing me such pain. The poor dude just didn't understand.

How I Spent My Summer Vacation

Edward

1980, age 13

My balls dropped the summer my parents divorced. The first tufts of brown hair sprouted around my dick and, fumbling with myself late one night while imagining Scott Baio in a jockstrap, I reached my first orgasm. A year later, at age thirteen, I masturbated three or four times daily while a parade of jockstrapped celebrities — Erik Estrada, Tom Wopat, and Greg Evigan — strutted with bulging pouches.

I was still underdeveloped for my age — rail-thin with a skinny dick, but a handsome boy-next-door face that saved me from being a complete geek. After the divorce, my mother moved to Indianapolis and that summer she used the Baxter YMCA as a convenient place to dump me and my sisters while she went to work.

One day in late August 1980, I met Bill, a carrot-topped, freckle-faced boy. Though only fourteen, and my height, he was well developed and packed with muscle. We struck up a conversation by the pool and I couldn't help noticing the man-sized bulge in his swimsuit. Bill said his mom worked for the Y and asked if I wanted to explore areas not usually open to the public. While roaming, Bill grilled me about my younger sister, Liz. He asked if she was a virgin, and if I'd ever done anything with her. Then Bill led the conversation to a more general discussion of sex and finally to masturbation.

"Do you jack off?" Bill asked.

"Sometimes." (*At least twice a day.*)

"What do you think about when you're doing it?"

"Girls." (*Lies!*)

"Have you ever jacked off with anyone else?"

"No." (*I wish.*)

"Do you ever think about guys when you jack off?"

"No. That's sick." (*That's all I ever think about!*)

Bill didn't believe my lies and led me into an unused kitchen area on the second floor to seduce me. When the door closed, darkness enveloped us. Bill panted heavily and began pawing me, running his hands all over my body. I responded, grinding against him. Bill kissed me hard, shoving his tongue deep into my mouth. All the while he explained what bitches girls were and what fun a guy could have with his buddies. He yanked down my suit, and my scrawny boner smacked against his thigh. When he tried to shove an unlubricated finger up my ass I got scared and pulled away.

The idea of sex with another boy thrilled me, but I didn't want to be caught naked in a kitchen. I suggested we go to the locker room, where we would at least have an excuse for being naked if anyone caught us. I didn't consider the fact that the locker room would be a more dangerous site because of traffic. But the hard cock of a horny thirteen-year-old knows no reason.

On the way downstairs Bill negotiated our encounter.

"Will you suck my dick if I suck yours?"

"Sure." *(I'd LOVE to.)*

"Will you let me fuck your asshole if I let you fuck mine?"

"I guess." *(Will it hurt?)*

"Will you lick my asshole if I lick yours?"

"That's gross." *(That's gross!)*

"No, no, it's not. It feels great, buddy. I'll do you first and you can see how good it feels."

"I don't know..."

"Come on. It's great!"

"I guess. If you do me first." *(I'll try anything he wants.)*

"You'll love it."

I'd always been sexually aroused by the sight of naked men but unsure what we could do together. I had an idea about the cock sucking and butt fucking, but the concept of ass licking was completely foreign to me. I was so horny and Bill was so self-assured that he could have made me do whatever he wanted. And he did.

When we entered the locker room we had the added thrill of seeing the Y's hottest, humpiest lifeguard standing completely naked. Bill knew the guy (who was probably only seventeen or eighteen), and spoke to him. I couldn't tear my eyes away as he dried off his fat, dark Italian dick. What a day! My first kiss. My first grope. And now the lifeguard of my latest j/o fantasies rubbing his cock and balls. He bent over to pick up his suit, giving us a clear view of his hard swimmer's ass. Thanks to Bill's earlier suggestions, all I could think of was dropping to my knees and licking the lifeguard's hairy ass crack and tongue-fucking his asshole.

After he dressed and left, Bill and I peeled off our suits and walked to the shower. My first glimpse of Bill's dick amazed me. I'd never seen another guy with a hard-on. It was huge — bigger than I'd imagined a cock could be. Actually, it was probably just over eight inches long and average thickness, but compared with the teenie weenie I had then, Bill was gigantic.

We stood in the shower ogling each other's cocks under the rush of hot water. I tentatively reached my hand toward Bill's veined pole. He didn't hesitate. He grabbed my little-boy cock and balls in one hand and jerked me toward him. We jacked each other's boners and just as Bill asked me to suck his dick we heard the door to the locker room open. We spun around. I didn't have any trouble covering my boner with my hand, but Bill had to face the corner.

After a cursory shower the intruder headed toward the pool. Bill motioned me to follow, and led me to the last stall of the rear bathroom.

"Pull down your suit and turn around," Bill ordered. I obeyed and he slathered conditioner in the crack of my ass, then proceeded to lube up his dick.

"Okay, now bend over."

I did, supporting myself on the toilet seat. Bill stood behind me with one hand on my hip and the other guiding the head of his dick to my ass pucker. Suddenly, in one swift motion, he slammed his dick in me up to his balls. I screamed and pulled off. My dick went instantly limp from the pain.

"Stop! That hurts!"

"Sorry, sorry. I went too fast. Let me try again."

"No way."

"Please."

"It hurts."

"I know. It always hurts at first but then it feels good. Trust me."

"Let me do it to you first."

"No, Edward, man, come on, I'm too hot. You gotta let me fuck you."

"Well..."

"You'll love it. Then you can fuck me."

Reluctantly I turned around and bent over the toilet, offering Bill my throbbing asshole. I clenched my teeth when I felt his knob press against my opening. Bill entered me more slowly this time but it didn't stop the searing pain. Fortunately he came on the sixth or seventh thrust. He quickly pulled out and I spun around and sat on the john, feeling like I had to take a massive dump but all I felt was Bill's cum oozing out.

It was my turn. Bill bent over and reached behind, spreading his cheeks for me. I'd never seen an asshole close up before, and Bill had a cute pink hole and smooth hairless crack.

"Come on. What are you waiting for? I'm ready."

Unfortunately, at the moment I'd dreamt of all my life, the source of all my j/o fantasies, at the instant I yearned for always, I couldn't get it up. Me. A thirteen-year-old with a perpetually hard dick presented with a great-looking fourteen-year-old asshole to plow and I couldn't do it. The trauma to my own ass had made me limp and the most I could manage now as I pumped myself furiously with my hand was a pathetic semi-erect hard-on.

"Come on and do it," Bill said, spreading his legs and cheeks even farther apart for me.

I pressed my dick against his butt, but I wasn't hard enough to penetrate. Bill reached around and grabbed my dick. After a few rough yanks I sprang to attention. It felt heavenly entering his hot moist crack, but I felt my dick going down after a few thrusts and I had to pull out.

"Did you cum?"

"Oh yeah," I lied.

"Great, isn't it? We'll definitely have to get together again. Maybe you can sleep over and we can do it all night long."

"Cool."

Since we'd both (allegedly) cum, we didn't get to any dick sucking or ass licking. It's too bad, because I never saw Bill again. The summer ended and I went back to my dad's house in Bloomington and he moved to Indianapolis.

Since then, my body filled out and my dick plumped up real big and I'm almost exclusively a top. But sometimes I reminisce about my first sexual experience and need a strong, bigger man. On those occasions I tell the guys not to be gentle, but just to ram their dicks up my ass in one swift slam. Just like Bill did.

I'm Not Shy, I'm Ruined

J.T. Colfax

1979, ninth grade

Sometimes I grandiosely joke that *"I invented embarrassment."* Much of that sentiment stretches all the way back to April 25, 1979, between 4:30 and 5:30 p.m. (Mountain Time). That is *exactly* when I had my first sexual encounter.

What led up to it was this: One day in late March or early April, when I came home from school, I found a book about sex in my brother's room. I already knew I was gay, hated that fact, and still hoped it was a phase. I was in the ninth grade. Flipping directly to the segments about homosexuality, I read that gays sometimes meet in the bathrooms of bowling alleys. As it happened, there was a bowling alley nearby. I went there immediately.

I did find some gay graffiti in the restroom but the chances of somebody coming in seemed dismal on a weekday afternoon. I hung around awhile before adjourning to the lobby, where there were pinball machines. Another young boy was the only one there. It may be hard to believe but I walked right up to him and asked, "Do you want to suck my dick?" I've never found this blunt sexual courage again.

The boy seemed to think about it but in the end he wouldn't do it. He did, however, know someone who would. The boy said he was gonna meet the guy at Terrace Park on an upcoming Thursday afternoon. I could come.

I went. Terrace Park was directly across the street from my mother's house. I put on clean clothes after school and paced in front of our picture window until I saw the boy enter the park.

Soon a van pulled up. The driver was overweight and in his fifties. This was in no way what I wanted. He had a sarcastic and mean attitude but I couldn't think of a way out. We got in.

The man drove us to an abandoned factory on a dirt road in North Denver. I specifically remember seeing in the van's magazine rack a new issue of *Time* magazine with the headline, "How Gay Is Gay?" When we stopped, the driver adjusted curtains on all the windows and had the other kid and me sit in the back.

He knelt in front of us, fondling our crotches. I grimaced out the window and made sure both of them knew I was doing it. Quickly the man began sucking our cocks, going back and forth. I couldn't get even

174

the slightest bit of an erection. He made a derisive comment about not having all day. When the other boy came, the man gave him twenty dollars. I got nothing. I was deeply ashamed.

When I got home I washed my dick with soap and water, then plopped in a chair in the living room, brooding. I guess I didn't stop mulling this over for years. I began a cycle of running away and hustling, continually repeating the experience, trying to get it right. After high school I became a full-scale transient prostitute: Denver, Los Angeles, New York, Chicago, Atlanta, San Francisco. Even in Salt Lake City I could tell you where the hustling spot is located.

I never saw the man with the van again.

For the rest of that year, the other boy made a series of harassing phone calls to my home. Often when one of us answered, all we heard was some sort of toy that belched out a maniacal laugh. I would hop on my bike and rush to the boy's house, where I circled his front yard like a shark.

I became angry and withdrawn, but I was brought up well, so people labeled my behavior as "shy." I began saying, "I'm not shy, I'm ruined," to correct them. Luckily the boy moved away in my sophomore year, so the threat of exposure diminished. I escaped into the world of drugs and punk rock, which was just starting to explode. My cute little punk name in high school was Dreadfully Tired. It fit like a glove.

I don't feel I'm qualified as a victim of molestation. I was the one who went out looking for sex that day. I do wish the man could have been a little more encouraging and less jaded. I don't just wish this, in fact, I resent the fact that he acted the way he did toward someone so young.

Rising Sun

Anonymous

I remember my first time clearly. While I was a child I seemed to always know there was something different — or maybe *special* — about me. It wasn't limited to just a lack of interest in girls ... I knew that it had something to do with my place in the world. By the age of twelve, I had either read about sex, heard about it on TV, or put two and two together to figure out that I wanted to experience it, and furthermore I knew that I wanted it with other boys.

If only I could turn back the hands of time, knowing what I know now, I might have been more proficient at getting around to having sex at an earlier age. Alas, it was not until I was fifteen that the "blessed event" happened to me!

In 1982, my high school band was invited to perform a concert in New Orleans. I was excited about this trip, as I had rarely been outside my native Georgia, and the thought of seeing the magical city of New Orleans left me giddy with anticipation. Little did I know that something else magical would happen on the trip — something that would change my life forever.

I had known Michael for about two years. He was just a few months younger than me but for some reason was one grade behind me. We weren't close friends, just dudes who were in band together. Our high school band was, at the time, one of the finest in Georgia, and we all took great pride in it. When it came time to sign up for hotel rooms, I was absent but later learned that Michael had signed for me to be in his room, along with two other guys, Mark and David. Michael played alto saxophone and the rest of us played trombone.

We arrived in New Orleans and immediately went sight-seeing. That night in the hotel room (we stayed at the Clarion on Canal Street), it came time for us to decide who shared what bed. Mark made some cute statement like "I'm not sleeping with that fag Michael," so that meant he was with David, because I had already claimed the bed by the window. Mark didn't mean anything bad by what he said; it's just how some teen guys like to talk. But, I thought, where there's smoke, there's quite often fire, and I felt excited about sharing a bed with Michael.

That night, we had to go to bed fairly early because our concert was the next morning. After the lights were off, we were all talking quietly until one by one we drifted off. I lay wide awake, almost trembling at the prospect of actually — finally — having another dude lying next to me!

After a while Michael shifted in the bed and his arm ended up across my stomach. I moved and my leg pressed against his. This went on for a good bit until finally his hand moved over on top of my shorts. (I was wearing gym shorts and a t-shirt; he wore only boxer shorts.) I rolled slightly and my dick started to get hard, but he didn't move his hand. Then I "accidentally" pressed my hand on his boxer shorts — only to be greeted a rock-hard dick standing straight up from the fly! Not a word was said. We quietly masturbated each other but neither of us came. I guess we fell asleep, because that's all I remember of that night.

The next day involved the concert and more sight-seeing. All during the concert Michael glanced at me and I glanced back. We didn't say a word to each other. I guess our minds were really spinning and sorting out all those feelings. That night, after midnight we turned off the lights, watched TV, and then Mark and David were soon snoring. Michael and I were lying on top of the blanket, both wearing only bikini briefs this time (his were blue, mine white). I turned the TV off, made a point of saying, "Good night, dudes," in case Mark and David were still awake (they weren't), and rolled facing away from Michael.

In time the same stuff as the night before started, but this time I got tired of beating around the bush, and just reached under the covers and pulled Michael's briefs down, and off. Then I removed my own. We progressed through a relatively varied sexual repertory as the night went on: beating off with each other, sucking each other, feeling each other's bodies all over, and kissing and hugging. Of course, we had to be as discreet as we could because of Mark and David, and we couldn't make any noise. Michael and I both came two times and had to change shorts when it was all over. The bus ride back to Georgia the next day was an emotional one, as Michael and I sat together but said little.

For the rest of that school year, and part of the next, Michael and I became the closest of friends. We experimented with sex quite a bit, and once had a three-way with a dude from another school. Eventually we moved on to other partners, and Michael moved away with his family in the middle of his sophomore year. I never heard from him again, but I will always, always remember that special time in New Orleans.

Sex Education

Gary Riley

It was the fall of 1980 and I was a seventeen-year-old high school senior. I had noticed a cute new sophomore around campus the first few weeks of the school year. He was about five feet seven, and had big blue eyes and blond, curly hair. I wanted to get to know this guy. Unfortunately, I was always the shy type.

One Friday afternoon while leaving a football pep rally in the gym, I noticed the boy, whose name turned out to be Todd, and another sophomore getting ready to fight. They were both yelling and pushing each other like guys that don't really want to fight but won't back down. It didn't take long for a crowd to gather and then for the teachers to take notice. When someone hollered, "Teacher!" I somehow got the nerve to step between them, break up their fracas, and lead Todd away.

Todd and I talked together for the next half hour until we caught our rides home. After that we seemed to gravitate to each other. We spent time together — our lunch hours, football games, and Friday-night roller skating. I had never been quite so attracted to anyone as I was to Todd. Oh, I'd had crushes on cute and popular guys through junior high and high school, but not as strongly felt, nor did I ever feel that it was mutual, as I did with Todd.

That winter, I asked Todd to spend the night. He got permission from his parents, and came home from school with me that Friday afternoon. We went to a football game after dinner, then back to my house. My younger brother and I shared a small room, so Todd and I slept on cots in the den that night.

Once we had watched some TV and eaten snacks we prepared for bed. We stripped to our briefs, and lay down on the cots. As with any young people, we talked before going to sleep. This was a nervous time for me. I knew what I wanted — to have sex — but I wasn't sure how to go about it. How would Todd react? Would he reject me? I had played doctor when I was seven or eight years old, and I had masturbated with a friend or two in junior high, but I wanted more this time. I had dreamed of having a lover, of sucking dick and having mine sucked. Would Todd be the one? I wanted him to be.

I steered the conversation to sex. Not gay sex but straight sex to start with. We discussed magazines like *Playboy*. a while back I had found a girlie magazine in an old box in our garage. It was the first one I'd seen, since I come from a strict Christian family.

I asked Todd if he knew all the positions for sex. He didn't. At least he claimed all he knew about was the missionary position. So I proceeded to explain what I had read about. Then I came up with the idea that it would be easier to show him rather than explain. Todd agreed and I started with the "doggie" position.

I told Todd to get on his hands and knees, then I moved in behind him on my knees and pushed my crotch up against his ass. We still had our briefs on. But at that age it doesn't take much. So after showing Todd a few more positions like that, we both had raging hard-ons.

For the last position I put Todd on his back with his legs up over my shoulders. By this time I couldn't contain myself any longer. I reached down and fondled Todd through his underwear. He didn't seem to mind.

A minute later we were both buck naked, comparing cocks and fondling each other. Todd had a beautiful five-and-a-half-inch uncut dick. I'm cut myself, and he was actually the first uncircumcised guy I'd seen. His foreskin didn't quite go back all the way when he was erect and I loved playing with it.

We stroked each other for a while, then I told him I wanted to try sucking him. Todd lay back and I took him in my mouth. It was wonderful! Better than I'd ever imagined. I thoroughly enjoyed the feeling of warm flesh with the life pulsing through it in my mouth, running my tongue all over it and up under the foreskin.

After a few minutes we switched places. When he first took me into his warm, moist mouth, I thought I would die. It took all the control I had not to explode right then. I had always expected it to feel good — a little better than jacking off with some lube — but this was exquisite.

I stopped Todd before I came, to make things last, and we relaxed briefly. Then we tried some different ideas. We got into a sixty-nine for a few minutes, we humped against each other, both face-to-face and against each other's ass cheeks. I finally sucked Todd to a climax, his cum sweet and warm in my mouth, though I choked on it a little, if truth be told. I got my rocks off by rubbing against Todd's ass — masturbating between his ass cheeks — since he wasn't thrilled about sucking dick at the time.

At that point I knew I was gay, that this was the life for me. I believe that this was both Todd's and my first time. But Todd seemed to enjoy it as much as I did.

Todd and I got together a few more times for sex, but he and his family moved away later that year. He came back into my life two years later and we were lovers off and on for about three years.

I realize now that I really did love Todd, and his actions later made me believe he felt the same way toward me. However, we never discussed our feelings. I guess we were both too afraid of what might be said or happen. I was never able to talk with anyone else at the time either; homosexuality was just too taboo for the time and the place.

Spin the Bottle

Russell Ben Williams

1982, age 17

My first physical experience with another boy happened when I was seventeen. My best friend "Billy" was one year younger, and he was my idol. We had been friends since childhood and had everything imaginable in common, including our virginity.

We did everything together, and we shared such a bond that people often joked we were homosexual lovers. Billy got upset about it, but for me it was a secret dream unfulfilled. I knew early on that I was attracted to boys — to Billy, in fact. He was a gorgeous boy, and we both knew it.

We played a game called "Spin the Bottle" in my room when he spent the night. We sat on the floor next to my bed and took turns spinning the bottle. If the bottle pointed in my direction, for example, I would be forced to take a dare from Billy.

Dares usually consisted of things like having to make crank calls to the fire station or lip-synching to a Village People song. Before long the dares grew more risque. Shirts and shorts were coming off, and moon-shots of each other's butts became common. What was simply a game to him was a forbidden turn-on for me.

One night he dared me to get completely naked. I hesitated for a moment. "This isn't a dare anymore. I'm asking you to do it. Who's going to know but us?" he added, pulling his underwear down to expose his hard-on. Before I knew it, he had my underwear down to my ankles. I was so turned on.

"Do you want to mess around?" he asked, wrapping his fingers around his own hard-on.

"I guess," I replied, glancing down at his dick. It was rigid and upright, and his balls were like two ripe plums in a sack of smooth skin.

"You can touch it if you want to," said Billy. I cupped his balls with one hand and stroked his penis with the other. "Yeah, that feels good, Ben. I want to show you something," he whispered as he pulled me into bed. He started kissing my neck and worked his way down. I squirmed with pleasure. He sat up, grabbed my penis, and told me to close my eyes. I did as he said.

I felt his lips touch the tip of my penis and in seconds his head was bobbing up and down on my hard-on. I moved my hips to match his pace. A wave shot through my body as I erupted in his mouth. I collapsed.

"My turn," he said. He straddled my chest, facing me. He grabbed his penis and said, "Okay, baby, open your mouth."

I obliged, and he leaned forward to slide his penis into my mouth. He started humping with his hips, thrusting his cock deep into my throat. I grabbed his buttocks and pulled him, forcing him deeper into my mouth. I sucked his cock while my fingers found their way to his asshole.

My eyes watered as I sucked harder and harder. His breathing intensified and his moans filled the room. I felt his cock throb and soon I tasted the salty goo on my tongue. He pulled out, spraying the last of his load on my face.

Billy collapsed on top of me, and after he caught his breath, he asked, "Are you okay?"

"Yeah," I replied.

"Are you mad at me?"

"No."

He draped his arm across my chest and said, "Good. Let's get some sleep. You wore me out."

We fell asleep and when we awoke the following morning, we made no mention of what had happened. We carried on with our lives as if we had never shared each other's cocks. The games of "Spin the Bottle" continued, but they never reached the point of eroticism that had resulted that one night.

He eventually found the girl of his dreams and settled down with her. I went off to college, where I met a guy who helped me come out. Coming out in a small town like Kingsville was hard, and when I did, my world seemed to come to an end. Billy broke off relations with me. Suddenly I was the town queer and rumors came out of nowhere that he had been my childhood lover all along.

His anger and hatred toward me intensified as the rumors persisted. He felt betrayed that his best friend turned queer, and I was crushed by the hypocrisy in his attitude. I eventually left town, unable to deal with the hardship of losing Billy because of my sexual preference.

That was twelve years ago, and those wounds have since healed. When I think about how happy and content I am today with my sexual preference, I think back to that night with Billy. That experience changed the course of my life. It changed the way I felt about myself, and I am all the better for it.

I've run into Billy a few times during occasional visits to Kingsville. He'll stop to talk to me, but his eyes dart around to see if anyone has spotted us together. There is still that fear in his eyes that the world will label him a queer if he's seen with me, and I feel sorry for him. It saddens me that in these times, a person would be so terrified of that which he does not understand or that which he refuses to accept as human sexuality. Billy was my first sexual partner — my first love. I miss him dearly, and it is still painful that I had to choose between our friendship and acknowledging my sexual preference. But if I had to do it again, I would still be gay today.

Finally

Kevin Curry

1979–80, age 18

I had just turned eighteen a month earlier. Daniel was halfway through his sixteenth year. As president of the high school French Club for the 1979–80 school term, I had to attend all club functions.

When Daniel asked for a ride to the barn we were using to construct the club homecoming float, I jumped at the chance. I had lusted for his steel blue eyes, shaggy brown hair, and tight tennis-team body for two years, and had suffered heart palpitations when he joined the French Club his sophomore year.

As had become common practice for me and the other officers, "post-float" time was used to drink heavily, smoke cigarettes, and farcically conjugate French verbs. Daniel was friends with most of the group so I invited him along. All evening we had made eye contact. That kind of eye contact that lasts a little too long, that kind of eye contact exchanged between experienced gay men. Later it would become so familiar, but was new to me that night.

The beer consumption had barely started when Daniel began to bombard me with comments full of sexual innuendo, the way that "straight" men sometimes play "the Homo" so as to reaffirm their heterosexuality. I had been jacking off since second grade, and had fantasized about another boy every time. I did not, however, know about gay pornography, bookstores, parks, or rest-stop sex. I knew I wanted sex with a guy, but I did not know that there were actually other guys out there — in Texas — that wanted it too. I had no idea what to make of Daniel's behavior, so I just played back. The more I responded, the more intense he became. Finally he was grabbing my crotch, claiming he was going to "take me," to the riotous laughing of the group. I grabbed back. Then that eye contact again.

It grew late and I told Daniel that if he wanted a ride home, we'd have to go. I approached his street, but turned before I got there and parked in the alley behind his house.

"What's up?" he asked, staring with those steel blue eyes.

"Earlier you said something about wanting to suck my dick. Were you serious?"

"Well, you said you wanted to suck my dick. Were *you* serious?"

"I'd be willing to suck yours if you'd suck mine."

"Well, I'll suck yours if you suck mine."

"Then whip it out." He did. And it was gorgeous. I wasted no time taking it into my mouth. They say that you can't remember sensory stimulation. But I can taste and smell that dick even now. It was like nothing I had tasted or smelled before, while at the same time it was familiar and *right*.

I sucked it wildly for several minutes, not wanting to take it out for fear of never getting it back in. Then he pulled me off and planted his mouth on my mouth, inserting his tongue. I was kissing a man. The energy pulsed through my entire body and concentrated in my engorged dick as Daniel grabbed it firmly through my corduroys. He fished it out and went down. I'd been blown before, by a girl, so the sensation wasn't entirely new. But to have that sensation provided by this hunky little stud was overwhelming.

We traded back and forth for a while, sucking, kissing, sucking, kissing, and finally I started really working his dick, hoping to taste that creamy surprise. I had tasted only my own cum before. His balls drew up, his dick head swelled, and I sensed he was close. Suddenly, he pulled me off and screamed, "Stop!"

"What's going on? I'm trying to suck you off!"

"I don't want to cum," he said, pulling his jeans back up and repacking.

"You don't want to cum? That's the whole point! What's the matter with you?" Suddenly I felt a strange fear replacing the ecstasy.

"I won't be horny anymore if I cum."

"I know. We'll cum and then we'll go home."

"No, I'll feel bad if I cum."

I then knew what was going on. There had been many nights that I had flogged myself, both physically and emotionally, after spewing jism while thinking about Rock Hudson or Burt Reynolds. But it had not occurred to me that if I were actually to have sex with them, and they liked it, and I liked it, that that horrible self-loathing would still exist. And regardless, I would certainly never have stopped the orgasm ahead of time in anticipation of the negative ramifications.

But Daniel did. And so I took him home, took myself home, jacked off, and shot like I'd never shot before. Only as I drifted off to sleep did the pleasure of the experience wane and the impact of Daniel's angst take its place.

He avoided me the next day and most of the next week. I dragged him aside in the hall one day to tell him that he needed to calm down. No one was going to know what had happened, and I wouldn't ever bring it up again. He took comfort in that and our pre-tryst friendship resumed after several weeks.

We had sex three other times over the next three years, before I lost track of him my junior year at Baylor. We sucked on one another that next spring before I graduated, and then got together two more times after he went off to university. He never allowed himself to cum until the last time, and then immediately feigned sleep so as not to have to deal with it.

I knew I didn't love Daniel, but I found myself then and now greatly concerned about him, and how he felt about his sexuality. Partly for his sake, of course, and partly for mine. Because he was suffering from the same guilt that would control my life for years to come. As I came to know that there were more of us out there, I found that different guys reacted differently, though the guilt was usually the same. Some just go on playing the hetero game. Others killed themselves because they couldn't resolve the whole thing. And it seemed that a few actually overcame it. Daniel and I started the expedition together. I wish I knew if he made it to the end of the trail.

Curious about George

Robert Roush

1983, age 19

When I was sixteen, I started working at an office supply store (now out of business) called Ulbrich's, in the Buffalo, New York, area. I knew what I liked at sixteen, and boys were sure one of those things.

Working at an office supply store with an art department and book department let me see a lot of cute guys. I was pretty fawning and effeminate, and I now realize how obvious my orientation must have been to most people.

I often got calls from a man named George in the art department at another branch of our store. His calls meant he was looking for a certain item a customer wanted. During a two-year period, George and I developed a relationship, and repartee over the phone, which I later would realize was "camp," mixed with (for me at least) a good deal of attraction to this voice.

Well, what had to happen? I got a transfer to George's store, as it was closer to my home. High school ended for me, and I hadn't yet decided on where to go or what to do, in college. I now have a master's degree in nonprofit administration, and have raised hundreds of thousands of dollars for things like heart disease and AIDS in my career, so this fear and indecisiveness seems somewhat foreign to me now. But I felt it then, and I know it had a lot to do with this sense of unrequited love and sexuality I felt for other gents.

I met George, of course, when I transferred. He was blondish with a fuzzy beard, and twenty-three to my eighteen years. He was a bit taller (maybe an inch) than my five-foot-seven frame, but had a long torso. His nose was quite large below blue eyes, but I rarely looked at that. He had a habit of rolling back the sleeves on his shirts, showing extremely defined arms which, back then, seemed huge to me.

I was at an excellent weight for fawning, about 120 pounds. I was thin, but pretty well proportioned. After high school, I had bought the weight set I always wanted, and started working at it. I guess you'd call me a late bloomer. Back then I had a bit of dark fuzz on my chest, and George had a magnificent even coat on his chest and abs (the man *had* a chest and abs, which was an endless source of desire for me). Our relationship was destined to become quite close after two years of a phone relationship. I thought he was gay, but didn't know how to talk about it. I didn't realize it, but he *knew* I was gay.

We wore work boots while slinging file cabinets and safes, and watching George's arms bulge just drove me wild. I'm not sure how much time passed, but I remember I was nineteen. Finally, one night after closing, we had our arms around each other's backs and we were walking up one of the aisles singing, "We're off to see the Wizard..." and I asked if he'd like to go to Perkins, the famous chain diner, after work. "Sure," he said. It was a Friday. I called my parents to say I'd be going out and not to wait up.

Despite my previously chaste nature, this was not a surprise to them, as I went out with high school pals all the time. I still sort of had a girlfriend with whom I hung out, and I had told her *and* my parents about my gay feelings two years earlier. My parents were coming to terms, though confused that I could "know" without any experience.

Off George and I went for a quick ice cream. Afterwards, we sat in his car. It was winter, and very cold. George lit a cigarette and at long last I told George I was gay. The next moment, he had slid over the black vinyl front seat of his white Plymouth Duster, planted his mouth over mine, and pulled me down on the seat.

Whoo-boy! That was fast! We were in the busy parking lot of a pancake house, and I was mortified. The man tasted like an ashtray, it was cold, and people leaving the restaurant saw us while getting into their cars. They drove away honking their horns. Some folks even pounded on the now-steamed windows. I am convinced that in the dark winter, with my face turned down and away from the windows, and the heavy winter coat, people probably thought I was a girl. No one would have looked for two men in such a situation, so I doubt that's what anyone saw.

After what seemed like an eternity, he let me go and asked if I wanted to go to a gay bar. I didn't know, but hell, I was in it now, wasn't I? The situation was not too pleasant, but the feel of his stronger body captured my attention. Off we drove into Buffalo, I was about to be introduced to the smoky rooms and the boom-thump of the disco era.

I met a couple dozen of George's friends and got the "My" and the hands over the mouths and the "They start them younger and younger" cracks. Everyone smoked. The bar's interior was painfully drab, and George and I got a couple beers and sat at one of those square tables that rock back and forth because they cannot be adjusted to a bad floor. The black glued-on formica veneer was chipped or peeled away in many spots, revealing areas where filth had caked on the glue beneath. He rattled on, and I had another beer or two, but didn't get drunk. I think I asked George to dance, but he said the music was wrong. To me it was either going BOOM! THUMP! THUMP! or THUMP! BOOM! BOOM! BOOM! I couldn't tell any difference.

Eventually I became tired of the noise and the endless stream of friends, "Dahling! How are you?!" Kiss, kiss, etc. I asked George to take me home. He did. Mind you, I still lived with Mom and Dad. George kissed me and asked to come in. I said yes.

Inside, we continued to kiss on the couch. My parents were asleep on the other side of the living room wall. I was nervous, but got tired of the ashtray-licking kissing that was going on. George was wearing one of his famous rolled-sleeved shirts, and I kept pushing the sleeve up and feeling his upper arm. He kept his arm extended, and every once in a while, he'd readjust his position and I felt his triceps ripple. I had no such muscles, but had loved to look at muscular men for as long as I can remember. It was a thrill to see what they actually felt like. Finally, I asked him to flex his biceps. (Corny, hunh?)

I became excited despite my skittishness. "All right," I said. "Quit fooling around and take your clothes off." Yes — I actually said that. It had been a "joke" phrase we used in high school when sexual overtones began to be expressed. He complied quickly. He stood up and I stood in front of him. When he removed his underwear, up willy sprung. I was amazed for several reasons. First, it was the first erect penis I had ever seen other than my own. Second, it remains, to this day and many men later, one of the biggest I've ever seen. I remember trying to take it into my dry mouth as I sank to my knees, but I was so nervous by this point, I was starting to feel sick to my stomach.

George, being more experienced, realized I was having trouble. He moved me back to the couch and told me to stop shaking. I was still hard as a rock myself, and with both hands, George faced me and started to jack me off. I remember getting to reach down and feel the bulging muscles in his arms. I was able to come, I think, because of this. After I lay a moment trying to recover, and trying not to be embarrassed while I used the tissues nearby to wipe off the sticky goo, I saw that he was dressing. I said, "But there's unfinished business." He said, "That's all right." One more kiss, and he was gone.

My parents were still asleep (it must have been 1 a.m. by then), but I was so confused and upset by the experience I almost threw up. I felt the way I did before having a test, or performing music on my viola at school, or going to a new class. Overall, it had not been a pleasant experience. My thoughts for the days following were mostly of the cigarette smoke and the vile taste of the kisses. (You may have guessed by now I'm a nonsmoker.)

Later, I would "finish the business" by sucking and jacking George off in my bedroom, also at a time my parents were home, but after that I began working days and seeing little of George. A couple times at work, he would grab my crotch like it was familiar territory. He also made some snide remarks about liking arm muscles, and grabbed my arms while I was moving and lifting some things. We went out a few more times to eat, and I bought him a stuffed little bear, which he put in his car. I asked if he cared about me and he said, "No, I don't feel that way." It hurt me, so finally I told him not to ever touch me again at work, and he didn't.

I went on to find a short-lived first lover from a personal ad, and finally, I moved out and went to college, where I truly came out and met many men. I have now been in a long-term relationship for the past six years.

Beer-Belly Mike

D.A. Bungay

I had seen Mike standing soberly in the corner of the bar. What attracted me to him most was his posture. He was erect, stiff, self-confident. Mike wasn't much of a looker but he had a strong square jaw framed by a beautiful dark mustache, long dark fur peeking out from the open neck of his red flannel shirt, and a beer belly that protruded over his belt line. I guessed that he was about forty, but I was only eighteen and at eighteen, everyone over twenty looked forty. I knew Mike was from out of town. Living in Smalltownia, you eventually know everybody, and I didn't know Mike, but I knew that I wanted to.

Somewhere between my fifth and sixth beer I found my feet dragging me over to where he stood. My heart was pounding and I could feel the blood rushing through my ears. I was hatefully inexperienced and had no idea what I was going to do once I got in closer to him. Except for some jacking off with friends, I was completely a virgin.

I stood next to him at the bar with my elbows back on the flat top and a beer dangling in my right hand. I was not even sure he had seen me move toward him, and I was terrified to turn to look at him to see if he was looking at me. I knew I could not maintain this position for too long. My dick was as hard as a brick and I feared someone would notice it.

I couldn't help but smile to myself. For years I had enjoyed fantasies of men in all shapes and sizes and various stages of dress and undress. In my mind I was confident that if I got with Mike, all these fantasies would come true. Of course, I reminded myself, I had no idea how to make love to a man, let alone play out my ten million fantasies at once. I felt pressure on my arm. It was Mike. He leaned in on the bar and planted his heavy hairy forearm on mine. I believe that was the first time I had ever been brought to orgasm by another man. He didn't move his arm. And I panicked. I dropped my beer on the bar and left.

Walking home, I cursed my chickenshit self under my breath. I wanted sex with another man in the worst of ways, but I was as terrified as I was eager and horny. AIDS was just on the horizon and like most folks, I was deeply afraid and ignorant of the disease. I remember looking down at my feet and seeing my shadow growing longer in the approaching headlights of a car. I moved to the side of the street to let it pass. The car, a white late-model LeMans, slowed considerably as it passed. It was Mike.

Three slow passes later, I found myself in the passenger seat going to his motel room for a drink.

Mike came out of the bathroom holding two beers, wearing just his flannel shirt and his underwear. Orgasm number two. Talk was sparse and mostly centered around his reasons for being in town. He kept adjusting his balls in his underwear and running his hand up under his shirt over his big hairy belly. Somehow I knew he had done this at least once before and I felt horribly awkward and virginal. The next few moments are blurred. I do remember getting up from the edge of the bed to get an ashtray and feeling something on my crotch. It was Mike.

Looking back some ten years later, I have to smile to myself. I remember being so afraid, yet so eager, and worrying a great deal over the fact that I was a virgin. When Mike took off his shirt, I began to run on instinct. The fear and apprehension just seemed to melt away. When I touched his dick for the first time, I immediately knew that this was right. It fit into my hand. Into my mouth. I was amazed how easy and natural sex with Mike was. There was no work, no effort. I glided into three orgasms. Mike knew what he wanted from me and showed me how to do it. I believe he sensed that I was inexperienced, so he slowly showed me what intense lovemaking between men was all about. Was it everything I had imagined? Skyrockets maybe? Most certainly yes!

I slept with Mike that night. In the morning, I quietly dressed and left his motel room as he slept. That night I went back to the bar to see if I could find him again, but without success. I almost walked to the motel to look for his car, I don't know why I didn't, but I didn't. I guess I knew that I'd never see him again.

I don't live in that town anymore. But when I return, Mike is never far from my mind. I look for him in hopes that our paths may cross again. In fact I look for Mike wherever I go. I firmly believe that he has been a major influence in my sexual preference and in my life.

White Satin

Steve Heyl

I was a late bloomer as far as sex was concerned. After graduating from a Catholic high school, I stayed in my hometown of Orlando and went to a commuter university. After the first summer on campus, I decided that if I didn't join a fraternity, I would have no social life at all, and I joined Delta Tau Delta. It was in the fraternity that I met Alan. He was twenty-one, and had dropped out of the university the year before, but still came to fraternity functions.

Alan was just shorter than my five feet eleven inches. I had always been fairly thin. He, on the other hand, had the sort of build I always noticed and admired: beefy without being overly muscular. Imagine a high school football player who is too small to play in college and you get the idea. He was also starting to go bald. He would probably catch my eye today, though not like he did then.

I didn't really recognize it as a sexual attraction, but I knew I enjoyed being around him. We instantly began to go places together. We found lots of common interests, including the fact that both of us were fans of the Moody Blues. We'd drive around town with "Nights in White Satin" blaring from his car stereo.

The night before the fraternity initiation was known as Hell Night. Pledges were given a series of tasks that took the better part of a night. For example, we were given a dozen eggs and a list of a dozen people who had to autograph them. On the list was 'a bartender at the Parliament House' — a gay bar. So it turns out my fraternity took me to my first gay bar before I knew I was gay.

When the weather warmed up in the spring, Alan and I found Playalinda Beach on the Canaveral National Seashore. Different sections of the beach drew different groups, but the section that interested us was the nude section, a half mile north of the sign advising us that nudity was illegal on Florida beaches.

I had fantasies about the men, but kept trying to suppress them because of my Catholic background. When Alan and I discussed such things, he said that he used to have fantasies about both men and women, but he outgrew it and I would too. I was nineteen and he was in his twenties, so I figured he was right.

None of the fraternities on campus then had houses, so I lived near campus in a small townhouse with two roommates. One Saturday in July, when my roommates were out for the weekend, I invited Alan and a few friends for dinner. As was common at these college events, we drank lots of homemade sangria. Even in my somewhat inebriated state, I could tell that Alan had imbibed quite a bit more than I, and I told him he was too drunk to drive home. After much protest, he finally agreed to stay and sleep it off.

He followed me to my room, and lay down on the floor. I climbed into bed. It was a hot and muggy night as we lay there naked. After a brief silence, he asked if I was tired, and I said no. We talked for a while and at some point the conversation got around to the current sleeping arrangement and the fact that he never is comfortable sleeping on the floor. I asked why he didn't take the bed and he said, "You didn't ask." I said I didn't mind the floor, and got out of bed onto the floor. He didn't move. Again, we were silent. He took my hand in his. Still no words. Finally, one of us commented on how this would look if one of my roommates walked in at that point. We agreed it was none of their business. Then we moved our hands to each other's cocks; to this day I insist he did it first, and the last time we spoke about it, he insisted I did it first. In any event, as soon as one of us did, the other followed immediately.

We stroked each other for a while. We didn't say much, except the occasional grunts to indicate that we each enjoyed it. He stopped and said that if we were going to do this, we might as well be in bed. We moved. He asked if I would give him a blow job, and I agreed to, if he would do me afterwards. I put my mouth on him and began to lick. He moaned and I knew I was doing a good job. Besides, I liked it. The years have taken some of the rest of the night from me. I know he sucked me, I know we eventually kissed, and at some point we each came, but the details are gone.

We woke up the next morning in each other's arms despite the heat. He asked if the previous night had been a dream. I replied that if so, I had the same dream. I told him I really enjoyed it; he hedged and said something about having wanted to try it but that he probably wouldn't do it again. He said it was better with a woman, but I knew from his voice that he was trying to convince himself.

I turned on the radio as we got out of bed. "Nights in White Satin" came on. Without a word, we embraced each other, lay back down on the bed, and began to kiss. We reached for each other's cocks and stroked until each of us had come.

For a while we remained close. Most of our friends never knew what had happened. I wanted to talk about it, but he always refused, until one of our weekend trips to Cedar Key, a small island that embodies what

Florida was before the mega–theme parks. I insisted we talk about what had happened that July night. Finally he admitted that he'd enjoyed it, but he thought it was a bad thing and he didn't want to do it again. We had sex that night.

About a year or two later, we had a falling-out. I saw him only once again, when he announced that he was engaged to be married. By that time I had quit the fraternity, and Alan and I had little in common. But to this day, when I hear "Nights in White Satin" a slight smile crosses my face.

Birthday Present

Anonymous

1978, age 20

As my twentieth birthday approached, in 1978, I did not yet consciously think of myself as gay. I had several gay friends, and saw nothing wrong with homosexuality (it probably helped that my parents were both atheists). I just didn't know the term referred to me. Sure, I thought men were attractive, but I'd never had sex with one of them — nor with a woman. If this all sounds confused and illogical ... it was.

My college roommate threw me a birthday party that year, and one of the guests was a slim, attractive biology major whom I'll call David. I'd seen him occasionally around campus and thought he was attractive, but had never spoken or paid him any special attention. That night, however, something was different.

We were introduced; he had come with a gay friend of mine, but they clearly weren't a couple. David and I ended up talking, and he quickly mentioned that he was gay. In a fumbling, liberal way, I explained that I wasn't bothered by that. We talked for a little while, and discovered our mutual interest in tennis, but then much as I was enjoying the conversation, I had to go socialize with other guests.

As the party wound down, he came by and resumed our conversation. Soon we were the only ones left, and David suggested we go for a walk to a wooded area near campus. As we walked, he told me about his own coming out a year earlier, and how he was hoping to meet someone he could have a long-term relationship with. I felt a special closeness to him as he told me all this, though I wasn't ready to share anything about my own somewhat confused feelings. Yet, in retrospect, I must have given off some clear signals.

We arrived at the woods, and walked down a path toward the river. My foot caught a tree root, and I started to fall. David quickly threw an arm around behind me, and gently squeezed my shoulders between his two hands to steady me. Without thinking, I put one of my hands on top of his, holding it against me, and we looked at one another. At that moment, I knew we had connected; we were crossing some unspoken boundary.

We sat under a tree, above the river, and talked. For half an hour, an hour, two hours? I don't know. For the first time ever, I put into words some of my confusion about my sexual identity. At some point I said, "All I know for sure is, I want to be with you."

David invited me back to his room, and I had no hesitation in accepting the invitation. It took us no time to get out of our clothes. My erection was stiff and calling for attention, yet I wanted to stretch out our time together. We rolled together in the bed, trying to bring as much of our flesh into contact as possible. I leaned on one elbow and looked down at him, entranced by the soft down on his chest, the faint outline of his ribs as his chest tapered to his waist, his firm stomach, and of course, by the first erection I had ever seen on a man other than myself. I vividly remember the pearly drop of precum (something I was unfamiliar with, as I don't seem to produce it) on the tip of his penis. It was a thrill to realize that this gorgeous and desirable man was so excited over me.

David didn't seem to believe that I was really, completely, a virgin. He kept asking if I'd ever been fucked, ever had oral sex, jerked off with a guy, slept with a woman, etc. Finally he seemed to realize that he was dealing with a complete (but eager) novice. Almost apologetically, he said, "I really like to fuck. Do you think you can handle me?"

"If you'll tell me what to do," I said. He got some KY jelly, slipped a pillow under my butt, put my legs up around his shoulders, then lubed up both me and himself. It might hurt a little as he entered, he said, but he'd be gentle, and if I ever wanted him to pull out, all I had to do was say so.

It did hurt a little, but not much. I was high on love, or lust, or something, that night. David entered slowly, then paused as I got used to the feeling. He relaxed me by pumping my erection with his free hand, then started slowly moving in and out. Soon the delicious sensation of fullness overwhelmed me, and I encouraged him to go faster and harder. He was noisy, something I hadn't anticipated. Soon he was groaning and moaning loudly in tempo with his thrusts, and I joined him. Triggered by his own orgasm, I came just a few seconds after he did, a complete body orgasm. We cleaned up and fell asleep in one another's arms.

That began a relationship that lasted two and a half months. For the first month, we had sex every single day, almost always in the same position as the first night. It eventually became clear that while we had certain interests in common, we were too different to be a couple. Still, while the relationship was short by some standards, it was important for us. By the time it ended, I knew I was gay, and was out to most people I knew.

We parted amicably, and we still exchange notes occasionally. His last birthday card to me said, "Still fondly remembering your birthday party of nearly twenty years ago."

Crossed Communications

Anonymous

1978, age 21

My first true sexual experience happened when I was a 21-year-old college student, early in 1978. My only previous encounters had been fooling around with guys in the isolated small-town neighborhood where I grew up.

I had dated little, and had never even kissed anyone in a sexual context. To say the least, I was inexperienced. However, I did know about most sexual acts and how they were supposed to work. Nobody had yet heard of AIDS, but I knew about other sexually transmitted diseases and how they were spread.

Almost by chance I had fallen in with a group of friends that included several gays, several straights, and a couple "question marks" like myself. We socialized a great deal, and frequently went out dancing at a popular gay club. So, as the months passed, I became familiar with, and comfortable being around, gay people.

"Tim" (not his real name) was part of the group, and when we first met, he was dating a female friend of mine. Tim was two years older than I. We got to know each other over time, and when he told me he was unsure of his sexual orientation, he was one of the first people I ever told that I, too, was unsure of mine. We spent more time together, and he gave me the impression that what he wanted more than anything in the world was for someone to love him. He also made his family sound like a bunch of maladjusted, uncaring, and cold people.

Tim's relationship with Meg eventually wound down. One evening, he and I were alone in his apartment, and he asked me to spend the night with him. I knew I wanted to, and while not scared, I was still apprehensive. I didn't repel his first physical overtures, but I didn't really respond for the simple reason that I just didn't know what to do. That night we slept together still wearing our shorts, just cuddling and touching. In the morning, Tim pulled my shorts off, and I experienced my first blow job.

In retrospect, it was a good blow job. At that time, however, I had no standard of comparison, and I felt assaulted by an enormous range of emotions and questions. One of my first realizations was that Tim was far more experienced sexually than I had known. The second realization was that I was in love with him, and would do my best to give him the love he wanted.

From that point on we had sex several times a week. Being twenty-one with a sexual outlet for the first time in my life frequently meant my cock stayed hard even after he had sucked me off. While Tim was a good sexual partner, he wasn't a particularly good teacher, and more than once complained about my lack of technique. I did my best to follow his example, and also read everything on the subject that I could get my hands on.

We had discussed the idea of becoming roommates several months previously, so we went ahead with our plans and found an apartment. But we were headed for disaster. The living arrangement lasted about three months. I was already looking for a single apartment or room when Tim announced that he was planning to move in with another guy, apparently as his lover.

My relationship with Tim certainly hastened my own coming out. However, I now realize that if any one of about three other guys I knew at the time had asked me to spend the night, I would have. I'm glad my "first" was with someone I knew in a private, comfortable place, and not with some faceless stranger in a stinking restroom somewhere. However, although my first sexual experience was very good physically, it was emotionally disastrous.

Panic vs. Desire

Brian J. Hamel

In January 1980, I was a sophomore at Central Michigan University and fast approaching my twenty-first birthday. I saw a notice for a gay liberation meeting in the school newspaper but missed the first opportunity to attend, rooted by fear to an easy chair in the corner of my dorm room. A week of dejected disappointment forced the issue. At the next meeting, as I entered the room, a young man in a black woolen overcoat turned to me and uttered the first words of my new homosexual life:

"Gay Lib?"

"Yes," I whispered and took a seat at the table, making a total of four attendees. A blonde woman was unhappy about the low turnout. She and Black Woolen Overcoat had a brief discussion, then decided to adjourn the meeting for lack of interest.

"Lack of interest?" I asked myself. I was so interested I thought my nerves might vibrate through my skin! Lack of interest? Was this it? Wasn't I going to meet any *men?* C'mon, there has to be more than this, I thought. I had been so nervous on my way there that I took a roundabout route so even people I didn't know wouldn't see me enter that room. All the blushing and watching my shoes as I walked there ... for a canceled meeting? I was truly disappointed.

Black Woolen Overcoat snapped me out of my reverie. He offered a ride to a friend's house, where members of the group often spent time together. I deliberated, then accepted, and we drove there in his yellow Volkswagen.

Black Woolen Overcoat was not exactly my fantasy man. He wore a hat to match his coat, and his voice alternated between male and female as he questioned me about various facets of my life. He was cheerful though, and funny. It really didn't matter what he sounded like; I was alternately full of myself for finally facing my fears, while also contemplating making a break for it at the next stop sign.

Like his voice, Black Woolen Overcoat seemed to walk a line somewhere between male and female. He wore a dark two-piece suit, white shirt, and dark tie. His hair was totally without shape or styling and hung unnoticed where it landed when he removed his hat. He was neither tall nor short, fat nor slim. Had he been born a shadow or a spy, he would have found unequaled success. Everyone at his friend's house liked him and responded to his campy humor. I left the gathering with him to get a ride home, but also hopeful of sex. By now we had determined each other's names, knew a modicum of each other's vital statistics, and I was somewhat comfortable with him in the dark and shivery confines of the tiny, freezing automobile. His name was Bob.

Bob resumed questioning me about my personal life, specifically about my sexuality. His breathing got noticeably short when I explained to him I had never before had sex or come out in any way.

"I'm not really gay," I said. "I mean, I might be, but I don't know for sure, I—" I stammered to a complete stop as I realized I had never before spoken the word "gay" to describe myself. My nervous system began functioning so fast that I saw and heard everything whizzing past us with extraordinary clarity. I grew dizzy and my fists clenched in my lap. Finally I lit a cigarette and cranked open the window for some fresh air. I was having serious doubts about what I was doing and thought again about making a break for it.

His hand slid gently onto my knee. I felt pinpricks of sensation at his touch and a tremor shook my shoulders. As I turned to see what I was feeling he smiled and offered quietly to be my first. With an exhale of blue cigarette smoke filling the space between us I answered, "Okay."

▼

At his apartment we sat briefly on either end of the sofa. I kept as much distance from him as I possibly could. I excused myself to use the bathroom and in my absence he spread a blanket on the living room floor. When I returned and saw him there I took a deep breath and joined him. He coaxed me out of my clothes, kissing me, fondling me, and patiently answered my questions. I had no trouble undressing him and was stupefied at the size of his cock. It was thick, long, and like nothing I had ever imagined. He had a low-hanging sac with balls as big as my thumbs. He knew exactly what two men could do together and was adept at instruction.

I followed his suggestion to suck his dick. It was much bigger than my own and I played with it, stroking, licking, sucking, squeezing. I loved how it felt in my mouth, swollen yet still pliable, and after a moment's awkwardness this new activity came almost naturally to me. He didn't come but seemed wholly unconcerned.

When he turned his attention to my pleasure I was not at all prepared for the intensity. Bob was a skillful sexual partner and as I lay on that blanket with my head rolling from side to side, hips bucking up and down, lost in the sensation, I gave myself over to desire. All the while he uttered encouragement and delighted in my responses to his attention. He repeated much of what I had just done to him, and added a few more acts that caused me to cry out in pleasure, satisfaction, relief, and shortly, incredible release. The grin on his face said volumes as he looked up at me from between my legs, wiped his lips, and said, "Well now..."

We cuddled and kissed for a few moments before he put some music on his stereo. Rejoining me on the blanket, he asked how I was doing, how I felt, and, coyly, if I liked it. Stretched out on my back, smiling, I closed my eyes and took another deep breath. I liked it.

The music: A woman sang in a good voice but the music was dated. I had never heard the song before and it broke my reverie of self-congratulation and satisfaction. Suddenly repulsed by the cuddling, I refused to let him kiss me anymore. I escaped to the bathroom again but couldn't look at myself in the mirror. Shaking, I examined my body for signs that I was a fag, that something might show, that I would become a nelly, lisping, drag-wearing queer. I was hoping like hell I could get out of this mess without anyone ever knowing. Stomach churning, I stooped over the toilet, convinced I would vomit. It was completely stained by rust. I flung open the door and stormed into the living room. Bob sat on the blanket, smoking, listening to his music. Naked, pink, plump, his black straw hair sticking every which way, he was at that instant the personification of everything hateful and ugly I had ever heard about fags. I wanted to kill him. I wanted to kill myself. My contentment of a few minutes before had dropped and shattered like a cheap dinner plate on a kitchen floor.

I asked him who was singing, and when he said Shirley Bassey I went over the edge, shouting about his shitty music and filthy toilet while I skittered through his apartment dressing myself, hell-bent on seeing the other side of his front door. He quietly reminded me that we were three miles from campus and said if that I would just wait a minute, he would drive me back.

It was the longest five-minute car ride of my life. He was silent, sullen, shaken by my outburst. I was incredulous at my actions, begging God to keep this a secret, to make me straight, to help me through this, to let me die that night in my sleep. I had Bob drop me at a different dorm, so he couldn't find me later. When he was gone, I walked back to my own dorm, into my suite, past my roommates, and lay on my bunk bed, fetal, facing the wall. My roommate Mike stepped in asking what was wrong. I told him I was fine.

The next day my two other roommates returned from dinner with a lavender-scented envelope addressed to me that had been left in our mailbox. They teased me, threatening to open it until I cursed so forcefully that they handed it over. Mike, who had not participated in the teasing, sat quietly at his desk looking at me as if for the first time.

"This has something to do with last night," he said.

"Yes." I opened the envelope carefully, sniffing the cologne and noticing the flouncy feminine handwriting. This could only be from Bob. It was a short note with his phone number and signed with the letter "B." I told Mike that "B" was a woman I had met in the campus library the night before with whom things had happened with a force of their own.

I fabricated a story about "B" so good I almost believed it myself, secretly vowing to never touch a man again.

Several months later, on the night that I told Mike I was gay, he and I shared a laugh over the true story of "B." Bob and I would have one more encounter but not for several years.

Bucking

Robert S.

In 1985 I was twenty years old and had just finished my second year of school at an old, established art institute in Brooklyn. I was a resident advisor in the dorm and would be staying on campus throughout the summer. My next-door neighbor, Ken, was also staying for the summer to work. Ken was a junior; tall, blond, and lanky, from Iowa. He smoked, drank, and was very funny. And he was a hell of a good artist. I had never been attracted to him in a sexual way, but always felt comfortable around him. I wasn't out at the time, although I'm sure he and most of the residents on my floor knew I was gay.

As the summer rolled on, he and I became closer almost by default. The population of the floor, which was sixty during term, was now four. He would stop by to see what I was up to and we talked late into the night. We never discussed gay issues or talked about sex. But I could tell something was happening between us.

One night I went to his room to chat as usual, but ended up staying longer than I normally would have. It was raining outside. I had always imagined making love while it was raining. I was sitting on Ken's bed, looking out over the brownstones of Brooklyn, when he turned out the lights. I was so nervous my stomach started to cramp.

Suddenly we were all over each other. We kissed so long and so hard that I noticed my chin was starting to hurt. I had never thought there would be a disadvantage to two men kissing. But all that stubble and friction! Nevertheless, it was wonderful. Nothing had ever felt so natural in my entire life.

I straddled Ken's chest and he ran his hands up and down my back and sides, something no one had ever done to me before. The sensation was so amazing and new that I began to buck up and down (whenever Ken wanted sex later he would ask if I wanted to "buck"). He thought this was hysterical.

We both had raging hard-ons that we rubbed against each other while we kissed. I was aching to give Ken a blow job so I unfastened his buttons and pulled out his cock. It was big, much bigger than I had expected. And I'll never forget how it smelled. All the porn magazine stories talked about that "musky, sexual aroma." Well, this was that very same scent and I had to admit I didn't care much for it. But the thought of finally giving head was so overwhelming, I overlooked the smell and got busy. For some reason I had always thought you were supposed to lightly rake the sides of a cock with your teeth (again from all those stupid magazines!). Well I guess I did a little too much raking, because Ken just about hit the roof. So throughout my entire first blow job all I remember hearing was the rain pounding the windows and Ken whispering, "Watch your teeth."

I sucked for so long my jaws started to hurt. Finally he said he was going to come and pushed my head away while he had a quiet but convulsive orgasm. Then he took me in his mouth and about five seconds later I came. I roared so loud I thought my head would explode.

And then it was over. I remember thinking while I was drifting off to sleep, *You did it, you had sex.* But I think what I liked most was falling asleep in another man's bed.

Ken and I were together for about a month. Then I became interested in someone else and realized (much to my horror) that I had only been using Ken for my own sexual awakening. He told me he loved me but I did not love him and broke off the affair. He was terribly hurt and we were never even friendly again.

But what goes around really does come around. After I left Ken, the guy I was interested in left me. Or maybe it had something to do with those toothy blow jobs!

May I?

Peter House

Early 1980s, age 21

All through high school I knew I was physically attracted to guys, yet I was a junior in college before I realized that this attraction meant I was probably gay. When I realized this, I wasn't upset — just surprised. I had never thought about actually having contact with a guy before. I didn't figure this out on my own though — Matt helped me to put the pieces together.

Matt was similar to me in many ways — we were the same age, we looked a lot alike, we had similar interests and similar backgrounds. Matt was in a state of sexual limbo similar to mine. Neither of us had ever had sex with *anyone,* male or female, though we were both twenty-one. Nor had either of us decided what our sexual orientation was. But we knew we were attracted to each other.

My attraction to Matt was the first one I'd ever had that was reciprocal. In fact, he was the initiator. We sang together in the college choir and after our regular Thursday-evening rehearsals we went to a college hangout for pizza and beer.

Matt always made it a point to sit next to me, sometimes so close we were actually touching. He then drew me into an intimate, private conversation. After a few weeks of this, he began introducing the topic of homosexuality into these talks. How did I feel about it? Had I ever had any homosexual attractions? Did I know anyone who was gay? Then he started asking me to drive him home each week. (I had a car — he didn't.) We would park outside his apartment for hours and talk about sex — mostly about the fact that neither of us had ever done it.

But Matt admitted that he was a frequent masturbator. He described in loving detail the different ways he masturbated, his favorite locations for doing it, and what he thought about while doing it. He also probed for details of my autoerotic life.

After a month of this, Matt came to the point. He told me he'd always wanted to jerk off with another guy and asked me if I'd like to do it with him. My heart was in my throat at this point. I wanted to do it more than anything I'd ever wanted. But I was nervous. Also, I had never jerked off with my hand before. I'd always done it by lying on my stomach and pushing and grinding against the bed. I confessed this to Matt and he suggested that we go to the 24-hour supermarket for some lotion and paper towels.

Then we drove into the park and found a dark place to park. It was November and in Syracuse, New York, that's a cold month. I left the motor running and the heater on.

Of course, we were both nervous, but Matt broke the ice with the trite expression "I'll show you mine if you show me yours." He unbuttoned his belt and pulled his pants down around his knees. He yelped as his bare butt touched the cold vinyl seat. I grabbed a blanket from the backseat and spread it under him.

Then I took a minute to look at what Matt proudly wanted to show me. His penis was completely erect and it looked a bit strange to me, as I had never seen anyone with an erection before. Matt pulled it down and released it so it smacked against his belly. Then he said, "C'mon, I showed you, now you show me."

I slipped my pants down. After staring at my erection for a few minutes Matt said, "Let's get started." He masturbated with his hand while describing what he was doing. Apparently I wasn't doing it right, because after a few strokes Matt's hand reached out and he asked politely, "May I?" Then he began stroking my penis.

I asked if I could touch him. It was a strange feeling and I remember the feeling of resistance in his hard penis when I pushed against it.

Matt masturbated me for fifteen minutes or so until his hand got tired. He wanted me to cum, but I was too nervous. He was too nervous to cum also. Finally we both gave up and went home. By this time it was 4 a.m.

Two weeks later we did the same thing again in the same place. This time we both came.

By now I was hopelessly infatuated with Matt. In fact, I was obsessed. He was all I could think about. I couldn't concentrate on schoolwork and I nearly failed every course that semester. I desperately wanted a deeper relationship with Matt. I wanted to hug and kiss and hold hands. I wanted to sleep together in the same bed. I wanted to cuddle together on the sofa and watch TV. I wanted to use the *l* word.

Finally one night I told Matt I loved him. He told me he knew that. He told me that he loved me, but as a friend only. He denied even having a physical attraction to me, and claimed that he was simply experimenting because he was a writer and thus needed to "experience" as much of life as possible.

This is still, to date, the most painful experience of my life. I was able to cope only by completely severing all ties with Matt.

Our tenth college reunion was this year. Matt and I talked for two hours. We didn't mention these incidents. But Matt alluded to having had relationships with men. He was fascinated with the details of how I met my lover of five years and expressed support for domestic partnership legislation.

I'll always consider Matt my first love and credit our relationship with bringing me to terms with my sexual orientation.

Dancing

Rick

1985, age 24

"I just need to tell you that I am totally, hopelessly attracted to you."

Such a simple statement, really — just a few average words strung together to form an idea. Yet given the intensity of this particular thought — the years of suppressed desires, the hiding, and the artificial posturing — the statement was monumental. The words actually were held together by a courageous glue born of desperation. The need to speak or burst was high; pressure cookers left on for ten or so years tend to malfunction.

I was twenty-four, working as assistant director of admissions at a small liberal arts college nestled in New York's beautiful Hudson River Valley. Rural, funky, and artsy barely *begin* to describe the scene. In addition to interviewing prospective students I coordinated our office's tour guides, mostly comprised of eager work-study students. When Tori (one of our summer workers) announced the arrival of a drop-in interview on a sultry late-August afternoon in 1985, I didn't have a clue as to how drastically my life was about to change.

I grew up in a town of five hundred people with one crossroads and no stoplight, in upstate New York. Isolated, conservative, white, heterosexual, and backward are some of the adjectives that help to draw a picture of what the place was like. I always knew I was different from most of the people there, and several memories of childhood discomfort remain burned into my mind: my teenage brother telling me not to play with my hair because it looked faggy, my mother frowning disapprovingly at the *Tiger Beat* pictures I chose to put on my wall (cute boys, like Shaun Cassidy, Donny Osmond, Mark Spitz), my baby-sitter telling me not to try on her necklaces and earrings because boys don't wear jewelry. It wasn't until puberty that I really conceptualized my differentness as *sexual.*

From this point on, the messages became frighteningly clear: a family friend telling me that he hoped the queer disease wasn't catching, because a faggot doctor from New York City had bought a house near ours; my inability to look any of my male classmates (many of whom I fantasized about constantly) in the eye during after-gym showers.

Freshman year of college brought a welcome break from small-town life, yet I still was afraid to explore the seemingly murky depths of my homosexuality. An unwelcome advance by the unattractive brother of a friend during junior year, and the come-on of an equally reprehensible

207

economics professor my senior year, forced me even deeper into the closet, for I feared attracting only those people who I found uninteresting. Summoning up my small reserve of courage, I came out to a few close straight friends, who all were supportive and could care less about my sexual preference. I was relieved and encouraged but still not ready to take the flying leap of faith necessary to seek out someone like me.

Back to 1985. I told Tori to send the drop-in to my office. When Carlton walked into the room, I nearly fell out of the window — the energy *leapt* between us. Initially I was undecided about whether to erect a protective wall or to welcome the flow and let it do what it may. By the end of the interview, I was hooked — he was tall and solid, an actor/singer/dancer, witty, spontaneous, and sensitive. Only nineteen, Carlton had been accelerated due to intelligence and talent and was ready to begin his junior year as a transfer student. There was no question as to whether he would be admitted. After conferring with my boss I called with our decision. He was excited but worried about costs; then he received a work-study stipend as part of his financial aid package. He expressed interest in a tour-guide position; after some deliberation concerning my motives, I hired him. Everything seemed to be moving forward, falling into place, and enabling the two of us to connect further.

The next two months were busy. I was gone most of the time recruiting, touching base with the office every other week for a few catch-up days. During those times, Carlton and I became friends. The tension between us was palpable, yet exciting and intriguing. I had him over for dinner and he freaked out both of us by telling me several specific details about three of my closest college friends after looking at their pictures. Apparently he had some psychic abilities in addition to his more visible assets. My crush was barreling down the road toward obsession, a point on the distant horizon where nothing else matters.

Needing to talk about the myriad emotions churning inside of me, I finally confessed everything to my roommate, Karen. She encouraged me to pursue things and not worry about getting caught up in the office dynamics of the relationship. Her support was invaluable at the time, for it made me feel like I wasn't alone and that at least someone understood. I knew the time for me to act on my feelings was *now*.

After Carlton declined my invitation to a Halloween party, we decided to spend the following Saturday together. We met in the early afternoon, saw *After Hours,* then drove around his hometown of Poughkeepsie, admiring the great Victorian architecture. Next we went to Vassar's amazing indoor Ecology Reserve, stopped for drinks at their alumni house, gobbled a pizza, found some clove cigarettes to smoke, and debated whether or not to head for New York City. Carlton wanted to take the one-and-a-half-hour trip, but I had other things on my mind.

On the dark and drizzly drive back to my apartment in Rhinecliff, I blurted out the opening line of this story. Carlton's composure crumbled as he began babbling away about his past, his feelings and fears about becoming sexual with me. He'd known he was gay for several years and had acted on it, but was in a somewhat celibate period trying to gather his thoughts and energy. He worried about how our relationship would change and cautioned me to think about the difference between two friends having sex and falling in love. I had no idea what he was talking about and was so far beyond caring that it didn't matter anyway; I only knew that I wanted to sleep with Carlton.

We arrived at my apartment and took a long walk along the Hudson, filling our lungs with the cool, moist air and clearing out our scrambled minds at the same time. Eventually needing some warmth, we went inside my apartment around midnight for some peppermint tea, walking up to my rooms on the third floor and settling into my couch. He automatically positioned himself some distance from me, making me feel more alone than ever. Was the first person I had been brave enough to come on to not *really* attracted to me?

I lit some candles to lend a gentle light to the chilly, darkened room — or maybe it was to ward off the gloominess growing inside of me. After more conversation about our respective pasts, Carlton asked if he could hold me. As his arms wrapped around my torso a total peacefulness suffused me, soothing, colorful, and filling.

I realized that *I* had been the strong one so far that evening and that Carlton had been very self-conscious. He said that he was used to being the person pursued and seduced, not the other way around, but was becoming much calmer as he felt my warmth. He asked if he could kiss me. As I responded affirmatively, he stroked my face while looking into my eyes, then kissed me, gently yet powerfully. The feeling of his bigger, fuller lips wrapping around mine hit me with a jolt. Finally, I was feeling the current flowing through my body, moving from all parts of it toward my growing dick. He asked what it was I wanted; I told him I wanted him to teach me everything I'd been too afraid to learn for so long. Looking like a scene from a bad movie he actually picked me up and carried me to my bed, at which point we both were laughing hysterically.

We gradually undressed each other, pausing often to travel the map that was our bodies. I spent the rest of the night enveloped in a dream — floating, spinning, moaning. The things Carlton was doing to my body suspended my conception of time, stretched it out by connecting me with another person.

Carlton brought me close to orgasm many times in many ways, but kept stopping short, telling me that it's much better when prolonged. As I in turn explored his body he told me not to do anything that made me uncomfortable. His big terra-cotta nipples fascinated me. I spent long moments lingering over their tender tips. As I moved my mouth downward he asked if I was *sure* I'd never done any of this before. I nodded my head up and down and replied, "Ummhmmm," my mouth being full at the moment. Removing my lips from his dick, I told him that it really *was* my first time, but that I'd done *a lot* of reading, fantasizing, anticipating. Satisfied with my answer, he guided my head back to where he wanted it, sliding himself along my tongue.

We twisted and turned, sometimes occupying most of the bed, other times small parts of it. We ended up on our sides in the sixty-nine position. Rocking back and forth, we synchronized our movements, hands caressing, lips sucking in, out. Like really good dancing the rhythm overtook us, became us. Carlton sensed that I was close and stopped once again. As I began to groan with frustration he smiled, took my hand, and pulled me up.

The sun was just coming up as we walked into the bathroom. Once under a warm shower, Carlton was on his knees immediately; I spread my legs and leaned back against the wall, eyes closed. By now *all* feeling was centered in my dick; the rest of my body merely supported its weight. I sensed movement and opened my eyes in time to see him replacing the bar of Ivory in its dish. Disengaging his mouth from me, he announced that it was time for the "soap trick." I smile-sighed and pulled his face back toward me, pelvis thrusting on its own by now. Sucking me harder and faster, he moved his hand in between my legs and simultaneously soaped my balls, perineum, ass. I felt parts of my body begin to separate, then coalesce and move downward and outward with great speed. Then it hit. My orgasm was so intense that remaining in a standing position would not have been possible if his broad shoulders hadn't been there to hold me up. As I gradually came back into my body, Carlton continued his mouth movements, now comprised of slow and gentle suckling, swallowing, sounds of satisfaction.

We ended up back in bed, cuddling and talking about what had happened. As spent as I was from staying up all night and having another human being take five hours to bring me to orgasm for the first time, I still wanted to reciprocate. Carlton told me that having an orgasm was not important to him at the moment, that he'd gotten more than enough out of the night.

As we drifted off to sleep, my absent roommate's alarm went off. Karen always woke up to music, but somehow the station had been changed from her regular funky choice, WBLS. A Sunday Christian sermon blasted up through the ceiling, spewing fire and brimstone toward our bed. We fell into each other's eyes for a long moment, smiles turning to laughter as we started to dance again.

6. Progress and Pain (1986-1994)

Today, gay issues are commonly discussed on television and in newspapers. Gay men and women are visible in nearly all walks of life. Old prejudices are not disappearing overnight, but clearly, they *are* disappearing. Teenagers who think they may be gay can find supportive books in their library, and can see role models on TV. Years of activism have paid off.

But AIDS is also everywhere. It's hard to find a gay person who has not lost a friend or lover. The words "AIDS" and "gay" have grown closely linked in the public mind. Teenagers who think they may be gay have something new to worry about.

I had expected that both our increased visibility, and the reality of AIDS, would play major roles in these stories. To my surprise, AIDS is rarely mentioned. No one seems to have held back for fear of becoming infected. No one worried that AIDS was God's way of showing disapproval. (Nor, unfortunately, did many of these writers take appropriate precautions during their earliest encounters.)

Gay visibility *did* have an obvious impact, even if it's not explicitly commented on by the writers. I don't know if teenagers are having more gay sex now than they did a generation or two earlier. But clearly, more are identifying as gay at a young age. Sometimes, their first steps out are taken in an environment that doesn't provide much support.

The first story offers a striking contrast in this respect. The writer himself comes across as remarkably self-confident. Though living in a small town, he's been able to acknowledge himself as gay. His first-time partner, on the other hand, simply couldn't handle the experience, and ruined it for both of them.

I hope this young contributor, and anyone else who is encountering difficulties as they come out, will take a lesson from all the stories in this book. Lots of men have traveled the road that you are on. Every one of us experienced some painful times on the way. The vast majority of us find that as we learn more about that road, and about ourselves, it gets much better. It will for you, too.

To Be Continued

Anonymous

1994, age 15

I'm a little under sixteen years old. I have never had a lover, or been in a long-term relationship. But I have made love once. His name is Don and he's fifteen years old, too. Before we took off our clothes, we held each other for a long time. I could feel his heart beating on my cheek. I have never felt so secure before.

He had fooled around before with other boys, but he had never had anal intercourse, and he wanted terribly to do so. We let our tongues travel up and down each other's bodies. He took my penis into his mouth, as I had done to him. Up to this point everything was what I had dreamed of, until...

Until he told me, abruptly to "turn over." I did as I was told, because he had more experience. Then he put his cock into me. The first thrust hurt like a bitch. Then again and again and again, it went on for what seemed like an eternity. Thrust after violent thrust. Finally, I pushed him away and told him that I was starting to hurt, so *please* stop. He stopped. Grateful, I kissed him on the lips and tried to cuddle, but he pushed me aside and went into the bathroom. When he came out, I had put on a t-shirt and silk boxers. He fumbled around in the dark, found his clothes, and dressed.

After dressing, he sat in my swivel rocker saying nothing for a long time, until he broke the silence by saying, "Aren't you going to say anything?" He said this so coldly, so uncaringly, so insensitively, that it felt as if he had stabbed me in the heart with an ice pick.

I replied, "What am I supposed to say?" as unemotionally as possible. He gave no reply, so after about five minutes of silence, I said, "Aren't you coming to bed?"

"No," was the last thing I heard from him that night. I felt like trash. I felt cheap. I felt hurt. I felt used. I felt like shit. I cried myself to sleep that night. I cried for a lot of reasons. I cried because my love for him would not be reciprocated. I cried for the loss of innocence. But I cried mostly because I finally realized how much I could be hurt.

I thought making love would be just that, making *love*. Holding each other, caressing each other, being tender. But Don turned my dream into something horrid. He made it animalistic and cold. I had done it out of

213

love, he had done it for self-satisfaction. With him it wasn't making love, it was having sex. Nothing more. He has hurt me forever.

Since that rainy Thursday, we haven't spoken much. When I brought up the subject of that one night we spent together, he just brushed it aside as if it hadn't happened at all. I never want to be with him again. Now I am looking for someone that will hold me all night long. Someday I will find him.

A Not-So-Sound Sleeper

Anonymous

1988, age 16

When I was sixteen, I was enrolled in a middle school in San Antonio, Texas. I had been with a girl before, and had just broken up with my girlfriend at the time.

I had a good friend at school, a boy a year older than me, and I told him about how I couldn't look my girlfriend in the eyes anymore, and there was no apparent reason for that. We started hanging out together a lot, and soon became best friends.

I had known I had gay feelings since I was four, but I didn't know there was a name for it. I liked him very much, but I never really thought of having sex with him. He came over one day while I was mowing my neighbor's yard, and we went swimming in my pool. Afterward, he asked if I was a heavy sleeper. I didn't know why he asked me that, but I told him that I was.

That night, he decided to stay over. My parents went to bed, and we went to my room. We played a board game for a while and went to bed on my king-size waterbed. I had had other guys spend the night and sleep with me on my bed, but nothing ever happened,.

About an hour after went to bed, he leaned over and whispered my name to see if I was awake. I ignored him because I wanted to get some sleep and didn't want to stay up all night talking. I was wearing a pair of shorts, and when I didn't respond, he placed his hand on my ass and acted like he was asleep. I knew he wasn't, but I didn't say anything.

I acted like I was asleep and moved around a little restlessly. I rolled over and placed my arm over his chest, still acting asleep. This went on back and forth, placing our hands on each other where they normally would not go. After a while, he rolled on his side and came in full contact with my body. I let my hand slip down on his cock. It was rock hard. I acted as if I were restless, which allowed me to move my hand up and down his hard cock once.

This felt great and I wanted to do more. I knew he was not asleep. Finally, I turned to face him, sat up, and told him that we both knew we were not asleep, now what were we going to do about it? He looked at me, and told me he didn't know. What *were* we going to do about it?

At that point we embraced in a passionate kiss. It was the first time I had kissed a guy, and I liked it. He was on the bottom, so I put my arm

215

around his waist and pulled him on top of me. We were still locked in this kiss.

I eased my hand down the front of his pants and started to jack him off. He put his hand down my shorts and glided it up and down my ass. We stopped kissing, and I pulled his pants off and moved down to give him a blow. My tongue started with the tip of his cock and it danced down the shaft of his enormous dick to the base of his balls. I took it into my mouth, but was not able to deep-throat it. I sucked him off for a while and he groaned with pleasure. I stopped before he came and then he began to give me a blow. By this time, we were both fully unclothed and we were going at it.

My parents were asleep in the next room, so we had to keep it quiet. We got off the waterbed, and I began to fuck him in the ass. He wanted to yell, but he kept it down to a mild moan. To this day, I don't know if my parents knew what we were doing. He was on his hands and knees as I was fucking him, and I came all over his ass and back. We had pulled a sheet down off the bed, and he laid back on it as I sat on top of him and he began to fuck me. I took it slower than what he did, and I glided my ass up and down his moist, hard cock. While I was being fucked, I began to jack off. This went on for a short while and then he came up in me, which was very unexpected, and I came on his chest.

This all took several hours. He went to the bathroom, which is right next to my room, and cleaned up, and I went in after him. We didn't shower because my parents would have woken up. We got back in bed, not saying a word to each other.

We fell asleep around 4:00 a.m. and I woke up around 7:00. He was asleep, and I tried to wake him up because we were both fully naked and I didn't want my parents to catch us like that. I had to wake him up enough to get his pants on so that my parents wouldn't find us together in the nude. It turned into a great relationship. We had sex many times after that, sometimes in my house, sometimes in his apartment, and other times in the car in areas that were not very populated. This happened in 1988, and because sex was new to us, AIDS was not on our minds, and we never practiced safe sex.

We dated for about a year, then finally broke up. I'll love him to the day I die. Two years later, I came out of the closet to my parents, my friends, and to most of the people that I met.

I still love him, and he will always have a special place in my heart.

Soda and a Smoke

Brian Moore

1980s, age not given

As I look back, I think I was in heat from the time I was eleven. My fantasies centered on the UPS driver and friends of my older brother. I also had a crush on my physical education teacher that made it difficult to stay less than excited during class, in the locker room, and in the showers. I was grateful for the fact that the supposedly straight boys also got hard-ons, which they explained away as "lack of pussy" or the result of recollections of the "pussy" they did have.

I stole muscle magazines, as well as one of the few gay magazines they sold at the confectionery store, by putting them inside the local newspaper. I was afraid of the looks I would get from the cashier. I also figured that they would never sell this stuff to me.

One day, walking home from school with my perpetual hard-on, I ran into Tony, an upper-class guy I had watched play basketball and football. The girls always hung around him, so I figured he would always be just my dream man.

Tony started talking to me about school and other boring subjects. He asked if I planned to go to the school dance, and I said I couldn't go because my girlfriend was sick. He asked her name and I drew a blank! Then Tony asked if I had time for a soda and a smoke. I didn't smoke, but Tony did and I was ready to try it. Tony invited me to his house because his parents worked late. I agreed happily.

We had a few smokes, then Tony said he wanted to change clothes. I didn't move, and he started to change in front of me. He was down to his Jockey shorts and I was going crazy. Then he said he couldn't find the shorts he was looking for. When I looked up, Tony was totally naked and had a big thick hard-on. So did I! He touched my shoulder and asked if I wanted to play around a little. I was almost speechless, but I managed to say yes. Tony asked if I had ever been fucked and I said I had not. He started rubbing his dick and asked if I wanted to find out what it was like. It was all happening so fast! I said I wanted to do it but I was afraid it would hurt. He laughed and told me to trust him — that he would be gentle.

Tony put pillows on the floor, turned on the stereo with some romantic music, closed the blinds, and stood in front of me with a sexy smile and a body to go with it — all mine for the taking. He slowly unbuttoned my shirt and slid it off. Then he unbuckled my belt and quickly slid down my jeans and underpants. I kicked off my sneakers and was left sporting only my white sweat socks.

Tony saw how scared I seemed and told me to relax and he would be gentle. He kissed me all over, and the kisses on my mouth were the deepest and wettest kisses I had ever dreamed of. I sighed as he explored the inside of my mouth with his tongue.

He rubbed his body against mine — his hairy chest and stomach against my smooth body. Maybe it was just the contrast, but I felt like a baby. He whispered in my ear that he wanted to fuck me and make me feel really good. He had a rubber in his hand and said he liked me so much that he would never do anything to hurt me. I was impressed and so horny I was ready to come.

Tony gently lowered me onto the floor with the pillows under my stomach and he put other pillows under my head so I would be comfortable. He fingered my butthole for a long time, then put some kind of cream all over my crack. As he mounted me he nibbled on my ears and kissed the back of my neck. He told me to relax and take a deep breath. My cheeks were spread and I felt his cock bury itself inside me. He asked if it hurt and I said it did. Tony laughed and said, "Guess what. It's only halfway in!"

I gasped and he turned into some kind of an animal. He was ramming his cock up my ass and slapping my butt furiously. I liked it and hated it. I was confused and angry and happy. I realized I was sobbing, and Tony buried my face in the pillow as he went right on plowing my hole. I guess I really didn't want him to stop, but he wouldn't have anyway. He kept this up for ten minutes and I realized that I had already shot a load all over the pillows.

Tony got more turned on by this and got rougher. My whole body was bouncing in response. Finally, Tony started yelling that he was coming and did something I didn't expect at all. He pulled his cock out of me and tore off the rubber and shot loads of cum all over my back and cheeks and legs. Then he kissed me and held me close and said he was sorry if he hurt me. I was confused. I asked why he whipped my ass if he didn't want to hurt me. No answer. He told me that now I had become a man. He vowed that there would be repeats on this scene because I was so good.

In the next few days, Tony always seemed to avoid me. I tried to get him to take me home again, but he acted as if nothing had ever happened between us. I had fallen totally in love with him, and he was ignoring me — probably looking for another new guy to dazzle.

Blind Date

M. Scott Mallinger

1988, age 18

I was twelve years old when I first wanted man-sex.

I didn't get it until I was eighteen.

Until that time, a terminal case of shyness and poor self-esteem stopped me. But good fortune struck in the beginning of my senior year of high school: I developed a brain tumor.

Brushes with mortality put life into new perspectives; love and affection suddenly seemed paramount, and attempts to squelch such desires seemed counter to living. My new goal in life was to come out and live as I had never done before. And I did. But I had an extra obstacle thrown at me, impeding progress in the romance department: brain surgery left me temporarily blind. Although I could identify some colors or shapes, I could not recognize my own parents. I ventured into the gay community looking for love and sex, unable to see.

In a way, it was a blessing.

For years I spent energy caring about how I looked. Was I too fat? How did my hair look? Were my clothes all right? As a blind man, I couldn't ask myself these questions. They were non-issues. Instead, miraculously, I directed energy into meeting people, getting to know them.

I joined a discussion group for gay men and listened to stories of coming out, yarns of unrequited love, and tales of pre–safe sex. All the stories were interesting, but what I found most intriguing was the voice of one man: Saul.

Saul was a cantor at a local synagogue; his voice was deep, rich, masculine, warm. The voice commanded attention, but in a gentle way. When he spoke, you felt like his voice enveloped you and held you tight. I wanted him to hold me tight. I wrote Saul a note, explaining that I was smitten. Before I knew it, we had plans for dinner.

My parents were shocked to see Saul greet me at the door — he was in his midforties, older than my own folks! It simply hadn't occurred to me to ask his age. Based on my parents' reaction, however, I thought it unwise to ask if he was sexy. Instead, I just allowed him to take me into his warm grip and lead me to his car. We didn't stop talking, although I cannot recall our conversation. My head was spinning — I was on my first real date!

As with all good things, the date was coming to an end when Saul invited me back to his apartment. After a sequence of awkward silences, I eventually consented. We sat on his sofa and tried to make small talk. When that didn't work, Saul offered me his hand again. Suddenly I was aware of his strength. His fingers were warm and pulsed with rushing blood. This, I thought, was someone who was really alive. I heard Saul sliding a little closer to me and I swallowed hard. Reaching over me, Saul brought a hand to my opposite shoulder, bringing us nearly face-to-face. I could feel on my neck his hot breath, sweet like the red wine we had imbibed over dinner. I closed my eyes, rather unnecessarily considering the circumstances, and allowed the sensation of his mouth at the base of my neck to overwhelm me.

Fingers were suddenly stroking my hair, and I was amazed by how erotic the feeling was. Next, fingers lightly stroked up and down my arms, tickling the dark hairs covering them. Soon his lips found mine, and I don't honestly know whose pressed harder against the other's. Before I knew it, my arms were wrapped against his broad torso and I was holding him tight. I could feel his firm nipples pressing into my chest as my tongue entered his mouth. I was intoxicated by what we were doing, as if I had transcended our actions and actually become sensation.

Saul took me to his bedroom, then he took his time undressing me, rapturously kissing me everywhere, his voice exalting the praises of a young man's body. I was self-conscious at first. But although I thought of myself as overweight, Saul enjoyed every inch of me. He smiled and cooed as he knelt, kissing the fur on my belly while his hands explored the rest of my body. And everywhere his hands went, that glorious mouth soon followed. He was classically trained! It was the most sensual and liberating feeling I've ever known.

Self-control was not a priority for me on this occasion. I had submitted myself to pleasure, and three times that night received all the adoration that this charming older man had to offer. It was not until I was totally spent that I realized that I had not once reciprocated. Although he lavished me with praise and massage and oral aerobics, not once had I touched him intimately. As it turned out, he'd orgasmed during the act without my assistance.

The evening was so wonderful, I could not believe that I had waited so long for it. The cliche about good things being worth the wait certainly held up.

We lay back in the bed, the sheets dampened a bit with sweat, and our chests heaved — just a little — as we reclaimed our breathing. Life seemed to be returning, the real world once again seemed real. And, oddly enough, I felt more comfortable with myself than I ever had before. This was home.

"Thank you," I said, placing my hands on his face for the first time. Lightly, deftly, I ran my fingers over his broad forehead, his high cheekbones, his wide nose, his soft, thick lips, his chiseled chin. I tried to picture what he looked like ... then decided not to bother. I didn't need to. I felt what he looked like; a visual image would not enhance the moment. It couldn't.

Sight would have only destroyed the magic of making love for the first time. And it was magical with Saul, and continued to be for several months.

Six years and innumerable boyfriends later, sex continues to be a pleasure sought out. Rarely, however, is it as intense as that first experience. And even more rarely is it as spiritual.

College Boys and Camel Lights

Eric L. Roland

1987, age 19

I had walked into King Library on numerous occasions, probably three to four times a week, but most of my journeys into this academic library were not to study, but rather to visit the first-floor restroom I had discovered late in my freshman year. When I had come to Miami University (in Oxford, Ohio), I was still suppressing my homosexual desires, yet I had never pursued a heterosexual life either.

My homosexual desires blossomed one day in 1987 when, as I sat on the toilet in the first stall, I noticed that the small holes to my left allowed me to watch men (usually gorgeous college men) piss in one of four urinals hanging on the wall.

Needless to say, I became quite a cock watcher upon my return to campus for my sophomore year. I saw all kinds of dicks — big, small, dark, light, cut, uncut (these were a rare, albeit prized, sight on this primarily upper-middle-class, white, midwestern campus). Cock watching soon took on a new dimension when I discovered that the small holes drilled into the right side of the marble stall wall were angled to give a view of the cock of anyone sitting in the second stall. Occasionally, I would witness a man slowly stroking his dick and, despite my arousal and anticipation of participating in some form of sexual contact with another man, I always quickly became nervous and fled the restroom.

But one Friday in late September, two weeks before my twentieth birthday, I entered that three-story colonial brick building and my life changed. Since the first stall was occupied, which meant the occupant watched me enter the restroom through peepholes and thus knew what I looked like, I used the second stall. For one of the first times, I began jerking off and noticed, through the holes, that he too was stroking his large, unusually red cock. Within minutes, I heard him whisper, asking if I knew of a place to go. Nervously (and surprisingly!), I answered yes. Indeed, I did have a more private place in mind — a single-toilet restroom in Upham Hall. I had fantasized about taking a hot man into this restroom, but I never thought I actually would do it.

222

After pulling up my pants and attempting to *not* look nervous, I exited the stall and got my first glimpse of him — tall, well built, early twenties, light brown hair parted to the side and gelled back, attractive face and smile, dressed in blue jeans, white t-shirt, beige fraternity jacket, and white Converse "Chucks." He wasn't a god, but he was a very attractive college frat boy.

We left the restroom and the library together, not speaking until we were outside in the quad. As he lit a Camel Light, he introduced himself as Jon and asked me where we were going. I introduced myself using my real name, told him we were going to Upham Hall, and asked if I could have a drag off his cigarette. He obliged, and the deep long drag of smoke helped calm my trembling nerves.

Inconspicuously, we entered the small restroom in the basement of Upham Hall and locked the door behind us. While he unbuttoned my shirt, he asked if I wanted the light left on. When I replied yes, he began kissing me, the first time another man's lips had ever touched mine. Within a few minutes we were both undressed, exploring each other's nude bodies with our eyes, lips, and tongues. His dick was actually bigger than it had appeared through the peephole, and its girth filled my mouth. The feeling of sucking on his cock was all that I had imagined, and his warm mouth on my cock gave pleasure beyond belief. We concluded our rendezvous by jerking each other off while deep-kissing. After wiping up and getting dressed, he left the restroom, but not before giving me a smile and a wink.

I saw him a month later in a bathroom in the Student Center. We had a repeat performance except this time we were together in a toilet stall in a busy, lunch-hour restroom. The possibility of getting caught was high; however, this heightened the thrill. These were the only two times we had sex, although I saw him walking on campus a few weeks after our second meeting. He convinced me to join a gay and lesbian support group on campus, where I met many of my college friends, as well as my lover of four years.

That first sexual experience was not only exhilarating but vital to my development into an "out" gay man who's always been a part of the gay and lesbian community. Interestingly, Jon did leave a few impressions on my subconscious mind — I still eroticize Camel Lights and a man wearing white Converse "Chucks" high-tops.

Queen of the Night

Sandip Roy

1987, age 20

The Indian postal system, never a speed demon, conspired against me that time. A letter that should have taken three days took over a week. So when I finally heard Ritwik was in town it was almost time for him to leave again.

I had never met Ritwik but we had common friends in Delhi where he lived. At that time I knew practically no other gays in Calcutta. My gay life was lived through long letters with men all over India and abroad. One of these friends knew Ritwik and when he heard Ritwik was coming to visit his parents in Calcutta, he gave him my address.

I called the number he had given me in his letter, wondering what message I should leave if he was not at home. Should I give my name? What if his mother asked who I was? What if he called back and my mother asked him who *he* was? What if...

But miraculously he answered the phone himself.

We agreed to meet the next evening at seven at my old school. Ritwik and I had gone to the same school but he was three years my senior. If he was who I thought he was, he used to be really cute. I doubted that he'd ever noticed me. Three years his junior, my classmates and I might as well have been cockroaches!

Next evening I waited on the steps in front of the sweeping main hall. It was only 6:45 but I was afraid if I was even a minute late he might not wait. He'd said he would wear blue jeans and white shirt. Everyone seemed to be in blue jeans and a white shirt. It was 7:02 by my watch and he still had not shown up. I should have brought his phone number. I felt a few drops of rain. Thank God, I'd brought my umbrella. I shifted from foot to foot, staring at the gate, trying to will him to appear.

Then someone tapped me on the shoulder and said, "Are you Sandip?"

I whirled around and there he was. I recognized him instantly — the tall lean frame, the lopsided smile that lit up his eyes, the thick mop of untameable black hair that fell over his forehead. Blue jeans, white shirt. I dropped my umbrella with a clatter and stuck out my hand.

"Hi," I said, and then rather redundantly, "I'm Sandip."

"Ritwik," he said, shaking my hand and grinning. "Have you been waiting long?"

"Oh no," I lied. "Just five minutes."

224

My mind was prodding me to make intelligent witty conversation. But I couldn't think of a thing to say. So I just stood there grinning like an imbecile, hoping he could not hear my heart thumping.

"Let's go sit near the playing fields where we can talk."

The fields were dark and quiet. I could see lights where evening classes were still on, and in the priests' cloisters.

"Did you know about Father Stillson?" he said. "We all used to talk about him. He'd always be asking boys up to his quarters. And once someone said he was only wearing a towel."

"And he used to love giving football players pep talks before the matches while they were changing."

It was like the sluice gates had opened. All the fantasies, desires, fears, questions bottled up inside me came tumbling out. We talked about school, boys we had secretly lusted after, parents, marriage, and frustrations. Ritwik had gone on to study in England and America before coming back to India. He told me about nights of poetry and wine and men in Cambridge, male porn movies in America about prison guards and poolboys, hunky villagers, and bitchy queens in Delhi.

He tried to explain to me how gay activism meant different things in India, how we should not ape the West. His words came faster and faster, almost tripping over each other in their haste to be heard. I listened open-mouthed, watching the moonlight play over his animated features. Although barely three years older than me, he seemed to have already lived several lives.

The evening classes ended. The students strolled across the field in twos and threes, their cigarettes punctuating the darkness like fireflies.

"Do you want to take a walk?" he asked.

We got up. "Come on," he said, slipping his hand in mine. Startled, I left my hand in his palm, not knowing what to do. His hand felt warm and alive. We walked through the old school, past the shuttered classrooms toward the little field at the back. We walked to the end of the field and peered over the wall at the archbishop's garden next door. I could hear the little fountain gurgling in the dark and smell the flowers.

"What is that smell — what kind of flower is it?" I said, because I could think of nothing else.

"I think it's called *raat-ki-rani* (queen of the night)," he replied, smiling. "Like us."

I was achingly aware of his leg touching mine. My heart was thudding. But I kept my leg against his and tentatively put my hand on his waist.

He looked down at me. His face was much softer now. Then very gently he said, "Are you scared?" I shook my head dumbly and just stared back at him, totally tongue-tied.

And then he kissed me. With those beautiful curved lips that I had been watching all evening. Those sexy lips that had been telling me all those stories. I gasped and opened my mouth and felt his tongue on mine.

225

I moved my body closer and put my arm around him, feeling the hardness and the slightness of his body. I could smell the flowers in the Archbishop's garden. Or was it his hair? He smelled so clean and freshly showered. My dick was straining against my jeans. I thought I would just explode as I tasted his warm smooth skin.

Suddenly he stopped and said, "If anyone comes, you run this way, I'll run toward that gate."

I nodded and said, "Oh, and don't let me forget my umbrella. My mother will kill me."

He grinned and started laughing. But when he knelt before me and took me in his mouth I knew even if the headmaster showed up I would not have been able to stop. When I knelt before him he said, "Are you sure, you are ready for this?"

Of course I was. I had been dreaming about this.

I pulled his jeans down. He had on dark blue underwear that stood out against the lightness of his skin. I ran my fingers over his thighs wonderingly, feeling the soft roughness of the hair. Then I slowly pulled down his underwear and tentatively touched him with the tip of my tongue. He gasped. I opened my mouth and tasted him — hard and velvety smooth, smelling a little of soap and sweat.

"Careful with the teeth," he said. "Open your mouth wide."

We came on the grass in long shuddering spurts. And then we clung to each other, our pants still down at our ankles. He kissed me and said, "Are you all right?"

I wished we could do it on a bed without looking over our shoulders. The real thing was infinitely more exciting than jerking off over underwear ads. I had unleashed riderless horses in myself. As we walked out of the school, we bumped into the old prefect of discipline.

"Sandip," he said in his booming voice. "And Ritwik too. What are you boys up to?" I turned bright red and stared at my pants to see if there were any stains. I was sure we smelled of come and bruised grass. I was twelve years old again, quaking before the twitching cane in his hands.

Over the years we met every now and then. We wrote long untidy letters full of passion and raunchy stories. I went on to America and he became more and more activist in Delhi. The last time we met we walked back to the old school again, to the little field, and this time I kissed him.

"Next time come to Delhi," he said. "We'll have a real bed." I never got the chance. One cold January evening I heard he had suddenly passed away in Delhi.

Sometimes, walking down the street in San Francisco, a laughing young man in a hurry will suddenly remind me of him. A look, a smile, a hand pushing back an unruly lock of hair. And I'll wonder if the raat-ki-rani is still spilling its fragrance with such careless abandon in the archbishop's garden. I don't know. I never went back there. Somehow I did not want to find out.

226

Is That All There Is?

Paul Schwartz

1988, age 22

I came out after AIDS did, so my perspective on man-to-man sex had always been from a safe distance. I did have sex with my girlfriend of five years. Many times while we had sex, however, I had fantasized about men.

She was the first person I had told that I was gay. We broke up nine months later, during my senior year of college. After I graduated in 1988, I moved across the country to rural California, fifty miles north of San Francisco, to start a new life as a gay man. I immediately searched for gay support and social groups to contact other gay people.

I first saw him at a local college's Gay and Lesbian Alliance. At thirty-nine, he was seventeen years my elder. He had some rather interesting and unconventional ideas about homosexuality. He was intelligent and masculine, and although he was not devastatingly handsome, I found him attractive. I was interested in this man on an intellectual level.

I wanted to approach him and talk with him further. But I didn't want to seem forward. I left when the group was over. And when I arrived the following week, he was not there.

A few weeks later, I ran into him again at a gay men's potluck. I expressed how I had wanted to talk with him after the meeting and was glad to run into him now. We talked further about his philosophies, which evolved into more discussions with other men. As I watched him, I felt an underlying current of sexual attraction. He had a demure presence shrouded by a strong, masculine body, with an undercurrent of erotic animalism. I was intrigued and confused by my own feelings. If I called this man and met him, I was not sure what to expect. I was not sure what I wanted.

I went to his home a week later, where we explored realms of logic about God, alienation, brotherhood, and our fathers. Perhaps this was intense conversation on a first date, but I felt comfortable with him. We sat on the sofa holding, stroking, and comforting each other. We played with his dog, who he joked "loves me only for my dog food." He had an uncanny ability to make me feel safe. We then headed out to the Cloverdale Citrus Fair.

It was late on the last day of the fair, and half of it had closed already. We purchased a few items from a gem dealer, he got a bite to eat, then we returned to his place. I was going to go home, and we started hugging, then kissing. Then he started caressing me.

"I should go."

"Why don't you stay?"

"Half of me wants to leave, half of me wants to stay."

"Which half?"

I looked into his gentle eyes, I sighed heavily, then smiled. "I've never done this before — with a man."

"I know."

We moved to the floor and I watched the fire, the ceiling, his dog, as he made love to me. And that's what it was. He made love to me. I told him I did not feel comfortable reciprocating some acts. He granted me as much space as I needed to feel good. He let me explore at my pace, and as far as I wanted. Again, he made me feel safe. At one time, I started laughing uncontrollably. "Is that all there is?"

I did not feel like staying with him that night, perhaps due to a lack of intimacy or my nervous thoughts of what might happen as I moved deeper into this new realm. I went home, and immediately told my best friend about losing my virginity again! But that was the last time I saw the man for more than a year or two. I called several times, leaving messages on his machine that I wanted to see him again, and waxing philosophic. I yearned to explore these ideas with him more than having sex with him.

He did not return my calls. I grew frustrated and angry. I couldn't believe that the safety I had felt in his arms was simply a seduction for a one-night stand. I remained bitter at the thought of him for a long time.

When I finally met him again in a local bar, I expressed my resentment. But I also thanked him. He had shown me some respect that night, having allowed me the space to comfortably explore my first time. Since then, our paths have crossed many times. We have become friends, and we have slept together on occasion but have not had sex again.

Overall, when I look back upon that first time, I feel good. There was a pleasant surprise about the whole event. Like a giant balloon deflating, my anticipation was expelled and yet its importance was diminished at the same time. For years I had been taught — whether directly or not — that sex with another man was wrong, so I had denied my own feelings and yearnings for such male intimacy. I created a monster from the tension around what "it" would be like. When I finally faced that demon, I realized that it really wasn't anything at all. It became insignificant and vaporized, and there was nothing to fear. My anxious anticipation was almost a letdown, and I was left feeling so calm and so safe, but still wondering, "Is that all there is?" Of course, I have since found out that the answer is a resounding, "No!"

The Fine Line between Nipples and Nuts

Randolph W. Baxter

1989, age 22

I still prefer backrubs as foreplay. The art of giving a stimulating full-body massage was the first thing Todd taught me, for which I'll always be grateful. That and a vision of innocent, youthful manliness are the two things I still love in any man.

Todd had just turned twenty-one, one year younger than I was. I'd loved him from the moment I laid eyes on him and heard the loneliness and sensitivity in his voice. We met, ironically, at a 1985 national conference for Christians who wanted to change their sexual orientation. I'd caught his stunning, sorrowful gaze after he introduced himself to the opening assembly. The next morning, we met.

We talked and ended up in his room between seminars. We didn't cross the line into anything overtly sexual, however; true to our spiritual interpretations at the time, we just caressed and massaged each other's bodies above the navel. He felt too guilty after I'd pushed him to kiss me on the lips, so we put lip-kissing off-limits. (Nipples, however, were not off-limits, by the convoluted rules of our intensely internalized homophobia!)

In any case, these trade-offs were well worth it to a complete amateur like me. It was still an ecstatic new world of manly love for a fearful kid who'd grown up in a repressed, northern California small town where my high school crushes were my best-kept secrets. I had not yet gotten past the negative images I'd seen of gays in TV coverage of San Francisco's pride parades — prissy, queenie "men" who seemed to hate their masculinity. Now, I was in the arms of a tall, blond, smooth, spiritual man, so different from my preconception of homosexuality that I wouldn't admit it was the same. After all, we weren't having *sex,* and were both determined *not* to do anything to hurt the other by pushing into forbidden activity.

Todd and I became best friends, and although he lived in Missouri, I flew out three times over the next eight months. We enjoyed long evenings wrestling, exchanging massages, and just holding each other in what to me was absolute bliss. Our jobs then kept us physically apart for over two years, but we wrote extensively and telephoned often. We knew the "attraction" issue had to change, and after we gradually admitted that our prohibitions were unrealistic, we agreed that we could incorporate overtly erotic activity into our friendship without "sullying" it by turning it solely into a sex-based relationship.

Once again, I flew to Kansas City, on the last weekend of February 1989. We saw the movie *Torch Song Trilogy* downtown, then went home to the country farmhouse he was renting outside of Independence — a fitting place-name for where I "came out" forever. We talked about the inspiring movie, reassured each other that it was okay spiritually to "cross the line," and then slid under the covers together for a sleepless night.

I was thrilled to feel a beautiful man's tool in my hand for the first time, as our full-body massages could now be conducted pants off. I longed to try to take him down my throat, but he was only ready for mutual masturbation that night and the next. He again hesitated when I stroked his crotch, claiming bad memories from the times he'd been fucked years before as a teenager. But we both enjoyed a tender, emotional weekend. I loved him like a brother; we thanked God together for each other's beautiful bodies and spirits. I left more empowered than ever in my life, never regretting losing my virginity since it was with the only man I'd ever physically been able to love. We planned another weekend soon, and I was sure that he'd then let me suck him off. Already I started planning to find a job in Missouri.

Then his letter came. He had "relapsed" and thought it wrong that we'd made out. He couldn't handle being gay and being in the Church, regardless of what we'd talked about; now he wanted a girlfriend and to be straight. He admitted to having fallen with other guys during our friendship (when he'd assured me he was "holding out" like I was for him). His weak explanations in later letters sent me into depression for several months. I was devastated as much at my self-delusion as at his fickleness and deceit. I had spent almost four years holding him as the pillar of my heart, and now it had crumbled. Perhaps *Torch Song* had been a fitting film to see before my first encounter.

Over the next two years, we tried to piece together what remained of our friendship amidst the tension of my being out and him not. His sexual encounters with guys continued apace with my increasingly open contacts around Sacramento. I discovered the joys of oral sex with another man, who was bigger in every way than Todd, but who was just not the same (and who dumped me after three weeks). I still find myself judging all my potential boyfriends by the passionate, emotional, sensitive, and spiritual yet still firmly masculine standard I found in Todd; I continually remind myself to let the others be human. Backrubs, however, are a standard I'll never give up — if a guy isn't into them, I can tell he's not going to last!

Todd finally came out in 1992. We saw each other again the following year, after we'd both moved to the L.A. area, when he and his first official lover had a housewarming party. I realized I still loved him; part of me always will. I was actually happy for him, to see him be able to kiss another man in public, but was grieved to find out that they're both HIV-positive (though still healthy). I was finally able to understand, thereby, why he hadn't let me suck him off that fateful night back in Independence — he'd been afraid that he might be positive. Even amidst his confusion, he'd still loved me enough not to hurt me.

No Hot Dogs

Robert R. Reed

My first time occurred just after dawn one Sunday in early December 1990.

I was restless, bored, and horny. I had finished work at 5:00 a.m. (I work nights and am a night owl by choice.)

It was about 6:15. I'd been cruising the streets for over an hour. I'd given up and was on my way home, when I finally saw what I'd been looking for: a transvestite. He was black (I'm white). He wore a bright yellow above-the-knee skirt with matching top and black high-heeled boots that stopped about three inches below the knee. Inappropriate for the weather, but a great turn-on for me!

He was about six feet tall and had a healthy physique that I found sexy as he sauntered seductively.

I'd fantasized about same-gender sex since the mideighties, but was hesitant about trying it, partly because of AIDS, but mostly because of the stigma. Also, I really wasn't gay, just curious.

Beginning in 1985, I practiced, using half-thawed hot dogs, since they seemed closer to reality than a dildo, even a lubricated one. In 1988 I began viewing she-male videos, but was mostly disappointed, as I was only interested in scenes depicting she-males in assertive roles, having sex with men in passive roles.

In 1989, I began going to female impersonator shows. I'd fantasize about having sex with several of my favorite performers. I wasn't sure if I could become emotionally involved, but the sex intrigued me.

I felt I was finally ready for the real thing. There was one obstacle in my path, however: I could only get excited about drag queens, trans-sexuals, transvestites, hermaphrodites, and the like. Masculinity did not turn me on. It didn't matter that the person was the same in or out of drag. The illusion of femininity had to be present to get me started. And there weren't any *available* she-males I knew of except prostitutes.

Even so, I found them to be as rare as dinosaurs. Until that morning in '90.

I drove adjacent to the person and stopped.

He got in and we drove off for our encounter.

I was getting more excited by the second. I couldn't wait to get my face between his legs!

We drove to an alley and parked. I told him I wanted to go down on him and then wanted to receive intercourse from him. We put our respective seats down, and he raised his skirt and pulled his penis out from the bodysuit he'd been wearing. I engulfed his shaft hungrily.

After several minutes of intense sucking and licking, I paused to admire my handiwork. He was about six inches long and his diameter was somewhere between a quarter and a half-dollar coin. I'm husky, so I had no reservations about getting it inside me. I stroked it a couple times, then I pulled my jeans and briefs down and turned onto my front. He quickly mounted me. I moaned in sheer ecstasy as he penetrated my yielding virgin anus and began pumping. At first the motions were slow. I found it simultaneously soothing and sensual. "Oh yes," I breathed with every other undulation. I took my penis in my right hand while steadying myself against the seat with my left. His thrusts increased in intensity but were not violent. After several minutes, I felt something inside me like a glob of paste. He withdrew from me and wiped the remaining drops of semen off his penis with a paper towel and announced, *"I'm done!"*

I came shortly after against the back of the seat. I pulled up my shorts and jeans and turned onto my back. For about a minute I just lay there, recounting the feeling of him inside me, savoring it in my memory.

I dropped him off where I'd found him and asked if I could call him. He told me he didn't have a phone, but could arrange a future meeting. I told him I wasn't sure when I'd be able to do it again.

I never saw him again. I realize I should've been more concerned with safety, but the cliche excuse of "spoiling the mood" prevailed. Neither of us had mentioned condoms, though I had several and would've used one if he had insisted on it. Fortunately, nothing unhealthy presented itself in several AIDS and STD tests I took over the next couple years. In 1992, I encountered another transvestite and had sex.

Again, I was passive. Again, we took no safety precautions. Again, AIDS tests were negative. I realize my behavior was irresponsible, but psychologically, I couldn't get as excited about sex otherwise. If I wanted to suck a balloon, I'd get one and fill it with water.

I turned forty in February 1994.

I've begun answering ads by *pre*-op transsexuals for long-term relationships. This is something I thought I'd *never* do! I certainly wouldn't have considered it a decade ago, though I fantasized about the sex.

The femininity still has to be present, along with that "extra" touch. And it has to be real. No dildos or other props. Certainly no hot dogs!

Don't Look Back

Jay Owens

I'd always sworn that I'd wait until I got married. When I realized I was gay and saw the option of "legal wedding as foreplay" dissipating before my eyes, I was faced with a frustrating set of circumstances.

In 1991, at age twenty-two, I was still a virgin. I found myself sitting across from my father at a hamburger joint in Hollywood on the weekend of my college graduation. I was a complete mess. "Confused" was the word I'd chosen to characterize my ambiguous sexuality, though "terrified" would have been more accurate. To make matters worse, I was soon scooping my chin off the checkered carpet after my father asked me point-blank, "Son, are you gay?"

What followed was a three-day discussion during which I learned a lot about my own sexuality and my father's. (I'll never forget masking my surprise upon learning that he's never gotten a blow job.) I realized that not only was I graduating from college, looking for a job, and moving out of my apartment, but I was also officially coming out of the closet. How could I let such a weekend pass without getting laid? It seemed like the only sane course of action.

The second my father boarded his plane back to the Midwest, I got in my car and headed for West Hollywood. I was entrapped by fear and inexperience. My sexual excursions had been limited to three unforgettable (but not exactly memorable) occasions: (1) in grade school, putting my hand down the pants of the girl next door; (2) in high school, fiddling with my car keys as my date waited patiently for the sexual advance that never happened; and (3) in college, awkwardly trying to have a kiss in a crowded airport as a last attempt at heterosexuality. That was it. Unless, of course, you count excessive masturbation since the age of fourteen.

I knew I wouldn't have any luck in a bar or club. I barely had the courage to look at a guy, much less talk to one. So I hopped in my car and did what any lazy, horny guy does in L.A. I drove around in circles, looking at other guys driving around in circles — the four-wheel cruise. I figured it had to work for me. I'd only have to look attractive from the shoulders up, and my shaking knees wouldn't give me away. One drive around the block, and I was hooked. The streets were packed with men of all shapes and sizes. It was amazing.

At nearly three in the morning, I caught the eye of a guy driving a red Jeep. After passing each other several times, he pulled over. I followed, got out of my car, and nervously approached the driver's side door. We didn't say much. He was cute. Not gorgeous, but cute. He asked if I had a place, and I said no. "So," he said, "does that mean you're following me?" I nodded, retreated to my car, and followed him home.

Once we arrived at his apartment building, he took me to the rec room in back. It was dark and quiet. We introduced ourselves. I used a fake name. We sat on the couch.

He was probably in his late twenties. His face was pockmarked and lined with muscles. His short, naturally blond hair was neat but not overly styled. His muscular body was covered with tight blue jeans, a snug red t-shirt, and cowboy boots. I couldn't stop staring at his bulging chest. My erection, which had arisen about four blocks back, kept getting bigger.

I had no idea what to do. I decided to let him lead. Whatever he did to me (short of fucking or exchanging fluids) I would simply reciprocate. He touched my leg. I touched his. He started kissing my neck and ears. I followed suit. As I leaned closer to him, I could smell alcohol, and I was instantly relieved. It wasn't going to be very good for him. Maybe if he were drunk, he'd think he was enjoying it.

He started stroking my dick through my jeans. It was the first time a man had ever touched me. I was so excited, I came in my pants immediately. He didn't seem to notice, so I decided to fake it. I'd come again later and maybe he'd never know the difference.

We took off all our clothes, and he sucked my nipples before working down to my crotch. As he went down on me, I knew that by my own rules, I would also have to go down on him. And when I did, two things went through my mind. "No female needs to be involved here" was one. It was immediately followed by, "My poor father has no idea what he's missing."

Everything got lost in sensory overload. I was excited and nervous and terrified and exhilarated all at the same time. I quivered every time he touched me. Eventually, we both came. He took his dick into his own hands, leaning back and stretching his body, his head thrown back in awkward pleasure.

"Were you scared?" he asked.

I nodded.

He got up to search for a towel. His body looked beautiful in the dark. The light filtering through the trees outside the window shed the most erotic shades over his chest and stomach. Then he turned around and bent over to open a cabinet, and I caught just a glimmer of a lesion in the moonlight. I wasn't shocked or surprised. Well, I thought, welcome to the world of the sexually active.

I'd always wanted my first time to be like a movie. It's a common fantasy — glistening muscular bodies, slow pans across gyrating flesh, lots of blue lighting. What I'd gotten instead wouldn't have made it into a third-rate porno flick. He was drunk. He probably had a lover upstairs. He did this sort of thing all the time. But I didn't care. It was like intergalactic travel. I'd just visited another planet that I'd spent so much time thinking about, and while it hadn't been just like I'd pictured it, neither was it disappointing.

A few months (and several men) later, I saw him again. I was driving down the street, and I spotted him on the sidewalk. I had to look twice to make sure it was him. His hair was bleached blond, almost white, and he was wearing tacky skin-tight cutoff shorts, a thirty-year-old lost boy, with the summer sun emphasizing what the moon had hidden. I didn't stop or pull over or even slow down. I just drove away, thinking how different he looked in my rearview mirror.

It's Happened to Everyone

T.P. Landry

1993, age 20

Sometimes I feel like a prude when I tell this story.
Do you promise not to laugh?
I was twenty years old before I lost my virginity.
No, really.

Not that I minded — I simply *chose* to wait until then.
Actually, I think I knew I was gay long before I knew I was gay.
Do you understand?
Scary, huh?

I remember being attracted to men way back in junior high.
How did I know?
It must have been the hours I spent loitering in locker rooms.
Or maybe the fantasies about Superman.
Anyway...

I never slept with anyone in high school.
I never even dated anyone.
The only girl I ever kissed just came out as bisexual.
It was odd.

At twenty I was working in a video store.
I took the job because they rented adult videos.
Sometimes at night I would smuggle one home and watch it in my
    room.
A few of them really scared me.

I also kept a mental list.
Every man who rented from the gay section went on it.
How could I keep track?
It was Pennsylvania, there weren't many.

One night a man made eyes at me.
I made eyes back.
When he was ready to check out, I took over the computer.

I was the manager; I could do that.
His name was on the list.

What happened next?
He stayed at the counter and we talked.
His hands shook from being near me.
That touched me.
I gave him my number and he called me that night.

To this day, over a year later, he claims he wasn't really nervous, but I
    remember.
How could I not?
It was those trembling hands that clinched it.

We had dinner a few days later after I got off work.
I kissed my first man at a country stop sign, surrounded by stars and
    cornfields.
We made out in the parking lot of the video store.
I laid my head on his chest and he told me he loved me.
I didn't know what to say.

He met me after work again on Friday.
We hugged in the dark of the empty store and I told him that I loved
    him.
The next step was obvious; we went to his place.

It was quite far away.
I was quite nervous.
Sometimes I still can't believe I ever got up the nerve to lose my
    virginity.
Didn't you find it scary?
Anyway, I decided to trust him.
It was the best move I ever made.

What was it like?
I remember kissing on his big, slippery couch.
I remember meeting his dog.
I remember going upstairs.
He took my shirt off.
I took off his.
He was white Calvin Klein's.
I was plaid Gaps.
He did everything I asked him to and a few things I didn't even know
    to ask for.
How could I?

He was ten years older — the one with all the experience.
He did everything he could to make me absolutely comfortable.
He touched me in places I couldn't remember ever being touched
  before.
He gave me the kind of intimacy I had always dreamed of.

I wasn't afraid in his arms.

He held my hand the whole way home.
I can still feel the warmth of it under mine on the gearshift.
Are all men so kind?
Do they all feel so keenly the needs of others?
I hope so.

My first time was an incredible time.
It changed my whole life.
It made me feel whole.
I understood at last that sex with a man *could* be exactly the way I had
  dreamed of it.

And I never even came.
That one fact still amazes me.

Don't laugh — you promised.
I just couldn't.
Nerves, I suppose, but it didn't change anything.
Besides, it's happened to everyone.
Hasn't it?

Other books of interest from
ALYSON PUBLICATIONS

❏ **B-BOY BLUES,** by James Earl Hardy, $10.95. A seriously sexy, fiercely funny black-on-black love story. A walk on the wild side turns into more than Mitchell Crawford ever expected. An Alyson best-seller you shouldn't miss.

❏ **BECOMING VISIBLE,** edited by Kevin Jennings, $10.95. The *Lambda Book Report* states that "*Becoming Visible* is a groundbreaking text and a fascinating read. This book will challenge teens and teachers who think contemporary sex and gender roles are 'natural' and help break down the walls of isolation surrounding lesbian, gay, and bisexual youth."

❏ **CODY,** by Keith Hale, $5.95. Trottingham Taylor, "Trotsky" to his friends, is new to Little Rock. Washington Damon Cody has lived there all his life. Yet when they meet, there's a familiarity, a sense that they've known each other before. Their friendship grows and develops a rare intensity, although one is gay and the other is straight.

❏ **THE GAY FIRESIDE COMPANION,** by Leigh W. Rutledge, $11.95. "Rutledge, 'The Gay Trivia Queen,' has compiled a myriad gay facts in an easy-to-read volume. This book offers up the offbeat, trivial, and fascinating from the history and life of gays in America." —Buzz Bryan in *Lambda Book Report*

❏ **MY BIGGEST O,** edited by Jack Hart, $8.95. What was the best sex you ever had? Jack Hart asked that question of hundreds of gay men, and got some fascinating answers. Here are summaries of the most intriguing of them. Together, they provide an engaging picture of the sexual tastes of gay men.

❏ **THE PRESIDENT'S SON,** by Krandall Kraus, $5.95. "President Marshall's son is gay. The president, who is beginning a tough battle for reelection, knows it but can't handle it. *The President's Son* is a delicious, oh-so-thinly-veiled tale of a political empire gone insane. A great read." —Marvin Shaw in *The Advocate*

❏ **TWO TEENAGERS IN TWENTY: WRITINGS BY GAY AND LESBIAN YOUTH,** edited by Ann Heron, $9.95. "Designed to inform and support teenagers dealing on their own with minority sexual identification. The thoughtful, readable accounts focus on feelings about being homosexual, reactions of friends and families, and first encounters with other gay people." —*School Library Journal*

These books and other Alyson titles are available at your local bookstore.
If you can't find a book listed above or would like more information,
please call us directly at 1-800-5-ALYSON.

a